FALLEN ANGELS

MATTHEW HATTERSLEY

VINCI
BOOKS

Vinci Books

vinci-books.com

Published by Vinci Books Ltd in 2025

1

A CIP catalogue record for this book is available from the British Library.
Paperback ISBN: 9781036700690

Printed and bound in Great Britain by Clays Ltd, Elcograf S.p.A.

Also by Matthew Hattersley

Acid Vanilla

Final Kill

Seven Bullets

The Hunt

Sister Death

Exit Wounds

Never Say Die

I am a Killer

Bad Blood

Fallen Angels

Annihilation Pest Control Series

White Heat

John Beckett Series

Darkness On The Edge Of Town

When The Kingdom Comes

A World Of Sun And Violence

A Bullet For The Past

Chapter One

It was Saturday night in London's historic Covent Garden, and the streets surrounding the famous Royal Opera House buzzed with activity. Not that this was unusual for the area. The opera house, with its classical columns and intricate stone carvings, often stood as a backdrop to such bustling scenes. Just around the corner, in the main piazza, locals and tourists alike meandered among charming boutiques and quaint eateries, drawn by the vibrant atmosphere and the myriads of buskers, clowns and performance artists. Even at this late hour, some street performers still captivated clusters of weary shoppers with their melodies, weaving a lively soundtrack to the evening.

Tonight, however, the air was alive with more than just the whimsical tunes of street musicians. Five minutes earlier, the opera house had released its audience after a stellar performance of Verdi's *La Traviata*, and the piazza now brimmed with excited chatter. The emotional intensity of the production lingered as elegantly dressed patrons drifted out from the grand arches, their conversations a mix of critique and praise for the night's entertainment.

Among them was Pali Rama, striding confidently out through the open doors, the vibrant chords of Verdi's masterpiece still echoing in his mind. Rama had always been a huge opera fan and tonight's performance had been a spectacle of passion and tragedy, of human emotion and musical genius. Violetta's haunting final aria, and her poignant struggle, resonated with him more deeply than he cared to admit.

He lingered briefly on the pavement, inhaling the fresh late-summer air, savouring the moment. Despite the warnings from his advisors, attending the opera alone had been an excellent decision. Experiencing Verdi without distractions allowed him a rare moment of solace, a fleeting reprieve from the relentless tension that defined his life. He took a right down Bow Street and entered the main piazza, his gaze sweeping over the scene, the soft glow of streetlamps illuminating his fellow opera lovers.

Wandering the city streets alone was a risky move for someone in his position, but he couldn't resist. Despite the weight of the secrets he carried, he still craved notoriety. Fame, even. He wanted to be noticed. As he walked down Russell Street, he drew admiring glances from a few attractive middle-aged women clinging to their husbands' arms. He smiled back, relishing the curiosity and slight lasciviousness in their eyes.

That was how he liked it.

He was a man who naturally commanded attention. Despite his advancing years, his presence was undeniably striking. Tall and dark-skinned, with a twinkle in his eyes and the devil in his smile, he'd never worried about the lack of female attention. He'd always had plenty of it. Even if his hair colour came from a bottle, and the thickness of his darkened mane was now the result of expensive hair-building fibres rather than genetics, he remained a handsome man. Tonight he wore a tailored charcoal suit and a pair of Italian leather Oxford's – the best money could buy. He had plenty of that, too.

Because, beneath the meticulously crafted facade of Pali Rama, the man who had this evening stood on the steps of the Royal Opera House was once Festim Martini – a name synonymous with the violent underbelly of the Albanian organised crime world. Martini was a cruel and brutal operator whose name alone could instil fear in the toughest of men. For twenty years he'd been both an enforcer and a *Krye*, the boss, of his own unit. Throughout his career, Martini had been a savvy operative, but even for someone like him – who prided himself on being like a ghost, existing in the shadows – time and destiny had eventually conspired to take him down.

For the past two years, Martini had been forced into semi-retirement after Interpol's net had grown too tight. They'd chased him across Eastern Europe and into Germany where he'd barely escaped their grasp in Düsseldorf. A subsequent facial reconstruction and a forged identity had brought him to England, where he now walked a tightrope of anonymity and paranoia.

Despite assurances from his advisors – who had been handsomely paid to secure his new life – he couldn't shake the feeling of being hunted. They told him no one would find him here in the UK, that the five hundred thousand dollars he'd paid them ensured that Interpol, MI5, or even advanced facial recognition software couldn't track him. But for Martini, paranoia wasn't just a symptom of his lifestyle –

it was his lifeline, the very thing that had kept him alive when so many men had fallen.

Now, he moved with purpose across the busy piazza, his eyes scanning the area for any familiar signs, any hint of danger in the ordinary. It was a beautiful evening; the scent of rich food wafted from nearby bistros, mingling with the subtle fragrance of blooming flowers hanging from the lampposts. The normalcy of the scene was almost disarming, but Martini's instincts remained on high alert.

More so when his car was not where it was supposed to be. He had specifically instructed Limani to park on the north side of the piazza, a strategic location that allowed for a quick getaway. Yet as his eyes darted from space to space, his vehicle was nowhere to be seen.

A hot rush of anger surged within him, the composure brought about by the opera evaporating as his mind raced through possibilities. Was this a mistake, or something more sinister? The absence of his car was more than an inconvenience, it was a breach in his carefully constructed defences. It told him something was wrong. It told him he was in danger.

He pulled out his phone to call Limani, suddenly regretting his decision to walk out alone. He'd been cocky, unreasonable. Foolish. Freedom, even in small doses, was a luxury fraught with danger. As he dialled he kept moving, his steps quick and soundless on the paved street, his eyes continuously sweeping the area.

The phone rang out. No answer.

Where the hell was Limani?

This wasn't like him. At all. As well as being a loyal bodyguard, Limani knew Martini from old. He knew one wrong move could cost him his life. Martini's grip tightened around the phone. His surroundings felt as if they were closing in on him, the energy and laughter from the crowds mingling with the distant strains of a street violinist playing a melancholic tune. Every conversation around him seemed to grow louder, every shadow became a potential enemy. The paranoia that had kept him alive for so long now screamed at him from every corner of Covent Garden.

Where the hell was his car?

He needed to make a decision, and fast. The underground was nearby, but Covent Garden station was an archaic relic of another time, with a cramped elevator the only transportation down to the platforms. He already felt threatened, so entering a cramped metal box with a herd of strangers was not an option. A taxi might be a viable option, but could he trust a random driver?

Martini was a seasoned criminal whose hands were stained with the blood of countless adversaries, but it had been a long time since he'd had to prove himself in battle. Could he still hold his own if someone was lying in wait for him? Extortion, smuggling and cold-blooded murder had been tools of his trade but now, with his car missing and his bodyguard unreachable, a chilling sense of vulnerability clawed at him – a feeling he loathed above all others.

He pushed through the crowds, trying Limani again, pressing the phone so tightly to his ear it throbbed.

"Come on. Pick up, damn you."

But it was the same outcome as before. Just a continuous, unanswered ringtone mocking his growing desperation. Martini had always been a cool operator. Whether slicing the fingers off a wayward foot soldier or opening the neck of a rival, his calm detachment was chilling and part of the reason he'd earned the moniker *Mbreti Psiko* – the Psycho King. Yet this evening he found his usual composure slipping as he jostled past dithering opera-goers. He knew better than to duck into less populated back alleys. His survival instincts, honed over decades of evading law enforcement and rivals, kept him in the relative safety of the crowd.

He pressed on, passing the Jubilee Market Hall and hurrying down Southampton Street. His destination was now the Strand, a well-lit and populated area even at this time of night, where he could hail a taxi and make his escape. The summer evening buzzed with energy, the Strand illuminated by the bright lights of theatres and the steady stream of London's nightlife, but Martini hardly saw any of it. As he walked he muttered to himself, fists clenched along with his jaw muscles. Limani better have a damn good reason why he wasn't here to meet him. Maybe he'd had an emergency at home. Or perhaps had encountered car trouble. Neither excuse was good enough. In fact, Martini doubted there could be a reason on earth good enough to quell his rage. Taking a finger might do it. Or two. How many fingers did a man need to drive a car?

He was so caught up in his thoughts, imagining the many horrific ways he might teach his driver a lesson, that his focus was abruptly shattered when he collided with someone walking in the opposite direction. It was a woman, a foot shorter than him. As their bodies made contact, her hand brushed against his.

"Get out of my way," he snarled, glaring at her.

She was wearing a black leather jacket over a hooded sweatshirt. The hood was up, obscuring her face, as did a wave of black hair. She hastily muttered an apology. "Sorry, sweetie."

Martini responded with an angry grunt, pushing her aside as he scanned the wide street for a taxi. His mind was a whirlwind of escape plans and contingencies, barely registering the obstruction as human. But as the woman stepped back, her eyes met his briefly. There was something in her expression, a flash of unplaceable emotion that bothered him. He scowled, about to say something, but she was already hurrying away, disappearing into the crowd as quickly as she had appeared.

Martini's initial irritation at the interruption morphed into a stab of panic as he processed the encounter. Had that bitch just hustled him? He swiftly tapped at his pockets, checking for his phone and wallet. Both were still there. Yet his survival instincts, honed by years navigating the treacherous waters of the criminal underworld, had flared to life.

Something was wrong.

He took a step forward, intending to follow and confront the woman, but halted as a strange sensation – a wetness – spread rapidly down his leg. For a moment he worried he'd lost control of his bladder, before a sharp, searing pain cut through the fog of his anger and confusion. He stopped dead, his hand reaching down to touch the source of his discomfort. His trousers were soaked but it wasn't urine. It was blood.

Staggering slightly, he looked down to see the bright red stain blooming across his tailored trousers and the two-inch slit where the fabric had been sliced open on his inner thigh. Cold panic washed over him as the realisation hit. The woman who'd barged him wasn't a petty thief after his money. She was an assassin.

He grabbed his leg, squeezing with all his might to try to keep the wound closed. But it was pointless. Martini was no doctor but he understood enough about how the human body worked – and how to make it stop working – to know she'd sliced through his femoral artery.

He turned in a futile attempt to catch sight of his

attacker but she was already gone, a silent operator, a deadly ghost. Just as he had once been. His legs faltered, his body already feeling the effects of rapid blood loss. Stumbling forward he looked around for something, anything, to lean on, but collapsed instead onto the cold pavement. He tried to yell but his words were strangled by the tightness in his chest and his lack of saliva.

All around him the sounds of the city continued, oblivious to his plight. The world blurred at the edges, the sounds distorting into a heavy-bass fuzz that no longer made sense. His hands were now covered in his own blood, thick, sticky, obnoxious. Seconds passed that felt like days before people started to notice, their expressions twisting from curiosity to horror as they took in the sight of a man bleeding to death in the heart of London.

He wanted to implore them to help but his voice was barely a whisper, his body already shutting down. Blood pooled around him, the life literally draining out of his body. Despite the warm summer evening, he felt the coldness seeping in. It was almost funny, a cliché. But no one was laughing, least of all him. Festim Martini, a man who had evaded capture and cheated death so many times, was now facing the ultimate defeat not in a dark alley or a desolate warehouse, but surrounded by rich theatre-goers and hanging flower baskets.

It didn't make him feel any better.

As the voices around him turned into screams, the figures above him faded to grey. A few seconds passed. Festim Martini lay back, feeling the hard pavement against his skull.

He said a prayer. He wished for forgiveness.

Then he succumbed to the darkness.

Chapter Two

With tourists and locals rushing to the aide of the fallen Albanian gangster, the commotion was such that no one noticed the slim American woman of half-Malaysian descent as she hurried away. A few seconds later and Spook Horowitz had melted completely into the flow of the evening crowd. Like rainwater slipping through the cracks of London's lively streets.

She walked with purpose, her movements confident and decisive as she blended effortlessly with the tourists, drunks and theatre buffs. Continuing up Southampton Street, she then took the first left and cut back down Bull Inn Court. Coming out further down the Strand, she crossed over the road and entered Carting Lane. Halfway down, she encountered two men walking towards her, their swaying gaits and red faces telling her all she needed to know about them.

As she got closer, one of them looked her up and down and smirked, no doubt readying himself to say something he thought was both erudite and amusing. Spook clenched her fist. If this prick wanted to dance, she'd certainly entertain him. She had enough residual fire in her belly and adrenaline pumping through her system to take him and his friend down without breaking stride. But as she passed by he looked away, her brisk pace and the determined set of her jaw signalling she wasn't someone to mess with.

Not Spook Horowitz.

Not any more.

It had been over a year since she'd left Acid behind in Rome. Since then she'd spent every waking hour not only honing her skills and hardening her body, but working on her mindset and focus. She was fitter and stronger than she'd ever been, but more importantly she was more self-assured. The process had been long and gruelling, with many times she'd wanted to quit, but she'd gritted her teeth and pushed on through. She'd been dragged against her will into Acid's world of chaos and destruction, but she was here now. Once you walked through that door, there was no turning back.

Spook had made peace with who she was – and what she did. She was a different person from the timid, nerdy hacker she'd been before she met Acid. But sometimes that was just how life worked. In her darker moments, she liked to remind herself that her situation wasn't better or worse, it wasn't good or bad, it just… was.

At the end of the lane she paused, glancing back towards the Strand. No one was following her, but there was no reason they would be. She was anonymous, just another face in the crowd. Dressed all in black, her wardrobe choice wasn't only useful for blending into the dark city streets; her clothes highlighted the dual parts of her life: functional and nondescript yet with a sharp edge that made her feel powerful and tough. She wore black boots, a pair of tight jeans that were all but moulded to her now muscular legs, and a hooded sweater worn with the hood up to further mask her identity. The black leather jacket was the final touch to her outfit.

And yes, Spook knew what Nate thought of her wearing the jacket – and she certainly knew what it implied – but it had cost her almost five hundred pounds in a vintage shop in Camden, and she loved wearing it. To Spook it was armour. It made her feel invincible and helped her step into the persona required for her new, grim profession.

Entering the quieter, shadowed pathways of Victoria Embankment Gardens, she found the solitude required to transition back into Julie Miles, the mild-mannered UK citizen who – to the tax man and anyone else who asked – was a self-employed IT specialist. After taking off her jacket, she removed the hoodie and examined it for blood before balling it up and placing it at the bottom of a tree. Hopefully, a homeless person would make use of it, but if not it would be gathered up by street cleaners in the morning and sent to landfill. Not that there'd be enough of Martini's DNA present on the material to place her at the scene anyway. Spook was meticulous about how she carried out her new work. Just as in her old life as a hacker, she was a perfectionist and did everything to the letter.

Well, *almost* everything to the letter, she told herself as slipped the leather jacket back on.

Next, she gathered her long dark hair and pulled it back from her face, securing it in a tight ponytail with a shocking-pink scrunchy. The warm night air felt good on the back of her neck as she removed the disposable contact lenses she often wore on jobs and slid on the thick-rimmed glasses she'd carried in her jacket pocket. Each stage of her restoration was systematic. This was her stripping away Spook the Assassin and reinforcing the guise of Julie Miles.

Making her way through the gardens, she approached the river's edge and pulled the Stanley knife from her jacket pocket. Her fingers lingered briefly on the cold metal handle, acknowledging the gravitas of what she had done. Then, with a flick of her wrist, she sent the knife spinning into the Thames, feeling the elation of a job well done.

This was the third mission Spook had completed since Nate had declared her training complete, but it was the first time she'd accomplished a job solo. The exhilaration of executing all that Nate had taught her pulsed in her veins, a visceral reminder of the life she now led. No longer was she a spectator in the world of high-end assassins and calculated violence; she was a willing participant, shaping events with the edge of a blade.

Yet despite embracing her new identity, Spook still required some justification to steady her nerves. Indeed, there had been many times over the last year when she'd doubted ever reaching the stage where she could carry out a hit alone. She'd endured hours of mental gymnastics and intense research to reach this point. Back at their makeshift base in Dalston, she had painstakingly compiled a dossier on Festim Martini, including all his crimes, both in his professional and personal life. Along with all the horrific things he'd done as one of the leaders of the Clan del Kruja, he'd raped and murdered his brother's wife and gunned down the children of a rival gang member. Spook had absorbed every grim detail, the knowledge fuelling her resolve. It was the awareness of these crimes that had spurred her on as she'd approached him minutes earlier and drawn the Stanley knife.

The cold bite of the wind off the river brought her back to the present. She glanced around, making sure she was alone, before allowing herself a few more minutes of reflection. She knew it troubled Nate that she needed such intense psychological preparation before going to work, and that he worried about the naivety of her approach. But for Spook, understanding the depths of her mark's evil was crucial. It transformed the act from murder to retribution, a distinction she needed if she was to hold on to her soul.

And her sanity.

Nate had implied more than once that there had to be a certain amount of cognitive dissonance in Spook's psyche for her to carry out such jobs, while knowing that many of their clients – the people who hired them to do their dirty work – were no angels themselves. But Spook tried not to think about that element of her new career. This was her life now; there was no going back to who she once was. While this realisation wasn't new, each job cemented it further. She needed the money, yes, but more than that, she needed a purpose, and this dark world she'd been thrust into after meeting Acid Vanilla offered her both.

As the distant wail of sirens sliced through the night, Spook's senses snapped to full alert. This was unexpected. The emergency services were on their way far too quickly for comfort. Moving out of the gardens, she headed towards Westminster, flagging down a black cab outside Embankment Tube station and sliding onto the back seat with a deep sigh.

"Dalston," she told the driver as he pulled away. "Just by the Junction."

"No problem," he replied, catching her gaze in the rearview mirror. "Had a good night, have ya?"

"I've been at work," Spook answered coldly, hoping he'd pick up on the subtext. She wasn't here to talk.

As the cab weaved through London's neon streets, she rested her head against the cool window and closed her eyes, feigning sleep to halt any further unwanted conversation. She worked on steadying her breath and allowing the torrents of adrenaline filling her system to subside. It wasn't long before the full extent of what she'd done hit her and, as it always did, it made her a little nauseous. But she was getting better. Maybe she wouldn't always need to do so much groundwork and preparation for each job. Or maybe she would.

Right now, she was too tired to think too much about it. It had been a long night. She was glad it was over.

Chapter Three

Spook hadn't intended to fall asleep but she must have done, because the next she knew, the cab had stopped and the driver was barking at her through her haze of confusion.

"Sorry – what?" she muttered, sitting up and looking around. Through the window she made out the lights of Dalston Junction station.

"I said we're here," the driver repeated. "That'll be twenty-five quid, love."

Spook reached into her back pocket, pulled out three tens and handed them over, mumbling for him to keep the change as she climbed out. From the Junction it would still take her another twenty minutes to walk to the warehouse at the end of Dalston Lane where she currently resided and worked – but it was best not to have taxis drop her too close. Besides, the fresh air would do her good.

While she walked, her mind drifted to her old friend, as it often did in times like this when she was without distractions. The last time she'd spoken to Acid, Spook had told her she hated her. And she did. In a way. But she also had a hell of a lot of other feelings for that frustrating woman and, regardless of what Nate kept insisting, she couldn't forget about her. Acid had been Spook's life for the best part of seven years. Their time together had been intense, terrifying and messed up. Those seven years had felt like seventy. Spook had probably aged at least seventeen years in that time. So what Acid had done – leaving Spook to join forces with Darius Duke – was unforgivable. Yet Spook couldn't shake the feeling there was more to it than Nate surmised.

"I hate you," Spook had told her.

"Good," Acid had said. "It's easier that way."

It's easier that way…

The words echoed through Spook's mind as she neared home. She shook her head, trying to dislodge them. Whatever Acid had meant, there was no point dwelling on it. Spook knew her former friend was still working for Darius, and she hated her for that. Darius was a sick, egotistical bastard. He'd killed The Dullahan, for Christ's sake. He'd tried to kill Spook. But Acid had only ever looked out for number one. It wasn't the discovery that Darius was her half-brother that had swayed her to join him; it was the promise of a route back to her old life. As a killer for hire in his new organisation, Kancel Kulture.

It pained Spook to think of these things but she couldn't help herself. She'd been naïve to think Acid would ever change, and she wouldn't make that mistake again.

"Screw it," she whispered to herself. "It is what is. You don't need her."

Reaching her building, she paused for a moment to compose herself. She didn't want Nate to pick up on any tension or reluctance. The building she currently called home was an old warehouse tucked away on the far side of a railway bridge, its exterior a patchwork of aged brick and graffiti that blended seamlessly into the urban landscape. To any passerby, it was just another relic of the city's industrial past, but behind the worn facade lay the heart of their new organisation.

Spook approached the entrance, a nondescript metal door with no visible handle or keyhole. Pulling out her phone, she opened a specially designed app and held it up to a small glass panel beside the door. The panel flashed green, and with a soft click the door unlocked, sliding open silently. After glancing over her shoulder to check no one was watching her, Spook entered the building.

Inside, the transformation from a dirty old warehouse to a high-tech headquarters was immediate. She entered a dimly lit corridor that smelled faintly of paint fumes, leading to a metal staircase at the far end. As she walked up to the next level, she could sense the electromagnetic fields from the banks of servers she'd installed and hear the whir of equipment.

Stepping off the stairs, she was greeted by a vast open space that matched the warehouse's entire footprint. The area closest to the stairwell was taken up by three large tables, each laden with computers and high-resolution screens displaying real-time CCTV footage and a series of digital maps showing London, the UK, and the world. Spook expected to find Lena Katz in front of the main computer terminal, but the new recruit was absent, her purple fake-fur coat draped over the back of one of the chairs.

Scanning the screens, Spook saw footage of the Strand where she'd taken out Martini. He was no longer where he'd fallen, but there was still a pool of blood on the pavement – a grey and grainy smear in the black and white security footage.

Stacked up on another table were twenty orange plastic boxes, each filled with wires and small items. Burner phones, modems, GPS trackers.

Spook moved further into the space. "Hey," she called out. "I'm back. Anyone here?"

The rest of this floor was dedicated to physical training, with mats laid out for combat practice and racks holding various types of weaponry and defensive gear for training and fieldwork. Despite its comprehensive set-up, the space still bore signs of ongoing development. Cables hung from parts of the unfinished ceiling, and some areas were cordoned off for future expansion.

Above her, another floor contained a bathroom and shower stalls, as well as sleeping accommodation. It would eventually be used by operatives working in London – when they got around to hiring any – but for now it was where Nate, Spook, and Lena were all staying until the organisation became fully operational. This first floor would also eventually house a control centre filled with more sensitive communications equipment, and an armoury stocked with the best and most up-to-date weaponry and surveillance tools. Spook was pleased with their progress, but they weren't there yet.

"Hello!" she called again, directing her voice to another metal stairwell in the back corner, leading up to the floor above. "Nate? Lena?"

"Spook. You're back." Nate's deep Welsh voice boomed down from above. Spook walked over as he and Lena descended the stairs. "We were just discussing installing a meditation space on the top floor. How did it go?"

He reached the bottom of the stairs and faced Spook

with a serious expression. He'd recently had his hair cut back into a buzz cut, but was still a handsome man with dark eyes and chiselled features. Tall and imposing, he had an athlete's physique and a certain grace that belied his steely toughness. He was wearing a black t-shirt and a pair of baggy linen trousers with a drawstring waist, giving him the look of a yoga instructor or spiritual guru. They were the sort of trousers Acid might have scoffed at, if she were here.

But Acid wasn't here, Spook reminded herself.

"So…" he continued. "All good?"

"It went exactly as planned," Spook replied. "You can tell the client it's done… and start the invoicing procedure."

This was a pointed comment. Nate was always harping on about client satisfaction and their bottom line, and she'd begun to tease him about it. But it was fair enough. If their organisation was going to succeed, they needed someone money-minded with a vision towards expansion and growth. Plus, Nate was a decent man and a good trainer. He'd taught Spook everything he knew and, after she'd returned from Rome, had spent every available hour rebuilding her physically and mentally into a force to be reckoned with. He'd done well. They both had.

"I'll contact them now," Nate told her. "Good work, Spook. This could really get the ball rolling in terms of the word-of-mouth publicity we need. Get cleaned up and we'll have a debrief."

"Okay, thanks," she said, glancing from Nate to Lena, the latter hovering a few feet away, the overhead strip lights reflecting off her piercings as she self-consciously rubbed her palm over the tattoo sleeve on her opposite arm. "Did any CCTV pick me up?"

Lena shook her head and made her way back to the

computer screens. "No. You did well to hide your face. I've played the scene back a few times – you can't even see the blade or really make out what happened." She smiled. "It was great work. Textbook."

Spook followed her while Nate pulled a phone from his pocket and turned away. "I heard sirens," she said, lowering her voice so Nate wouldn't hear. "A minute or two after the hit. What the hell happened?"

Lena gritted her teeth as she sat, her fingers pausing above the keyboard. "There was a slight hiccup," she said. "Issues with the drone. I'm so sorry."

Lena had recently designed what she called a 'scrambler drone', which could create a blackout zone around an area by intercepting and blocking any outgoing emergency calls. When it worked, it ensured an operative had a critical window to escape after a hit without law enforcement being alerted.

When it worked.

"It is still in beta," Lena added. "I'm testing it live and tweaking as we go. It's almost there." She looked up at Spook, her big dark eyes full of hope and perhaps a little trepidation.

Spook nodded. Two years ago no one would ever have looked at her with the sort of respect she now commanded. It was a strange experience, but one she liked.

"It's fine," she replied.

But Lena didn't seem to hear it. "See here?" She pointed at a line of code highlighted in red on her screen. "The algorithm was supposed to reroute the signal through multiple nodes, creating enough noise to confuse the cellular towers. But there was a sync issue. I think it's the timing sequence in the firmware."

The young woman's eyes shone with a mix of frustration and excitement. Spook knew that feeling well – frustration at the glitch, but excitement at the challenge of solving it. "But it's fine," Lena added. "I've been monitoring police bands. Martini bled out before they even understood what was happening."

She grinned. A little too eagerly, Spook felt. But Lena's need for reassurance was understandable. She was new to this world of high-end assassins and shadowy morals, uncertain of her place in it and how she should act. Spook knew that feeling well, too.

"Festim Martini, huh?" Spook said. "Sounds like the name of a bad cocktail."

It was an attempt to lighten the mood, but Lena either didn't get it or didn't find it funny. There was an awkward silence for a moment as the two women stared at each other.

"I'm glad he's dead anyway," Spook muttered. "He was a terrible man. He deserved everything he got."

She wasn't entirely sure who needed the reassurance more, but Lena seemed to relax. "We did good," Lena said. "And I will get the scrambler working correctly. Promise."

Spook nodded, the way a wise old sage might, relaxing into her role as mentor. "You'll get there," she said. It was clear that Lena admired Spook a great deal. Sure, the constant need for reassurance and praise might get a little cloying after a while, but it was nice to be admired for once.

"And what about... the other thing?" Spook asked, casting a surreptitious glance Nate's way. "Any updates?"

Lena bared her teeth in an awkward grimace. "Well... yes. There is something," she said. "But I'm not sure you're going to like it."

Chapter Four

Spook had found Lena Katz on the dark web and monitored her work for three months before she and Nate even attempted contact. From Hackney originally, Lena had been using her advanced hacking skills to infiltrate and expose human trafficking networks across London and Europe. She'd sent down some of the most dangerous thugs in Eastern Europe, all while avoiding detection by both the criminals and the authorities. Her talents were evident, and once Spook was sure Lena had what it took, she'd sent her an encrypted message presenting herself as a fellow white-hat hacker looking to collaborate.

They'd met in person at the start of the year and hit it off immediately. Lena was impressed with Spook's prowess and had even recognised some of her old handles. This initial meeting was followed by an intensive three-month vetting process where Spook and Nate monitored Lena from a distance, analysing her coding and assessing her personality to ensure she met their stringent criteria. Both of Lena's parents were dead and she had no real friends to speak of, which helped matters a great deal. At the end of the process, Lena had passed all of Spook's tests and had met the data-based criteria Nate required. So, five months ago, they'd met up again and revealed their true mission, before inviting her to join them.

Initially Lena had been wary, but by this stage she and Spook were close and Spook was able to sell her on the organisation's goals in a way that appealed to the young hacker.

"We'll only target those who deserve it," Spook had assured her. "I know morally it's a grey area. But if you think about it, all we're doing is ridding the world of bad people. We're making the world a better place."

Spook genuinely believed this. She had to. She couldn't do what she'd been doing for the last year if she didn't. To her, their work was for the greater good. They were avenging angels, working to take down bad people...

Making the world a better place.

It was Spook's mantra. Not Nate's.

She kept one eye on him now as he continued his call, informing their client that the mark was dead. Spook didn't know who the client was – she assumed it was the head of a rival gang or perhaps even someone at Interpol – but that was how they made this work. Nate handled these matters, allowing Spook to distance herself from any information that might clash with the carefully constructed narrative she needed to maintain.

"Go on," she told Lena. "Tell me. What have you uncovered."

Lena continued to stare up at her with those almost cartoon-like eyes that Spook tried not to stare into for too long. Lena Katz was certainly intriguing. Her appearance alone was as striking as her tech skills. She was one of those young people who was naturally rather beautiful but who tried to hide it as best she could with piercings, tattoos and hair dye. The collection of silver rings adorning her eyebrows and lips glinted as she leaned forward, her eyes darting across the four screens in front of her. Her dark skin and eyes hinted at a mixed heritage, but she'd never explained and Spook hadn't asked. Her hair – dyed a vibrant shade of electric blue – was cut into an asymmetric bob that hung down around her small, pointed chin as she leaned over her keyboard and opened up a new terminal window.

Spook watched her as she typed, impressed and perhaps a little jealous too. Lena's ability to manipulate technology and write complex but effective code on the fly was nothing short of genius. Each line of code she wrote, every system she engineered, pushed boundaries and redefined what was possible in their shadowy line of work.

Apart from a few instances, Spook had been out of the tech game for a while now. She missed it, but she'd made her bed and she accepted that. Despite her previous unease and vocal contempt for what Acid did for a living, Spook Horowitz now saw herself in the same light. She was an assassin, a hired killer. It still felt surreal, but it was her choice.

"See here," Lena said, pointing at one of the screens. "This was the last time we got anything concrete regarding Kancel Kulture. Almost three months ago."

Spook narrowed her eyes at the screen, which showed a blurred image of Darius Duke and Acid Vanilla walking alongside Rome's River Tiber. It was the facial recognition software Spook had developed that had picked them up, and since then she'd had Lena working every spare hour on finding out all she could about Kancel Kulture's operations.

"But there's been new developments?" Spook asked, still watching Nate. He didn't know of Lena's extracurricular activities and Spook worried he'd be angry if he did. He'd told her more than once to forget about Acid. He was probably right. If only she could.

"Kancel Kulture's activity has dropped significantly in Rome over the last month," Lena whispered, her voice steady. "It looks like they've moved operations but I couldn't pinpoint where. Then, two days ago I uncovered a thread of encrypted chatter on one of the client forums we use. One of their operatives, an assassin known as Nokizaru, was found dead recently in the USA. After some digging, I found evidence suggesting that Kancel Kulture has possibly relocated to the States. Specifically, to Los Angeles, California."

Spook couldn't help but smile at Lena's superfluous addition – as if just LA wouldn't have sufficed. But this overly keen, overly informative aspect of her personality was one of the reasons Spook found herself warming to her new colleague.

"Do we know where exactly they're based?" she asked, refocusing her attention on the screens.

"Not yet. But I'm working on it."

"Good work," Spook said, leaning closer as Lena showed her the forum thread she'd hacked. "See if you can find any information about their recent jobs or clients. They have a good tech person and they'll be using cloaking software, but there's always a way around. Go deeper on the dark web."

"What are you two whispering about?"

Shit.

Spook had been so engrossed in what Lena had shown

her, she hadn't noticed Nate approaching. She looked up to see him standing on the other side of the desk.

"Well?" He folded his muscular arms, resembling an angry gym teacher momentarily. "What's going on, Lena?"

"Oh... I... erm..." She glanced up at Spook. "We just..."

"I asked Lena to look into Kancel Kulture's where-abouts," Spook said, crossing her arms to mirror him. "I wanted to—"

"Fucking hell, Spook! We've discussed this. Many, *many* times. You need to let Acid go."

Spook's jaw tightened at the mention of her old friend's name. "It's not about her."

"Isn't it?" Nate shook his head, softening slightly as his anger morphed into dismay. "Look, I get it. I wanted her to be part of what we're building here, too. But she made her choice."

"It's not about her," Spook insisted, trying to keep her voice calm, aware of Lena's eyes on her. "It isn't! Kancel Kulture is a rival organisation. They're the enemy. It makes sense that we monitor their actions. Lena's just discovered they're now operating out of LA."

"*Possibly* operating out of LA," Lena added unhelpfully.

Nate looked from one to the other, heavy creases across his brow. "I'm sick of talking about this," he said. "We need to focus on setting up our own organisation. We might have completed a handful of assignments but we're far from the finished article. No one knows about us yet. Hell, we haven't even decided on a name."

Spook opened her mouth, ready to offer up her sugges-tion of Avenging Angels once more. But she decided against it. Nate had already vetoed it, and it wasn't the time.

"I understand where you're coming from," she told him. "But if I can talk to her and—"

"Enough!" he snapped. "I mean it, Spook. You need to concentrate on the job at hand. We all do. We're building something important here." He glanced at his watch. "I've got a meeting with a potential client in an hour. I have to get ready. But you two need to cool it with this. Let's build ourselves up before we start thinking about rival organisations and old... adversaries."

Spook went to react but bit her tongue as Nate held his hand up to her. She gripped the back of Lena's chair, holding his gaze.

"Clean yourself up and get some rest," he told her. "I'll see you both later."

Spook watched him walk away, her grip tightening on the chair until her knuckles turned white. Nate, ever the pragmatist, made a valid point, but she couldn't shake her determination. Acid was her friend. She was concerned about her. Despite all that had happened, Spook still clung to the belief that she could persuade Acid to abandon Darius and join her and Nate.

But she also had to convince Nate of that, too.

"Keep digging," she muttered, placing a hand on Lena's shoulder. "I need confirmation on Kancel Kulture's centre of operations and Acid Vanilla's whereabouts."

Lena twisted in her chair, uncertainty flickering in her eyes. "But... Nate said..."

"It'll be fine," Spook replied. "It doesn't have to interfere with your work. Just keep an eye on that forum, look for patterns, and do whatever you can. This is in all our best interests. Trust me."

Lena nodded and turned back to her screens. "On it, Boss."

Spook stepped away. Her body was aching with exertion but she knew sleep was out of the question. She needed a release, a way of taking her mind off all that she had done and all she had yet to do.

"I'm going out," she muttered. "Don't wait up."

Without waiting for a response she headed for the stairs, hurrying down to the ground floor. It was almost midnight, but for people like her the night was just beginning. Her resolve hardened as she swiped her phone to unlock the door and stepped out into the cool night air. Nate was a good ally, and she knew he was only looking out for her and their new organisation, but he was wrong about this. She had to find Acid. She had to face her one more time. It was the only way Spook could move forward.

She needed answers, once and for all. And if Acid Vanilla was not for turning, then Spook would find a way to forget about her. For good.

Chapter Five

The room stank of antiseptic and stale air. A chill made the small hairs on her arms and neck stand on end. She'd hardly slept in the last twenty-four hours, but she was past sleep, more wired than tired. Her eyes darted around the plain, sterile room, reminiscent of a medical facility or a police interrogation room. The walls were a soulless shade of grey, unmarked and unremarkable, with a heavy metal door opposite her and a large mirror to her right. Overhead, a single fluorescent light buzzed, casting a harsh glow on the metal table in front of her.

Across the table sat a peculiar little man, who was currently scribbling in a notebook. He'd been introduced to Acid a few months earlier as 'The Scientist' and this was their fifth meeting in this room. The Scientist was small and rotund, with a perfectly round head and thick round glasses perched on his wide snub nose. The glasses magnified his eyes to an almost comical extent, yet the look in them was anything but humorous.

Acid Vanilla leaned back in the uncomfortable metal

chair, sighing as she waited for him to continue. Her gaze fell on the polygraph machine on the table between them, sitting there like a therapist, waiting to cast doubt on their relationship. Electrodes clung to her skin like unwelcome parasites, and as she flexed her hand, the dials and needles responded accordingly. She'd had enough of this shit.

The Scientist coughed once and looked up from his notes. "Okay, Ms Vanilla. Let us continue." His accent was curious. Predominantly German, perhaps, but it was hard to tell. "What have you had to eat so far today?"

"Today?" Acid smirked. "Let me think. Ah, yes. A bowl of bran with oat milk, accompanied by a turmeric shake." The needle on the polygraph machine jumped erratically. Acid laughed, a sharp, joyless sound that echoed off the walls. "Fine. I had an energy drink and a croissant," she announced. "I'll be healthy at lunch."

The Scientist adjusted his glasses, unamused, and moved on to a series of mundane questions to recalibrate the machine – her age, her last place of residence, her real name and confirmed alias. Then, without a change in his tone, he dropped a heavier question.

"Did you kill your colleague, Nokizaru?"

Acid took a deep breath. "This again?" She exhaled slowly, maintaining her composure. "No, I did not kill Nokizaru." She eyed the needle. It was stable. Of course it was.

She was sick to death of coming here and answering these inane bloody questions. By this stage her loyalty should have been accepted, not needing to be proved by a steady pulse. Yet it seemed trust was not freely given but painstakingly earned, especially here.

"What happened to your colleague, Nokizaru?" The

Scientist asked, peering over his glasses at the needle as it wavered on the readout.

"I've already told you," she said, turning to look into the two-way mirror that dominated the wall to her right. "Nokizaru was shot by Simian Maplethorpe's bodyguard as we were exiting his studio. It was simply bad luck. We had no intel on the security presence. You know this. And I had nothing to do with it."

She didn't need to look at the needle to know it would indicate she was telling the truth. She lowered her chin, eyes fixed on the mirror, speaking with quiet intensity, her frustration simmering just beneath the surface.

"Darius, I've passed so many of these bloody tests. When is this going to damn well end?"

No answer came, just a snuffling sound from The Scientist as he scribbled more notes. But Acid knew Darius was watching her behind the two-way mirror, analysing her every expression and tone for a sign of deception.

Why the hell couldn't he trust her?

After everything she'd done for him.

She squinted into the mirror but the only thing she saw was her own reflection.

And, well… shit.

To say she looked like hell warmed up would be an understatement. Her thick wavy hair was messy and unwashed, and her usual olive skin appeared a sickly shade of yellow in this unforgiving light. Her wide glassy eyes, ringed with days-old mascara and smeared eye shadow, gave her a haunted, hollow look. She shuddered. The old Bikini Kill t-shirt she was wearing hung loosely on her slender frame.

She sniffed loudly, the sound slicing through the tension in the room. The Scientist shifted uncomfortably in his seat.

"Have you any other questions, sweetie?" she asked, giving him a hard stare. "Maybe you want to know my bra size? Or my body count, perhaps? Although you'll have to be more specific. I know the kids use the term to mean people they've bedded these days." She grinned, enjoying his look of discomfort as she lifted her hands in the air as if weighing up the idea. "Bedded or body-bagged? I'm afraid both numbers are rather high, and I'll be honest with you – both will be guesswork at this point."

The Scientist adjusted himself. "Ms Vanilla. If we can please stay on track."

"I don't think so. I'm done." Without waiting for a response, she began to rip the polygraph sensors from her skin. The adhesive tugged at her, leaving red marks, but it only fuelled her anger.

"Sit down! We are not finished," The Scientist spluttered, glancing at the mirror. "Mr Duke, sir, I—"

"Oh, give it a rest, will you," Acid spat. She stood, the metal chair scraping against the floor with a harsh grating sound. Picking her leather jacket up from the floor by her feet, she shrugged it on and headed for the door. "Come on, D," she yelled, banging her fist on the metal. "Let me out. I've had enough of this."

There was a pause, then the sound of the lock clicking open. Yanking the door wide, she stormed out of the interrogation room and took a left down the corridor, coming face to face with Darius.

"You need to stop this," she hissed. "It's boring."

Darius hit her with a wide grin. His teeth were unnaturally white, almost as if he'd painted them on. But living in LA had that effect, especially on someone with already dubious self-esteem.

"You did well," he told her. "I'm proud of you."

"Proud? Really? Well, you have a pretty fucked up way of showing it. *Bro.*"

He snickered. "Come on, Acid. I only want to make sure. For my own peace of mind." He leaned back and grinned.

Those teeth. Jesus.

But they were only a part of Darius' transformation since setting up shop in Los Angeles. His hair, once jet black and swept back, was now cut in a classic Ivy League style with streaks of blond in the front, complementing a fresh-faced look further enhanced by the absence of stubble.

"That's got to be the last time," Acid told him.

"I just need to be sure."

"You need to grow a pair and trust me."

Darius rubbed his chin thoughtfully, clearly revelling in his position of power. He was wearing a leopard print silk shirt – with a few too many buttons undone, in Acid's opinion – tucked into a pair of sleek tuxedo trousers complete with the classic stripe down the leg. The look was finished with a pair of worn Converse, scuffed at the toes.

But she had to admit, the overall look suited him. He even had a tan, for heaven's sake, suggesting that he, at least, had spent time under the California sun rather than in clinical interrogation suites. If she squinted, he looked like he'd just strolled off a movie set, a perfect embodiment of the world he now navigated. One foot in the glamorous LA lifestyle, the other in the shadows of the criminal elite.

"Are we done here?" Acid asked, making to move past him towards the exit.

But Darius held up a hand to stop her. "You know why I'm doing this."

Acid halted, taking a moment to compose herself. "You don't have to interrogate me like I'm the enemy," she said.

"I'm on your side. I'm on *our* side. Hell, you're my only family, Darius. Of course I'm with you. Not only are you my brother, but you're also the head of the fastest-growing assassin network in the world. I'm back doing what I love. The only thing I've ever been good at. You can let me off the leash. I'm all in, I swear."

Darius studied her, his expression unreadable. "Trust is earned through actions, not words, Alice."

She tensed. She hated him calling her by her real name. Whenever she challenged him on it, he said it was a familial thing, but it always felt to her like a power move. "Then let my actions speak for themselves," she replied. "I'd suggest they already have. Many times."

Darius' features softened, the corners of his mouth turning up in a rare genuine smile. "Maybe you're right," he said. "Go freshen up, then come see me at HQ. I've got a new job for you."

"Fine."

As Acid walked away her shoulders relaxed slightly, the promise of a new job slicing through the residual tension like a blade. Another assignment. Hopefully, this one would finally silence the whispers of doubt in her brother's mind. She smiled to herself. A new job was exactly what she needed right now. Not only would it appease the bats and calm her restless soul, but it was a chance to prove herself.

And to remind everyone that she was still one of the best.

Chapter Six

Dalston at midnight was a different place to how it was in the daytime. Neon signs flickered and streetlights cast long spiky shadows, turning the area around the warehouse into an ocean of darkness, the possibility of danger lurking in every corner. Even the high street, usually bustling with life, was almost deserted, occupied only by the occasional figure moving swiftly through the night or those who lingered in doorways, their faces briefly illuminated by whatever they were smoking.

Spook ignored them all, moving with purpose as she headed towards the main junction. She didn't know where she was going. Or why. She just needed to walk, to breathe, to clear her head. Her pace was brisk and erratic, almost aggressive, her inner world made physical.

She was pissed off. More than she wanted to admit. But it was more than just anger twisting at her insides. Confusion, paranoia and despair could be added to that list. She pulled in deep breaths, trying to calm herself, but Nate's dismissive attitude toward her concerns about Kancel Kulture kept playing out in her mind.

What was his problem?

Why couldn't he see the bigger picture?

Yet, as angry as Spook was at Nate's indifference, she also understood there was a good chance she was deflecting her rage.

Because no matter how angry she was at Nate for telling her to cool it with her search for Acid, she was angrier at herself for still caring so much.

She reached a crossroads and stopped, considering her next move. A black cab drove past, heading north, and she watched its taillights fade before it disappeared entirely around a bend. It was the quiet at this time of night that unsettled her most. Apart from the white noise of police sirens, ever-present in this part of the city, Dalston was a ghost town.

A stray cat, its fur matted and eyes glinting with reflected light, scurried out from beneath a parked car. It paused, eyes locked on Spook, before darting away into the maze of trash bins in a graffiti-covered alleyway.

Spook resumed walking, peering into the dim alleys, searching for a distraction. It was probably a good thing she didn't find one, but it didn't feel that way. Tonight it was just her, the stray cat, and her frustrated, confusing thoughts.

Why did she care so much about that infuriating woman? Acid Vanilla sure as hell didn't care about her. She might have spared Spook's life that day in Rome, but she'd also sent her away, telling her she didn't want to see her ever again. Worse, she'd joined forces with Darius Duke, a man who'd spent the previous year trying to kill them both. The man who'd killed The Dullahan. Acid clearly didn't give a shit about Spook or anyone but herself.

But, hey. What was new?

Acid Vanilla or Alice Vandella, whatever she called herself, she'd always been the same, focused on herself first and foremost.

So why was Spook surprised?

Why did the pain of Acid's betrayal cut her so deep?

There was a quote she'd often heard, attributed she believed to Maya Angelou: 'When someone shows you who they are, believe them the first time.' It made a lot of sense, but she'd never taken it on board in terms of her relationship with Acid. Maybe it was time she did.

Spook had begun to wonder if, after all these years playing second fiddle to Acid's impulsive and violent nature, she'd developed some kind of twisted Stockholm Syndrome. Or had Acid been grooming her all this time? Gaslighting her, even?

On the flip side, she'd also played with the idea that deep down she was in love with Acid.

Yet in reality, Spook suspected the explanation was far simpler. She just missed her friend. She missed her catty humour, her eye rolls, her pursed lips and dismissive shrugs. She missed feeling incredibly safe but also that anything could happen whenever she was with her. Acid Vanilla was a whirlwind of chaos and charm – volatile, yes, but undeniably magnetic. Her disappearance had left a void in Spook's life, a space filled with unanswered questions and unresolved feelings.

She didn't truly believe that Acid had been brainwashed. It wasn't like her to be swayed so easily. She was too strong, too fiery. In fact, if Spook was completely honest with herself, she could understand why joining Kancel Kulture was appealing to someone like Acid. She had only ever known one way of life and Darius had exploited that fact – offering her a better version of that life on a silver platter.

The sting of the cool night air brought her back to the present. Driven by a need to escape her spiralling thoughts, Spook quickened her pace. But there were no answers to be found here on the cold streets of north London. She needed a drink. Somewhere warm.

And all of a sudden she knew just the place.

Stepping into the road, she flagged down a passing black cab and climbed into the back.

"South Kensington, please," she told the driver. "Near Old Brompton Road."

Forty minutes later, the cab rolled to a stop on the corner of Queen's Gate. Spook swiped her phone against the pay meter and got out. It was now 2 a.m., and the streets here were even more deserted than in Dalston. Few bars would still be serving alcohol at this hour, but she knew of one place.

Having never visited, it took Spook ten minutes of searching the dingy back streets before she finally found The Bitter Marxist, marked by an old neon sign flickering above a rickety Victorian stairwell. Grabbing the metal handrail, she made her way down to the basement bar, feeling nervous and excited in equal measures. This was Acid's place and she'd talked of it in almost reverent tones. If Spook could get into her old friend's mindset, she might understand why she had done what she did. But more than that, she craved the numbing embrace that liquor offered. With a deep breath, she pushed the door open and stepped inside.

Immediately she was hit with the harsh unfiltered blast of heavy rock music. She didn't know the song, she couldn't make out the words, but it was the kind of music she'd often heard emanating from Acid's room. As the door swung shut behind her, she stood for a moment, scoping out her surroundings. This was no polished inner-city establishment, but a real dive bar in every sense of the word. It was raw, real, and throbbing with danger. She could see why Acid loved it here. It was exactly the kind of place that would appeal to someone like her – unpretentious, defiant, rough around the edges but brimming with character. It felt like stepping into another world, one where the usual rules didn't apply.

The layout was simple and Spook was surprised at how small the place was. There was an enclosed raised area to the right of the entrance that was even darker and more threatening than the main space. A furtive glance into this gloomy alcove was met with snarls from a group of men hunched around a table, their faces lost in shadow. Spook turned away and made her way to the bar.

Along one wall were three small round tables, whilst the bar itself took up most of the floor space. She counted three stools at the bar, and dangling above her head three paper lanterns cast everything in a soft, sinister hue that somehow made the space feel even more secluded. Three tables, three stools, three lanterns. All threes. She wondered if it meant anything. Probably not.

Spook leaned against the bar, taking in every detail – the scuffed countertop, the ripped seat covers, the faint smell of beer mixed with the sharper tang of liquor. It wasn't hard to imagine Acid here, her sarcastic drawl loud over the music.

"Good evening," the barman said, coming over. He was tall and good-looking with dark skin and a gentle demeanour that felt at odds with the rest of the bar. But maybe that was just Spook's prejudices coming into play, relying on cliché with one foot still in the civilised world.

She now understood that life was more nuanced than simply labelling a situation – or a person – as good or bad, safe or dangerous.

"Whisky," Spook said, her gaze drifting over the vast array of bottles standing against the back wall. "Whatever you have."

She pulled up a stool as the barman turned and reached for a bottle. Pouring a shot of amber liquid into a clean glass, he slid it across the bar towards her with a knowing smile. "Try this. It's a good sipping bourbon."

Spook wrapped her fingers around the glass and knocked it back in one go, immediately regretting her decision. The drink was harsh, burning its way down her throat with a ferocity that made her eyes water. Fighting through the pain, she set the glass down.

"Give me another," she said. "A double."

"As you wish."

Spook hated whisky, but she hoped she'd eventually acquire a taste for it. That's what happened, wasn't it? Surely no one enjoyed this stuff straight off the bat. It was foul. Yet, lately, Spook had found herself forcing down more glasses of this harsh liquid than she cared to admit. The alcohol didn't solve anything, but it dulled the sharp edges of her thoughts, slowed the relentless pace of her mind. When you killed people for a living, finding some way of distracting yourself from that fact was essential. She could understand why Acid drank so much. Still, she decided to sip her next glass, trying to savour the warmth as it spread through her body.

But any solace was short-lived. From the corner of her eye, Spook noticed a man return from the bathroom and take a seat two stools down from her. She could sense him watching her and tensed as he leaned closer.

"How you doing?" he asked, in a rough East End accent.

Spook shot him a glance and nodded. "Just having a quiet drink. Trying to relax."

"Ah, you're a Yank!" he exclaimed. "Nice. I used to go out with an American girl. A long time ago now, mind."

He looked her up and down, making no effort to hide it. His eyes were small and too far apart. Spook might have said it gave him a sloth-like appearance, but that would be unkind to sloths. His pallid skin looked cold and damp, as if he'd been lying on a mortician's slab for most of the day. His hair was slicked back with an excessive amount of gel, giving it an artificial sheen.

"Can I buy you a drink?" he asked.

"No. I'm good," Spook replied, her tone polite but firm. "I'm going after this one."

The man edged closer still, bringing with him an unpleasant scent of cheap cologne and stale cigarettes.

"Oh, come on. Just one drink. I'm a nice guy." He lingered, his smile fixed and unconvincing, as if painted on.

Spook's gaze dropped briefly to her half-empty glass of whisky before she noticed his bony, pale hand snaking under the counter towards her thigh. Her instincts now on full alert, she lashed out, her fingers clamping down hard around his wrist. She squeezed, her grip iron-tight, her eyes locking onto his with a fierceness that would have been absent twelve months earlier.

"Don't even fucking think about it," she whispered. "That will not end well for you."

For a tense moment they glared at each other, Spook's expression unyielding, the man's smile finally crumbling under the weight of her stare. The background noise of the bar faded into a distant hum as the standoff drew out until, finally, he relented.

"Alright, fine," he muttered, the words barely a grumble as he pulled his wrist free and retreated to the safety of the shadows at the far end of the bar.

Prick.

Spook released a slow breath. She was now wondering what Acid had found so appealing about this place. But they were very different people and it was dawning on her that she hadn't ever really known Acid at all. Perhaps it was time for her to accept that and move on, like Nate wanted.

Finishing her drink, she paid the bartender and slipped off the stool. The night air was refreshing as she emerged onto the street, a welcome relief from the cloying atmosphere inside the bar. She pulled out her phone. A missed call from Lena. There must have been no reception in the basement.

"Shit. What is it now?"

She set off walking towards Fulham Road, calling Lena back on the way, but the phone rang for a while and then went to voicemail.

Fair enough. It was almost 3.30 a.m., and Lena had been working hard all week. She was likely asleep already. Spook was about to pocket the phone when it buzzed, notifying her of a recent voicemail. She called it up and stopped as she heard Lena's voice.

"Hey, Spook. It's me. Lena. Hope you're okay. I wanted to let you know that I think I've got a lead… regarding you-know-who! I'm going to try and confirm it for definite but I'm pretty confident we might have a confirmed location. Give me a call back if it's not too late. Otherwise I'll see you tomorrow. Okay… umm… bye then. Bye."

Spook smiled to herself as she reached the main street and headed for a taxi rank a little further down towards

Sloane Avenue. Lena's awkward phone manner aside, a lead was a good thing. As she jumped in a cab, she could already feel her eyelids growing heavy, her exhaustion, along with the whisky, battling a fresh wave of anticipation. Lena had done well, but it could wait another day. If this lead panned out, Spook would need to be well-rested and prepared for what came next. And maybe, just maybe, she would finally get the answers she needed regarding Acid Vanilla.

Chapter Seven

In LA the night was young, and the streets buzzed with the city's usual blend of excitement and menace. On Silver Lake Boulevard, a black Cadillac CT5 weaved through the traffic with Acid Vanilla behind the wheel, driving with the ease of someone who'd done this a thousand times. Beside her, Grimaldi was hunched over, his broad frame barely contained by the passenger seat. His thick fingers swiped carelessly through his phone, a smirk playing on his lips as he absorbed the latest gossip columns featuring their mark, Joey Peterson – a B-list actor with a penchant for making headlines for all the wrong reasons.

"Listen to this one," Grimaldi chuckled, his voice rough like gravel. "Last month he supposedly cornered one of his co-stars in her trailer whilst he was only wearing a towel. And, what do you know, he 'accidentally' let that same towel drop, revealing his semi-engorged penis. Those are the exact words they used in the article – 'semi engorged'. Peterson said it was supposed to be a joke, to help lighten the mood before a sex scene. Yeah, I bet it did that."

Grimaldi let out a rasping laugh that quickly turned into a harsh phlegmy cough.

"Fucking kill me," Acid whispered to herself, unable to hide her distaste, both for the news and the man beside her. She could feel her irritation simmering just beneath the surface, her grip on the steering wheel tightening. Joey Peterson deserved what was coming to him, no doubt about it, but Grimaldi's incessant commentary was making her mission harder to bear.

"Can we just focus, please?" she snapped, her steely gaze fixed on the road ahead. "I don't need a full rundown of all the tabloid gossip columns. I get it. The man's a prick, he's pissed off a lot of important people. And in the next few hours he's going to pay. Enough said."

Grimaldi snorted, unfazed by Acid's brusqueness. "Lighten up, it's funny. These pampered celebs think they're untouchable. I'm glad we get to teach them a lesson."

"A lesson?" she replied. "Doesn't that imply that they learn from their mistakes and move on? Because if so, I think you might have woefully misunderstood the assignment."

Grimaldi turned to stare at her, shaking his sweaty head. "Don't get cute with me, darling. I know what I have to do. I'm the best at it." He returned to his phone, muttering something about the Me Too movement she didn't catch.

Small mercies.

She chewed on her lip as she drove, trying not to let her colleague's presence get to her. Grimaldi was a necessary evil tonight, a horrid, uncouth thug whose presence she tolerated only because the job required it. He'd tried to kill her once, a fact that always hung in the air between them despite it never being discussed. But that was the industry they were in. Enemies became allies in the blink of an eye. And vice versa.

She pulled up at traffic lights, her lip instinctively curling as she glanced over at the big man. He was an ugly bastard, inside and out. The slicked-back greasy ponytail only accentuated his receding hairline and rough, pockmarked features. His mangled ears told the story of a man who'd lived a life of brutal confrontations. Yet despite his monstrous exterior, there was a shrewd gleam in his eyes as he continued to swipe through his phone, hinting at the calculating mind beneath.

"Tell me you don't find it ironic," he said, oblivious to her irritation. "We might be the closest thing to karma that someone like Peterson is ever going to meet."

"You've been in sunny LA too long if you're starting to talk about karma," Acid told him. "You're turning into a hippie. I mean, fair enough, you've already got the unwashed part going on. Now you just need some tie-dye and crystals. I actually think it'd be a good look for you."

Grimaldi shot her a glare, but the light changed and she set off driving before he could respond. The less she engaged with his banter the better. She needed to clear her thoughts. Tonight's hit was for a new client who had the potential to become a regular, and they needed to carry out their work to the letter. Darius was counting on it.

Taking a left onto Sunset Boulevard, she headed towards Hollywood Hills, driving past Chateau Marmont and pulling down a side street just after the Laugh Factory. She drove to the end of the street, took another left onto North Fairfax, then pulled into an alley, bringing the car to a stop on the corner of Sunset. From here, they had a clear view of The Bella Boudoir Club opposite.

"There it is," Acid muttered to herself. "Looks like a fun place."

Grimaldi squinted through the windscreen at the large, brightly lit building. "Sure does," he replied, not picking up on her sarcasm. "I hear the bottle service alone costs more than most Angelenos earn in a week."

Acid ignored him, focusing instead on the side entrance of the club. They had it on good authority that Peterson would be inside. Their source had also informed them that he normally arrived at the club early and left before 10 p.m., especially mid-week. Peterson's coke dealer moonlighted as a busboy at the club, and the actor only visited to score and get his face seen among the Hollywood glitterati.

"Come on, Joey," Acid whispered. "Let's have you."

Ten minutes ticked by, then twenty. Acid shifted in her seat, trying to push down the chattering bat chorus in her mind as they waited in silence, watching for any sign of their mark. Tonight her chaotic bipolar personality felt more brittle and unstable than ever. The bats were in full flight and they wanted blood. She sucked in a deep breath as she glanced up and down the Strip. The shimmering allure of LA's nightlife did little to ease her unrest.

This was not what Acid had imagined herself doing when she joined Kancel Kulture. Darius had talked about a network of elite assassins, whose purpose would be to eradicate organised crime gangs, traffickers and corrupt politicians in all corners of the globe. It sounded exactly like what she'd been doing at Annihilation Pest Control, only for more money. But then Darius had seen a gap in the market and – attracted by the potential to expand his reach within the cutthroat underbelly of Hollywood – had moved the organisation en masse to Los Angeles. The movie industry would prove fertile ground for their less-than-legal services, he'd explained to the team.

And wouldn't you know it, there really was a hell of a lot of people in Hollywood requiring their services.

Darius' shift towards the entertainment capital wasn't just strategic, it was opportunistic. For him, Los Angeles was a goldmine for their kind of work, and he'd embraced the city's glamorous facade wholeheartedly. There were plenty of wealthy clients with dirty secrets and the money to keep them hidden.

But for Acid, the move was a slow, soul-crushing descent. Her work had once been varied and exciting, taking her to exotic and unknown places. Now, she was stuck in a world of health fads and plastic smiles, working predominantly for film producers and movie executives. Kancel Kulture had morphed into fixers for the rich and powerful, performing the dark tasks no one else would touch. The money was good, and business was booming, but day by day Acid felt her dark soul eroding under the relentless California sun.

And now here she was sitting beside this hulking mouth-breather as she waited for Peterson to show himself.

"Just another night in paradise, hey?" Grimaldi growled, tilting his head to one side as two young women in incredibly short skirts walked in front of the car.

Acid didn't speak. She just ground her teeth together.

"You've got to admit, LA's got its charms," he continued, as if reading her thoughts and choosing to piss all over them. "The weather, the parties... the women. What I wouldn't give..."

Acid gave him a sharp look. She could have responded with something pithy and sarcastic, but she didn't have the energy. The constant battle within her – the resentment, the disgust, the yearning for something real – left her drained.

"Keep your eyes on the job," she told him.

Just as Grimaldi opened his mouth to retort, Peterson made his appearance, emerging from the side entrance of the club. He was instantly swarmed by a flurry of young girls and the flashing cameras of eager paparazzi. He navigated the chaos with a sloppy grin, his movements slightly uncoordinated as he laughed off the attention and staggered towards a waiting Uber.

"There," Acid said, starting the engine and pulling the car slowly out of the alleyway. "That's our cue. Once we get him alone, he's ours."

Chapter Eight

Acid kept her eyes glued to the taillights of the Uber as it made its way along Sunset and took a right up Laurel Canyon. The weight of the night's work pressed down on her as she leaned on the gas, her eyes wide and alert, the muscles in her jaw and neck tense. The vibrant chaos of Sunset Boulevard quickly gave way to the secluded, winding roads leading to Mulholland Drive. LA was so much bigger than Acid often realised. Below them the neon city stretched out to the horizon like a vast circuit board of light and colour. It was kind of beautiful. From a distance.

As they drove into the darker, more foreboding curves of the hills, Peterson's Uber was occasionally obscured by the lush foliage that thrived in this part of the city. Acid kept a good pace, matching the car in front turn for turn.

"You need to keep your distance," Grimaldi grunted. "We don't want to spook him."

"Peterson's clearly out of it," she replied. "He won't notice us following him, and even if he does he'll think we're paparazzi. The Uber driver doesn't care either way. He'll get his fare and a good story to tell his buddies."

But Acid had other concerns. Mulholland Drive was notorious not only for its sweeping views of the city, but also for its fortified private estates that stood like fortresses against unwelcome intrusion. The plan was to jump Peterson outside his residence, create the narrative of a mugging gone wrong, or – worst-case scenario – a hit and run. But this relied on getting Peterson alone, out in the open. It was going to be tight.

As the road climbed, the houses became fewer and further apart, each with high gates and security cameras. Acid's mind raced through possible scenarios, each more complex and risky than the initial set-up. She imagined Peterson's inebriated stumble, the sudden flash of head-lights, the brutal efficiency required to make it look like a terrible accident.

After another ten minutes, the Uber at last slowed to a stop outside a large, walled property at the top of the hill. Acid pulled up twenty feet away on the lip of a bend, watching as a tall metal gate slid open and the Uber drove into the compound.

"Shit," she muttered, easing down on the accelerator to coast past the compound's entrance without drawing atten-tion. She parked a safe distance away and killed the engine.

"What's the plan now?" Grimaldi asked with a chuckle, enjoying this new turn of events. "Something tells me it's going to get messy."

"It'll be fine," Acid snapped. "Nothing I can't handle."

"Oh, sure. I forgot – you're the best."

Acid bit her lip, choosing to ignore the comment. She peered out the window, scoping out Peterson's property and thinking. Grimaldi continued to mutter negativity beside her but she wasn't listening. Over to the west was 10050 Cielo Drive where, in the sixties, Hollywood's glamorous facade had crumbled into the dust of darker realities when three members of the Manson Family committed the Tate murders. A home invasion, a terrible slaying; and whilst Acid didn't equate what she did with how Manson's disciples conducted themselves, they proved it could be done. Only her way would be cleaner, and more professional. She wouldn't get caught.

"Stay here," she told Grimaldi. "Keep a careful watch. If he bolts, he's yours. Same plan as before."

"No problem." He grinned, his eyes lighting up in anticipation. "I'll destroy the pretty boy."

But Acid knew better. The mark was now holed up for the night. This job required a stealthier touch, courtesy of her.

"Don't get too excited," she told Grimaldi. "He won't run. He won't get the chance."

She leaned over and grabbed a backpack from out of the rear footwell before exiting the car. In just a pair of black leggings and a long-sleeve top, she felt the night air up here on the hill cool as it carried the faint sounds of distant traffic and rustle of wind through the trees. She hurried down the side of the compound wall, eyes alert for security cameras and an entry point.

Finding a section shadowed by the thick drooping branches of an old eucalyptus, she used the tree as leverage, scaling the wall and lowering herself into the lush garden on the other side. Before her, Peterson's white-rendered property shone in the moonlight. It was a nice enough place and probably cost well over ten million, but it wasn't to Acid's taste. It was too big, too modern. And there was no pool, from the looks of it. What sort of psychopath owned a huge property like this in LA and didn't have a pool? Along with all the sick and sordid details Grimaldi had been reading out for the last hour, it only made Acid's dislike for Peterson grow. But that was a good thing. She'd need to hang onto these feelings for what came next.

Sticking to the shadows, she moved around to the rear of the property. Still no pool, but there was a large patio area complete with expensive-looking furniture and a purpose-built bar made to look like a Hawaiian beach hut. The structure, with its thatched roof and garish neon 'Joey's Bar' sign, was tacky as hell but also the perfect height to allow Acid to reach the wide balcony spanning the back of the building. A set of sliding doors halfway along on the top level were sitting slightly ajar.

Perfect.

A rich person's confidence in their security system's ability to keep out unwanted guests never failed to amuse her.

She hesitated for another few seconds. There were two cameras back here, but both were trained on the wall surrounding the property rather than the area close to the building. After a swift assessment of their angles and scope, she was confident she could reach the balcony without being picked up.

Wasting no time she climbed up onto the beach hut's roof and jumped for the edge of the balcony, getting two hands on the tiled flooring and hoisting herself up. She crept along the side of the building then slipped inside, finding herself in a huge kitchen-diner with white walls and a large mahogany table. Music floated out from another room – the kind of slow jazz that people who thought they were cool pretended to like.

Acid moved silently through the kitchen and emerged onto a mezzanine landing. A mottled glass screen ran along its edge, overlooking a large room housing an eclectic array of vintage and modern furniture. The floor was polished cream marble, and the double-height ceiling created an airy but somewhat disorienting feel. It looked like the sort of room no one ever went into. Just something to show off to visitors.

As she made her way along the landing, she found the layout became even more odd. Peterson's mansion seemed to be one of those weird upside-down properties with the bedrooms on the ground floor and the living areas up top. This inversion felt like a metaphor for her own twisted life, a constant battle against the expected order.

The far end of the mezzanine landing opened out into another vast lounge area, this one complete with a cinema-size television on one wall and an impressive sound system. The fact that it was being used to play discordant oboe music was another nail in Peterson's coffin.

And there was the man himself, slouched on an immense leather couch in the middle of the room. Acid hesitated, observing him for a moment. His eyes were closed and his breathing was slow and heavy, indicative of a deep, alcohol-induced slumber.

She slipped the pack off her back and retrieved a small leather pouch from within, unzipping it to reveal a syringe filled with a clear liquid. Heroin. Strong enough to stop a horse. The narrative of an accidental overdose had become one of her go-to methods since moving to LA. It was the perfect ending for these tortured, troublesome industry folk whom people wanted offed for whatever reason.

She removed the syringe, resting her thumb on the plunger as she approached the couch. Peterson was a good-looking man – he had to be, he was a terrible actor – yet up close his appearance was almost too perfect. His nose, in particular, looked to be the result of several visits to one of Hollywood's top surgeons rather than genetics. The guy was also Hollywood-ripped, with muscle packed on muscle. Judging by the bulging vein snaking down his bicep, he was most likely juiced up on steroids. Acid smiled. It seemed almost too easy.

As she was just about to inject him, Peterson shifted, his head lolling to one side. Acid froze. Suddenly his eyes snapped open, wide and panicked. With a primal yell he jumped up and lunged at her, his movements wild and erratic, fuelled by whatever drugs were already coursing through his veins. The unexpected aggression caught Acid off guard. She stumbled backwards, the syringe slipping from her grasp and skittering across the floor.

"Get out of my house!" Peterson screamed, swinging his fist at her head.

Acid dodged the blow and ducked under a second one, then shoved him away to put distance between them. Assessing the actor's frenzied state, she surmised he was fuelled by more than just alcohol or cocaine. Angel dust, PCP, it had to be. It made him unpredictable and danger-ous. He lunged at her again, fists thrashing through the air. With the bats screeching in her head, Acid side-stepped the attack and countered with a jab to his kidneys. But it hardly seemed to register. He grabbed her by the shoulders, trying to push her towards the glass-panelled balcony.

Acid twisted out of his grasp, using his momentum against him and delivering a sharp kick to the back of his knee. He stumbled, momentarily thrown off balance, but recovered with a feral snarl.

"Who are you?" he spat. "What do you want?"

"Come on now, Joey. Do you really think I'm going to tell you my name? Let's just say I'm a bad dream. I'm karma."

Jesus.

She winced internally at her lame comeback. And using Grimaldi's words, too. It was a new low for her. She hoped she'd have time to rectify the situation as Peterson, drugged and desperate, scrambled to his feet.

"I'll fucking kill you," he yelled, swinging at her with a wild, uncoordinated ferocity.

Acid tensed, her training taking over. With a burst of manic energy she charged at Peterson, slamming her elbow into his chest with all the force she could muster. He cried out and staggered back, stumbling awkwardly. Seeing her chance, Acid surged forward, driving her shoulder into Peterson's midsection and sending him crashing into the glass panel. The glass shattered, shards flying around him like a deadly halo. With a cry he disappeared over the edge and fell into the room below.

She halted as a sickening crack echoed up the high walls of the atrium. Moving to the edge, she peered through the broken panel, her chest rising and falling erratically. Peterson lay motionless below, his head twisted at an unnatural angle. Blood was already pooling around the back of his skull, which had been smashed open on the unforgiving marble floor.

"Oops."

This wasn't how it was supposed to go, but the deed was done. The mark was dead. No more pestering young starlets, no more trying to blackmail their client. Joey Peterson was high, and in his impaired state he'd slipped and fallen to his death. For someone like Peterson it was a believable enough narrative. Now it was the job of the LAPD to sign it off as a tragic accident and Peterson's press officer to paper over the cracks as best they could.

But Acid was done here. There was a bottle of rum back at her apartment that was practically begging to be drunk. Rolling her shoulders back, she retraced her steps through the house. Time to clock off.

Chapter Nine

Grimaldi was still droning on about how they'd messed up and how Darius would be angry with them as Acid pulled the car into the underground parking lot concealed beneath the large building Kancel Kulture now called home. Tucked away on the edge of Echo Park, near the Arts District, the building had a long history. Originally a meat packing plant, it had morphed into a nightclub in the early nineties and now served as the covert headquarters for Darius' organisation. From the outside, it looked like nothing special – a deliberate move to keep things discreet. Inside, though, it was a fortress, fitted with a high-tech security system that had cost more than most people saw in a lifetime.

Stig Saga had masterminded the build, using a crew of shady contractors to install everything, most of whom were now buried under the concrete floor of the parking lot. They should have known they wouldn't be allowed to live after learning what went on inside, but for these small-time criminals, the lure of money outweighed the risk to their lives.

The parking lot was as fortified as the rest of the building: steel doors, LED lights, and security cameras wherever you looked that tracked the car as they drove in. Acid parked in her usual spot, killed the engine, and exchanged a glance with Grimaldi. She'd been trying to ignore his grumblings on the drive back here but she supposed he had a point.

"Don't worry," she told him. "Just another day at the office. I'll smooth it over with Darius."

Grimaldi grunted. "You think because you're his little sister he's going to put up with your shit always?"

Acid held his gaze. "No. I think he's going to accept that things took a turn and we dealt with them the only way we could. The mark is dead. No one saw us. All's well."

She climbed out of the car and slammed the door, then headed for the elevator, a shiny steel box embedded in a wall of rough concrete. Without a word, she and Grimaldi stepped inside and rode up to the main complex. The building comprised four floors, each one decked out in state-of-the-art equipment, everything a covert assassin network could need. The first floor housed interrogation rooms and holding cells, where they could extract information from targets and keep them confined until their fate was decided. The second and third floors were dedicated to a huge gym and training area, stocked with the latest combat equipment and tactical technology. Tonight, however, their destination was the top floor, which featured a collection of high-tech meeting rooms for planning and strategy sessions, as well as Darius' office.

Acid and Grimaldi stepped out of the elevator into a long corridor lined with large canvases covered in violent splatters of paint. Many of the pieces looked more like parts of a crime scene than modern art. But perhaps there was a point being made, Acid considered. Her darling brother did like making bold statements. They moved down the dim corridor, the muted lighting enhancing the gallery-like atmosphere as they approached the epicentre of Kancel Kulture's power.

At the end of the corridor stood Darius' office, the door heavy and imposing, designed to make another statement. Here be the king. Enter at your peril.

Acid knocked and waited. "Let me do the talking," she told Grimaldi.

"Be my guest."

Seconds ticked by. No one came. Acid was about to knock again when Darius' voice boomed from the other side. "Enter."

She pushed the door and walked into the room with Grimaldi a step behind her. Darius' set-up was less an office and more a gentleman's club. Everything on view was designed to intimidate and impress, from the lavish fur rugs to the antique weapons displayed in cases around the room. The centrepiece was Darius' desk, a massive slab of polished obsidian, paired with a high-backed chair that more resembled a throne than a piece of office furniture.

Darius was sitting with his feet up on the desk in a well-practised pose of hip nonchalance. Beside him stood Stig Saga, his right-hand man. With his stark white hair and pale, almost translucent skin, Saga looked like he'd just stepped off a vampire movie set. His tall, wiry frame was clad in a sharply tailored suit that did nothing to soften his severe appearance.

"Well...?" Darius asked, raising his meticulously plucked eyebrows. "Is he dead?"

Acid stood firm in front of the massive desk, her posture

rigid as she prepared to deliver her report. "Yes. I took him out. However… it didn't go quite as planned."

Darius sighed dramatically and swung his feet off the desk. "What happened?" he asked, his whimsical air replaced by an intense, unblinking gaze. "Am I going to get it in the neck from the client? Because this was a new studio, Alice! We needed to impress them—"

"Hey! It's all good," she interrupted, holding her hands up. "They'll be happy with the work. I just had to ad-lib a little, that's all." Taking a deep breath, she recounted the details, her focus shifting between her brother and his zombie henchman.

When she finished, Darius leaned forward, steepling his fingers under his chin as he processed her words. A moment of heavy silence followed, then he frowned, the lines on his forehead struggling against whatever toxins he'd injected to smooth them out.

"It was supposed to be an overdose," he said, his voice low and controlled. "That's what the client wanted. Clean. Simple. A tragic end to a shining talent. But what you've just described to me sounds like a goddamn shitshow." His London accent had slipped into a Californian drawl. It was happening more frequently the longer they were in LA, although Acid had first noticed it on the plane over here.

"The guy was high on PCP. Things escalated," she said. "He tripped. He fell. He's dead. Same outcome for the client. You know the coroner won't report what happened the way it actually did. It'll be covered up by fixers and the best PR people Hollywood can buy."

Darius' eyes narrowed, his dissatisfaction apparent as he exchanged a glance with Saga.

"The client wanted it to play out a certain way," Saga added. "This isn't what we agreed on."

"No. But it's what they're getting," Acid shot back, unable to control her annoyance. What did they think she was, some wet-behind-the-ears rookie? She'd been doing this job her entire adult life. Shit happened. "It wasn't a textbook situation. He fought back. I adapted."

"You adapted?" Saga said, with a sly smile. "You threw him off a balcony. That's a bit more than adapting, don't you think?"

She glared at him. "I thought on my feet. I got the job done. I always get the job done."

Darius rubbed his temples and groaned. It was all very melodramatic, in Acid's opinion. "Alice... Alice... It's not just about doing the job. It's about perception. The client wanted it done their way. Where were you, Grimaldi?"

"She wanted me to wait outside," he offered, stepping forward. "It made sense, I suppose. Back when we thought it was going to be a stealth job."

Acid turned and gave him a hard stare.

Thanks for the backup, partner!

She was getting sick of being made to feel like an amateur or a problem that needed dealing with. This wasn't what she'd signed up for. This wasn't why she was here. She continued to stare down Saga and Darius, her gaze flicking from one to the other. She was exhausted and needed a drink but she was damned if she was going to be cowed.

Darius leaned back in his chair, his expression shifting from frustration to a reluctant acknowledgement. "Fine. It's done," he conceded after a tense pause. "But next time do better, Sis, yeah? We're playing in a different league here in Hollywood. We have to impress. Every time."

"Sure, we wouldn't want to upset those movie industry wankers," she muttered.

"What was that?" Saga asked, raising his head.

"Nothing. I'm just tired. Been a long day." She gave him her best Hollywood smile.

"All right. Go," Darius said, gesturing for them to leave. "I'll speak to you both soon."

Acid didn't need to be told twice. She nodded and turned to leave, catching the grim look on Saga's face and the flicker of suspicion in his eyes.

Yeah, yeah. Whatever, Casper.

He could go to hell, along with the rest of them. Acid was pleased with her work tonight. She might not be the trim, clinical assassin she once was, but even with all her personality disorders she could still cut it with the best of them. Darius needed her. He should realise that. She was still one of the deadliest assassins in the business, and she always found a way through. It was what she did. It was who she was. And no amount of Hollywood sheen would change that.

Chapter Ten

Darius remained at his desk as the office door clicked shut behind Acid and Grimaldi. He didn't speak for some time. Lately, he'd been experimenting with silences, seeing how long he could stretch them out, how uncomfortable he could make his subordinates or whoever else had the displeasure of his presence. But this wasn't that. This time, he was silent because he was thinking. Hard.

Minutes ticked by, prompting Saga to move away and stand by the window, his lean silhouette outlined against the backdrop of downtown Los Angeles.

A cyclone of troubling thoughts swirled in Darius' mind. Had he made the right decision to move to Hollywood? Did he really have the abilities and personality to lead his band of elite killers to the big leagues?

And, more pressingly, could he trust Acid Vanilla?

The question wasn't new, but he was yet to come up with a definitive answer. He glanced at Saga, trying to read the Swede's stoic expression. Both men knew the stakes; verbalising it seemed redundant, yet Darius felt the need to gauge Saga's insight. Trust was currency in this game, and right now Acid's stock was volatile.

Without breaking the silence, Darius rose and walked to the window, standing side by side with Saga as he stared out at the night-time city. His reflection in the glass stared back at him, a man on the brink of attaining everything he wanted – if only he could trust the people around him. The interrogations and polygraph tests told him what he needed to know, but he still wasn't satisfied. Maybe he should push Acid further, test her loyalty in ways that would reveal her true allegiance. It was a risk, but one worth taking before they got too deep here in Hollywood. He turned to Saga, who watched him with his usual calculating calm.

"She's a loose cannon," Saga said. "I told you this from the start, Darius."

"Yes, I know," he snapped. "But I still want her to be part of this. She was once brilliant. She still can be. We need her."

Saga's expression didn't falter. "And what about all her... issues?"

Darius sighed and returned to his throne. Sliding open the shallow drawer under his desk, he pulled out an old, dog-eared photograph. It was a picture of Oscar Duke, his father, a man he barely remembered. In the shot, he was sitting on a patch of grass with a cigarette in his hand and a wicked grin on his face. He looked young, full of life. Yet he'd been nothing but a shadow for most of Darius' life, dead before his son's tenth birthday. The young Darius had grown up on stories filled with holes, on tales punctuated by worried expressions from the adults telling them.

The fact that his half-sister, Alice Vandella, had murdered his father – *their* father – was a detail that was never far from his mind. It was a betrayal and a salvation all at once. She'd made him who he was.

And now he had the world at his feet. Kancel Kulture wasn't just a business to Darius, it was a way to rewrite his history, to achieve the infamy his father never could. Maybe some would say he had daddy issues, but for him this was about proving something – not just to the shadowy figures of the underworld, or his father's memory, but to himself. In just two short years he'd built his organisation into something monumental, something undeniable. Power was not just his ambition; it was his validation.

And he'd get there.

He was certain of it.

He leaned back in his chair, unsure what to do with his hands suddenly. He placed them palms down on the desk as Saga turned from the window.

"Any updates on the Stardust job?" Saga asked.

Darius sniffed. "Not yet. I'm working on it."

Stardust was one of the big new studios in town. Ambitious and powerful, they understood what it took to run a business in this seedy world of blackmail and backbiting. Hence, they were on the cards to become Kancel Kulture's hot new client – just as soon as Darius could prove their worth.

"They *do* want to work with us?"

"Of course they do," Darius replied, not quite sure if he was even convincing himself. "Why the hell wouldn't they?"

His words hung in the air as he locked eyes with Saga, but the unspoken doubts were stronger. If Stardust discovered that Kancel Kulture had a weak link – someone in their ranks who was unpredictable, who didn't always stick to the client's carefully constructed narrative – it could be a problem.

Darius rubbed at his chin. He knew Saga was contemplating the same dilemma, and the atmosphere felt tense, each man careful not to reveal too much. He shifted in his seat, the leather padding creaking slightly under his weight.

"It's going to be fine," he said. "We're close. Very close."

But again the unsaid was more powerful… *but we're not there yet.*

Working with Stardust was exactly what Kancel Kulture needed to secure their footing as the go-to firm for Hollywood's shadowy elite. Encrypted message forums on the dark web were all well and good if a client knew where to look, but most business in the murder-for-hire industry came from word-of-mouth endorsements and referrals. Impressing Stardust was imperative. Their representative had hinted to Darius that Kancel Kulture could become Stardust Studios' in-house crew for every little problem that needed ironing out. It would mean a lot of work and a hell of a lot of money coming their way.

"This job could change everything for us," Saga said, reading his thoughts. "It will position us at the very top of the food chain."

"Yes, I do know that, thank you."

"But we haven't secured the contract?"

"No. They want a demo of our capabilities before they sign off on the retainer. They need to know we can handle things professionally. That means this next job has to be flawless."

Saga gave a measured nod, his face giving away nothing yet revealing everything. "I see, and I say again – what about Acid? It's been a year, Darius. She's proven herself in every test we've given her so far, but you know my stance. It's not just about completing tasks. It's about where her true intentions lie."

Darius' expression hardened. "I haven't forgotten who she is, or where she came from. I'm keeping an eye on her. If I sense any hint of betrayal or hesitation I'll handle it. She's my responsibility. Now leave me. I need to think."

"Of course."

Saga straightened, his pale eyes never leaving Darius as he bowed his head. The message was clear: no compromises, no sentimentalities. As Saga headed for the door, Darius spun his chair around, looking out at the dark cityscape. As always, his mind was a jumble of dreams and concerns. Acid was his sister, the only family he had left. He liked her. He'd even admit to himself that he admired her. It was important for him that she be a part of this operation. But did he trust her? Could he ever? He wasn't sure.

He heard the door to his office creak open but noticed it didn't close again. Turning around in his chair, he saw Saga hesitating in the doorway, a pained look on his face.

"What is it?" Darius asked.

Saga looked down and to the side, doing his usual tortured-intellectual routine.

"Just spit it out, will you?" Darius ordered.

Clearing his throat, Saga stepped forward, letting the door swing shut. "I can't shake my concerns about Acid," he said. "She's unruly... untamed. Even if her loyalty to you is without question – is she someone we can rely on once we reach the next level?"

"I told you I'd keep an eye on her," Darius yelled, leaning forward. It was late and he didn't need Saga holding a mirror up to his thoughts. "I brought her in, she's my problem to worry about."

"And if she becomes a problem you can't solve?" Saga pressed.

Darius lifted his chin, meeting the question with cold

resolve. "Then I'll take the necessary action," he replied. "No one here is indispensable, my friend. Not even family. If she's going to jeopardise our shot at the big time, then I'll do what needs to be done. Sister or not."

Saga smiled, a rare event. "Excellent," he said. "I was hoping you'd say that."

Chapter Eleven

After leaving Kancel Kulture's headquarters, Acid hailed a cab and had the driver drop her off at the corner of Sunset and Larabee. It was late, well past 11 p.m. But on the Strip, the evening was just getting started. The pulsing heart of Sunset Boulevard was alive and kicking, the streets filled with people, the sound of music, and that intoxicating blend of freedom and danger.

Acid should have headed straight to her apartment – it had been a long day and home was just a ten-minute walk away – but as she paid the driver and climbed out of the car, she felt a sudden restlessness. Her mind was racing and she could almost feel the needle teeth of a thousand invisible bats nibbling at her psyche. She preferred being alone. But not that alone. Not tonight. The bottle of rum would have to wait.

Instead of heading down Larabee toward Santa Monica Boulevard, she turned left, letting the Strip draw her in. Most of the other operatives working for Kancel Kulture lived near the organisation's headquarters in Echo Park, but

Acid had insisted she set up home near Sunset Boulevard. This was her concession for moving to LA – being close to the places that still pulsed with the music she loved, even if they were just shadows of the past.

Tonight, the area buzzed with the energy of a city that never really sleeps. Neon signs painted the sidewalks in vibrant hues, each bar and club she walked past vying for her patronage. Excited tourists snapped photos as they queued, mingling with locals who navigated the bustle with practised indifference. Heavy rock music throbbed from every corner, the drums and bass driving the rhythm of the night.

This was Acid's spiritual home. The bars and music venues of this legendary street weren't just landmarks to her; they were refuges, places where she could connect with the music that had shaped her past and try to forget about her future.

In front of her stood the legendary Whisky a Go Go. Further along was The Roxy, and down on Santa Monica Boulevard stood The Troubadour, another staple of the LA music scene. Each venue was a landmark in its own right, dripping with myths and legends concerning the biggest rock bands of the last fifty years.

Acid had frequented all these spots over the last three months, but tonight, like most nights, it was the Rainbow Bar and Grill that called to her. Back in the seventies and eighties, the Rainbow was *the* hangout for local and touring bands alike. With its dark ambience, red leather booths and walls covered with rock memorabilia, it was where Acid felt the most at home. It had become her anchor in the chaos of Los Angeles. As she approached, she noticed the usual cluster of tourists around the bronze statue of Lemmy from Motörhead outside, camera phones flashing as they captured their moment with the rock legend's likeness.

Even mid-week, there was a queue outside. But Mike, the burly doorman, spotted Acid's familiar silhouette against the neon backdrop and waved her inside. He'd been doing that ever since her second visit. But it wasn't just her shaggy dark hair and leather jacket that did it. Like knew like, and Mike had seen it in her eyes, in the way she carried herself. Alice Vandella was a rocker and a rebel through and through. Acid Vanilla was just the physical embodiment of that spirit.

"Nice to see you again, Sid," he told her, in a gruff Californian drawl. "You play nice now."

"Pfft. Always," she replied, giving him a wink.

Inside, the Rainbow was alive with energy, the air thick with the scent of spilt beer and fried food mingling with a faint hint of leather and sweat. The familiar din of the bar enveloped her as she stepped through the door. At this hour the Rainbow was packed with its usual eclectic mix of rock enthusiasts, industry veterans and curious tourists, each drawn here by the allure of a place that had hosted generations of musicians and fans alike.

Led Zeppelin's *Kashmir* boomed from the speakers, underscored by the clink of glasses and raucous laughter. Every inch of wall space was taken up by autographed guitars, gold records, and photos of musicians who had made the Rainbow a part of their legend, showcasing decades of rock 'n' roll debauchery and glory. In the far corner, a group of Japanese tourists were sitting in Slash's booth. To Acid's right was the stairwell leading up to the lair of The Hollywood Vampires, the men's drinking club formed in the seventies by Alice Cooper, Ringo Starr and Keith Moon. Every corner of the bar told a story of wild nights and legends, each booth and stool a relic of the Rainbow's glorious past.

Acid made her way to the bar and ordered a double Jack Daniels from the tattooed bartender. She sipped her drink, allowing the music and chatter to blur into the background. In the Rainbow, she could almost escape her tumultuous thoughts. But as the initial warmth from the drink spread through her, a familiar pang of agitation returned.

Acid's inner world had always been a storm of difficult emotions. She longed for those moments when all she felt was numb, but tonight she had anger, sadness, confusion – all the usual feelings. Often her moods culminated in a prickly chaotic 'oneness' that drove her forwards, but for the last few months it had been different for some reason. She was troubled, rudderless. She needed a…

No! Fuck that!

She was fine alone. She was doing what she needed to do.

Yet even here, in the home of rock 'n' roll, where legends like Ozzy, Guns N' Roses, and Motley Crüe – plus hundreds of other guys with better hair and make-up than her – had hung out, she felt abnormal and out of place. Her mental gears felt like they were grinding, slipping, threatening to come undone.

But what was new?

Even though Acid found some solace here at the Rainbow, the bar wasn't the place it once was. It was like that first disillusioning visit to CBGB's years ago, in her early days with Annihilation Pest Control. The reality never quite lived up to the legend. The idea of something was always better than the reality. It was what she'd always told Spook whenever she tried to convince Acid she was a better person than she gave herself credit for. Spook had believed in her. Maybe that was what she was missing.

But there was more, she knew.

Much more.

She downed her drink and signalled the bartender for another. As he free-poured two fingers of golden liquid, her thoughts drifted back to the early days with Caesar and the rest of her old crew. Back then she'd been full of piss and vinegar, fuelled by ambition and the sheer thrill of her new career. She loved her life then. No two days were the same. Annihilation Pest Control was a band of renegades – untouchable, fierce, different to anything she'd ever experienced before. With Caesar mentoring her, the young Acid Vanilla felt as if she'd finally found somewhere she belonged. Not like in Kancel Kulture. Not like now. She recalled the pulse of excitement that used to race through her youthful veins, the feeling of invincibility and camaraderie. She'd had the world at her feet.

Maybe that was what she really missed – youth. The thrill of not knowing how the future would turn out but relishing the uncertainty.

Now Caesar, Spitfire and all the others were gone. Dead by her own hands. She knew it had to be that way, but it didn't make it any easier. Then there was The Dullahan's death, which still plagued her in quieter moments. But as always, she pushed that thought down and distracted herself with another gulp of Jack Daniels. She couldn't deal with that yet. Maybe ever.

A rush of cool air wrapped around her, and she turned to see a guy walk in, looking every bit a Hollywood caricature of a rock star. His long blond hair fell in loose waves around the shoulders of a cut-off denim jacket worn over a faded Sabbath shirt.

"Shit."

Acid averted her eyes but he'd already caught her looking. He sauntered over to the bar with the swagger of someone who believed his own press. She watched him from the corner of her eye as she took a slow sip from her glass. He was very good-looking, with just-rough-enough features and the kind of scruffy allure she liked. Possibly he was in a band, but she'd never seen him before. He carried on staring at her in a way that could spell trouble or an interesting night, depending on the point of view.

"You drinking alone?" he asked.

Acid clicked her teeth and didn't look at him. "Looks that way."

"I haven't seen you around here before." His voice was a husky drawl. She suspected it was probably put-on, but it fitted his rugged appearance.

She glanced at him, her eyes cool, her voice even cooler. "Normally at this time of night I've taken on my bat form."

He laughed. "Cool. Me too. Bloodsuckers, huh?"

"Oh yeah, I find it intensely more enjoyable than waiting around to be picked up by a bunch of wannabe rock stars."

The guy's smirk faltered for a second, his eyes narrowing slightly as he processed her words. Or was he noticing her eyes? That would be next, she assumed; it usually came up early. But the guy just kept staring at her with that smirk twitching on his lips. It was clear he was used to being noticed, his confidence bordering on arrogance.

Bor-ing.

She turned back to her drink but could feel his eyes on her still.

"Can I buy you a drink?" he asked, sliding onto the stool next to hers.

Acid raised her glass. "Got one, thanks."

"You mind if I sit here?"

She shrugged. "Knock yourself out."

He ordered a drink, a double Jack the same as her, and had a brief chat with the barman. They seemed to know one another, sharing a joke and a laugh, but Acid felt as if it was all for her benefit.

"I'm not a wannabe, by the way," the guy said, proving her point. "I'm in a band called Riot Canyon. I play lead guitar. We're gonna be huge."

He carried on, giving her the full lowdown, trying to impress her with tales of near success and support slots with bands she'd actually heard of. He seemed like a decent enough guy, but Acid wasn't really listening.

"So, you're pretty much famous then?" she quipped after his third anecdote, hoping it might shut him up.

"I'm getting there," he shot back with a cocky grin. "You might see me on a billboard one day."

Acid didn't bother to hide her eye-roll, turning her attention back to her drink. "Cool. Right next to the ads for used cars and cheap motels?"

He laughed, more forced than amused. "You're a tough girl to impress."

"What can I say? High standards."

"Ever thought of lowering them? Might be more fun."

"Fun…?" she repeated, with a frown. "Hmm. Remind me again what that is. I forget."

The guy tossed his hair over his shoulders. "Are you always this direct?"

"Only when I'm bored."

"Wow. Tough crowd."

They sipped at their drinks. Acid waited. She could sense the guy was lining up his shot for another try. They'd made eye contact a few times now, and she surmised it would be a comment on her pupils being different colours. Failing that, her British accent. In her line of work it paid to read people, to know what they were going to do before they did it.

"So you're from England?" he asked, eliciting a sly smile from Acid. "That's awesome. You know we played there last year on a mini-tour. London, Oxford and Brighton. It was only small venues but we had a real blast and—"

"Listen, pal. I'm sure you had a great time. But I'm not really that interested." She finished her drink in one gulp. "Do you want to take me home or not?"

The guy blinked, taken aback. He recovered quickly, though, his grin returning with a hint of surprise. "Well, that's direct."

She stared into his eyes. "Come on." She picked up his drink and finished it before slipping off her stool. "It's getting late. We might as well cut through the bullshit."

Grabbing his hand, she pulled him off his stool and headed for the door. She wondered if this had been subconsciously her mission all along tonight. If nothing else, it would distract her from her spiralling thoughts for a few hours.

Right now, in Acid's world, that was as good as it got.

Chapter Twelve

The famous pop song *Dancing Queen* by the Swedish group ABBA is usually thought of as a happy song, often played at weddings and birthday parties. Its lyrics describe a young woman enjoying herself, eager to lose herself dancing to the music. But the song can also be construed as having a much darker tone. Read a little deeper between the lines and you'll discover a hopeless tale of a young, lonely girl willing to throw herself into any old dance, with any old guy, just to feel… something. And of course, as with most pop songs, the act of dancing here is synonymous with sex. So, in essence, the song is actually about a seventeen-year-old girl, alone and desperate, trying to convince herself that everything is fine by dancing her troubles away.

And anyone will do.

Anyone…

Acid knew how that went. She might not be seventeen any longer but she was still searching for herself in all the wrong places.

She leaned against the cool leather of the car seat, her

gaze flitting between the passing streetlights and the animated face of the man sitting beside her as he continued with more anecdotes about his band's journey to the big time. She nodded along, her mind only half there, but like the Dancing Queen, she was glad of another soul to take her mind off her problems, regardless of who it was.

As they'd waited outside the Rainbow for an Uber to arrive, the guy had informed her, quite seriously, that his name was Rad Jaxon. "With an X," he'd said, as if this was the coolest thing ever. Even in her semi-inebriated, semi-aroused state, Acid thought this was beyond lame, but whatever floated the guy's boat. This was LA after all. Right now they were heading for Oakwood, a much further trek than her own apartment but she'd rather go to his place than hers. It wasn't the safest option, but for someone like Acid, safety wasn't the issue. Being able to make a quick getaway when the fun ended was.

Rad had been stroking his hand up Acid's inner thigh for most of the journey. Once he'd flung the door of his apartment open, Acid took the lead, pouncing on him with a passionate embrace. They stumbled inside clasped together in a frenzied rush of adrenaline and attraction. Rad's apartment was a typical bachelor pad, with takeout boxes, old magazines and guitar picks scattered around, all of which Acid noted in one snapshot glance, too caught up as she was in the whirlwind of Rad's eager hands and hungry lips. They kissed with a raw urgency, their breaths mingling as they tugged at each other's clothes.

Acid grabbed a handful of Rad's hair, twisting it around her fist as they fell onto one of the two old couches that made an L shape around a low coffee table in the centre of the room. The lust that had propelled them through the door intensified as they mauled each other. Spurred on by

Acid's rough play, Rad yanked at her hair, forcing her head to one side as his lips traced down her neck, biting at her skin. It felt good. It was passionate, animalistic, a dance of desire that found its rhythm on the wild side. And, more importantly, it was holding Acid's focus.

And anyone will do.

Anyone...

Her problems, her thoughts, even her sense of self, were gone for the time being. It was bliss.

Right up until Rad shoved his hand unceremoniously down the front of her leggings and yanked her head back viciously, constricting her breathing.

"Hey," she gasped, fighting to sit up. "Too much."

"You love it!" Rad groaned, unrelenting.

"No. I mean it." She elbowed him in the chest and he released her hair. "What the fuck? I don't know what you're used to, mate, but I'm not some sex doll you can toss around." She glared at him as he smirked back.

"All right! Chill." He adjusted himself and leaned forward, retreating his hand from her pants and scooping up a small vial from the coffee table. "You want some?" he asked, tipping a mound of white powder into the recess beneath his thumb and hoovering it up.

"No," Acid told him. "Not my thing."

"Come on, it's good stuff," he said, tipping out another mound. "It'll get you in the mood."

"I was in the mood!" she hit back. "I don't need that shit, sweetie. I'm chaotic enough, believe me."

"Just a taste," he insisted, shifting closer, shoving his dusted thumb to her nose.

"I said no!"

"Come on!" he yelled, his patience snapping in the face of her resistance. She shoved him away but his hand clamped around her wrist, not playful but authoritative. Acid didn't like that. At all. It wasn't fun. It wasn't sexy.

She twisted away but he yanked her back and slapped her across the face, leaving a cloud of cocaine lingering in the air.

"What the—? Are you serious?"

She touched her fingers to her cheek as she glared at him, the sudden shift from passion to aggression bringing with it a sharp rush of clarity.

Big mistake, Rad. Very big.

The slap had flipped a switch inside of her. Her training and her instincts, all the hard edges of her being, now came to the surface. She could handle rough, but not violent. Not without consent. And definitely not without repercussions.

Things were about to get extreme.

With an X.

She twisted her wrist, pulling free from his grasp and jumping to her feet. Rad got up too, trying to grab her again, but his judgement was clouded by alcohol and cocaine. And he'd never dealt with Acid Vanilla before. As he grabbed at her, she swerved out of the way and caught his wrist, twisting it back sharply and leveraging his body against itself until she could flip him over, sending him crashing onto the coffee table. It splintered under his weight, glass and white powder scattering everywhere.

"Dumb fucking bitch," he hissed, scrambling to his feet.

He lunged at her, driving her back and sending a lamp crashing to the floor. Acid hit the wall with a thud, her adrenaline soaring as the bats in her head screeched for blood. Bouncing off from the wall, she used the momentum to launch herself at Rad, wrong-stepping him at the last moment and landing a solid punch to his ribs. He cried out, swinging his fist in a wide arc, but his movements were sloppy and his coordination off. In contrast, Acid's response was smooth and instinctive, honed through years of necessity and survival. Stepping inside his arc, she slammed her fist into his solar plexus. As he doubled over, she delivered a heavy elbow to the back of his neck, sending him stumbling towards the small kitchen area off the main space.

The kitchen was cramped, filled with dirty dishes and half-empty takeout containers. Rad, scrambling for any advantage, pulled a knife from a drawer and waved it wildly.

That was his second big mistake.

"You want some of this, huh?" he snarled, eyes wide with a cocktail of fear and drug-induced frenzy as he sprang at her, blade first.

But Acid was already three steps ahead. Her body responded almost instinctively as she side-stepped his advance and her hand shot up to grab his wrist. Rad's own force betrayed him, propelling him forward too quickly to stop. As he stumbled, Acid twisted the knife around and drove it forward with a grunt.

"No... what?" A shocked gasp escaped Rad as he looked down at the blade protruding from his chest. "You've... You..."

His eyes, once fiery with anger and drugs, were now clouded with confusion and fear. He staggered into the living room, his steps faltering. His mouth opened and closed a few times in a silent plea for help. But there was no helping this guy. He was dead the moment he'd laid a hand on her. He made a guttural wheezing sound, then his eyes glassed over and he collapsed onto the floor.

Acid stood for a moment, her breath heavy as she watched the final signs of life leave Rad's body.

"Pissing bloody shit!" she hissed. "You complete idiot!"

She didn't need this. Not tonight. Pulling out her phone, her hands steady despite the chaos of the last few minutes, she scrolled through the only six numbers she ever called and hit Saga's. He answered after two rings.

"Ms Vanilla. What can I do for you this evening?"

She sucked in a deep breath. "We've got a problem. *I've* got a problem."

"Is that so? Do tell." He sounded amused, almost like he was expecting her call. She didn't like that.

She quickly informed him of the situation, giving only what he needed to know. "I had no choice," she added. "It was him or me."

There was a long silence, and then Saga's voice came through. "Fine. Where are you?"

Stepping over Rad's lifeless body, she found an unopened utility bill on a side table and read off the address.

"I'll send a clean-up crew out to take care of it," Saga replied, the repressed rage in his voice evident. "They'll be there within the hour, but you need to leave right now. The same way you came in. Don't let anyone see you."

Acid bit her tongue, resisting a pithy reply to this extraneous instruction. Who the hell did he think he was talking to?

"Don't tell Darius," she blurted before she could stop herself. "I'll do better. I swear. This won't happen again."

There was another heavy pause. "Make sure it doesn't, Acid. For your sake." He hung up.

Acid stared at the screen for a moment, then pocketed the phone and headed into the bathroom to clean herself up. Harsh LED spotlights flickered to life as she entered, their sudden brightness doing little to ease her mood. She leaned over the sink, feeling the cold porcelain through the material of her leggings. Twisting on the water, she let it run before splashing it over her face. The chill provided momentary relief as it washed over her skin, mingling with the sheen of sweat and spots of blood. Straightening, she watched in the mirror as the water dripped down her cheeks and over the hard lines of her jaw. Her pupils looked too big, like they'd seen too much. The bats were as loud as they'd ever been, sending her synapses firing, making her nerves feel raw and prickly.

She was on the edge. As close as she ever got. One step and she'd be freefalling. But would that really be a bad thing? It would mean she'd checked out completely, not responsible for her actions. It would be liberating. In a way.

Acid had always had a foil, someone to sound off to – to keep her in check when her volatile personality threatened to send her off course. Once it was her mother, then Caesar. Later it was The Dullahan, and then...

No...

She didn't need Spook. Those days were over.

She glared at her reflection. "You're just getting too old for this shit," she muttered to herself.

She knew it was a line. It sounded like one at least. A quote from some movie she'd seen in passing. But even if it was a cliché, it didn't mean it wasn't true. That was the thing about clichés, right?

"Enough playing, sweetie," she told herself firmly. "Time to get serious."

It was true, she had to get her head together. Although, the fact this realisation came via a discussion with her reflection wasn't the best of starts perhaps. But the next six months were important. She needed to focus on the job at hand. She turned from the sink. Maybe she should stop drinking, she thought, as she stepped over Rad's body and went to gather her things.

Maybe...

The idea made her laugh out loud. Laughing like it was the funniest thing in the world.

Not a bloody chance.

Maybe she'd stop one day. If she ever lived that long. But right now she needed a buffer to this sick, twisted world she inhabited. Without... anyone by her side, she needed that crutch more than ever.

She picked up her leather jacket and headed for the door. She didn't look back.

Chapter Thirteen

Spook had returned to headquarters around 5 a.m., collapsing into bed fully clothed and face down on her pillow. She slept for seven solid hours, waking up feeling relatively refreshed and eager to see what news Lena had for her. However, it was already lunchtime, and a note on Lena's door informed her that Lena had gone to pick up an online order of drone components from the local parcel shop.

Undeterred, Spook hit the ground running – quite literally – pulling on a pair of yoga pants and launching into a vigorous training session that left no room for worry. She began with callisthenics: push-ups, sit-ups and jumping jacks, and even forcing herself through three punishing sets of burpees. Spook used to hate exercise, but now she embraced the pain of exertion. The ache in her muscles and the sting of lactic acid made her feel strong and focused. She finally understood why Acid always got up early to exercise, even on days when she was hungover or feeling particularly despondent – which, for Acid was practically every other day.

Training regularly made Spook feel like she was taking control of both her mind and body. It made her feel as if she could take on the world.

Exercise completed, she transitioned to the heavy bag, channelling her deeper frustrations through fists, feet and elbows, slamming them into the thick leather with as much force as she could muster. The bag swayed and turned as she worked, the muted thuds punctuating the quiet of the large gym space.

The routine took her almost an hour in total, but it wasn't just a workout; it was a reaffirmation of Spook's dedication to her new role. She was sharpening her skills, honing herself for a world where vigilance meant the difference between life and death.

Now in the shower, she closed her eyes and let the water cascade over her head, washing away the ghosts of her worries along with the sweat and adrenaline. Once clean and dressed in black leggings and a matching hoodie, she left her room and headed downstairs to the main space to fix herself some coffee.

The kitchen area in the old warehouse was basic but functional. Essentials were crammed into one corner – a coffee machine, a toaster, a microwave, along with two plastic tubs containing loose crockery and silverware. A sink and a dishwasher stood to one side, along with a huge metal refrigerator whose low-level hum provided a constant backdrop. The set-up was enough for their current needs, though not what Spook envisioned long term.

It would do for now. Not forever.

The coffee machine had already been used that morning

and refilled with water. Spook scooped a few servings of ground coffee into the filter, and as the machine hissed and gurgled, she pulled a clean mug from out of the box and added a splash of milk. Once the coffee was ready, she poured herself a mugful and walked it over to the rectangular heavy oak table with seating for eight that served as both their dining and meeting space. She sat, allowing herself a moment to just breathe as the steam from the freshly brewed coffee awakened her senses.

As she sipped the hot drink, she considered Lena's message from last night.

I've got a lead... regarding you-know-who! I'm going to try and confirm it for definite but I'm pretty confident we might have a confirmed location.

Lena had found Acid. Or it sounded that way, at least.

So... what now?

The trepidation twisting in Spook's stomach hinted that perhaps a part of her hadn't wanted to find her old friend – and that opening this particular can of worms might be the wrong thing to do. And it definitely was trepidation rather than excitement or eagerness; there was no self-help-like reframing of this feeling. Yet, what was also true was that Spook strongly believed if she could meet with Acid – speak to her, make her see sense – there was a chance to alter the path they were all hurtling down. One way or another.

Her contemplation was broken by Nate's arrival. He was wearing a tight vest top and a pair of shorts. From the sweat dripping off his brow, Spook presumed he'd been out for a run.

"You're still alive then?" he said, moving past the table without really looking at her.

"Yeah. Sorry if I was a little off last night," she replied. "I just needed to clear my head. This is all new to me, you know."

"I know that, Spook." He moved over to one of the exercise mats and positioned himself for a calf stretch. "Mainly because you remind me at every opportunity."

Spook said nothing. She sipped at her coffee and watched as Nate stretched out his calves and quads before straightening up and flexing his shoulders. He looked good; a strict diet and training regime meant he had a hard muscular frame and minimal body fat. Spook caught herself watching him a little too closely and quickly reined it in. She didn't even like Nate that way. She never had done. Well... maybe she did at first. But not now. Not anymore.

"Have you spoken to Lena today?" she asked, aiming for nonchalance.

"I saw her first thing. She seemed excited about something. Probably those new drone parts." He rolled his head from one side to the other. "She should be back soon if you need to speak to her?" He phrased it like a question, narrowing his eyes at Spook as he walked over.

"Sure, right, it's just... she mentioned she had... Doesn't matter. I'll wait to see her first."

Nate raised his chin quizzically, but Spook turned away. There was no point discussing it further until she'd spoken to Lena and knew the situation. Out of the corner of her eye, she saw him shaking his head before pouring himself a mug of coffee.

"Any closer to coming up with a name?" she asked.

Nate cleared his throat. "I've had a few ideas," he said, bringing his coffee to the table and sitting opposite her. "What about Vector Consulting?"

Spook winced. "I'm not so sure about that one."

"Final Touch Remediation?"

"Bit of a mouthful. But I guess it's on the right lines."

"Crimson Asset Management? Meridian Logistics?"

"I don't think we're there yet," Spook said, imagining Acid's eye-roll. Imagining her sneer.

But Nate had been correct about one thing – they did need a name, and to establish their identity. The organisation was operational now and it didn't look good to be referring to themselves as simply 'the team'. Especially since there were only three of them. Nate had the right idea: the name had to sound like a legitimate business to any layperson but carry the right connotations for those in the know. The only problem was, Spook was still set on the name Avenging Angels.

She'd had the idea in the back of her mind for years, ever since she realised there was no going back to her old life and she had to make a go of it living in the shadows. Avenging Angels was her concession to this new world. She envisaged a group of vigilantes but with clear ethics and good admin. She still felt it was a good idea. She was a hired killer now and that was the way Nate wanted the business to go, but there was no reason why they couldn't combine the two fields somehow.

"Don't you think we need more operatives before we get too bogged down in a name?" she asked. She didn't look Nate in the eyes as she spoke, focusing instead on his large hands wrapped around the coffee mug. This was old ground they were covering and she suspected it might annoy him.

"I am aware of that," he snapped, right on cue. "But we need to find the right people. Those we can trust and who are ready and able to work as part of a team. I'm not sure we've met anyone who fits that bill. The industry has changed a lot in the last few years. Most of my old contacts have gone freelance."

"But we found each other," Spook added. "We found Lena. There'll be others out there who share our vision."

"And I suppose you have someone in mind."

"You know I do. But we need more people, regardless. If we're going to compete against the likes of Kancel Kulture we need to be a global network, with operatives in every country ready to be mobilised as the work comes in." She noticed Nate tense at the mention of Kancel Kulture but she kept going. "And yes, if Acid joined us we'd have a much stronger footing—"

"For heaven's sake!" Nate cut her off. "Give it a rest, Spook. She's gone. We don't need her."

"I think we do."

"We don't! And even if we did, she's with Darius now. She made her choice."

Spook shot him a look, forcing herself to hold eye contact. "It was made *for* her. She saved my life."

"She *spared* it."

"Same thing. Darius might be her brother, but he killed The Dullahan. I don't believe Acid would let that go. Plus, Darius is an egotistical prick who's only interested in money and power. That's not how Acid rolls. Not anymore. Kancel Kulture isn't her vibe. Those aren't her people."

"Yet she's doing good work for them. One of their top operatives, from what I hear."

"What?" Spook stared at him, her mouth dropping open. "What do you mean by that?"

Nate waved her away. "Forget it, I'm not discussing this. Acid works for a rival organisation and your loyalty no longer means anything to her. You've got to cut the ties, just like she has, or risk getting yourself killed. Grow up and face the facts, Spook. She's the enemy now, and I don't want to hear her name mentioned again."

Spook gripped the side of the table as a wave of indignation surged inside her. In the past she'd have let this go, bowing to Nate's superior knowledge and experience, but she wasn't the same person she'd been a year ago. She wasn't even the same person she'd been six months ago. Spook had killed people before, in self-defence, to save others. But now she was doing it as a career, forcing herself to act cold, methodical and calculating. Stepping into that role fundamentally changed a person. Spook was at the stage now where she didn't consider if it was a good thing or a bad thing, it was just her situation. Her life.

She shifted in her seat, ready to keep at it with Nate when footsteps on the stairwell changed her mind. A second later Lena appeared, her normally composed demeanour replaced by a sudden urgency. She was carrying two large holdalls, which she placed on the table.

"Hey guys," she said, widening her eyes as she took in Spook. "How's it going?"

"We're good," Nate replied, nodding at the holdalls. "Did you get everything you needed?"

Lena grinned and nodded. She was dressed in her usual eclectic attire – an oversized tie-dyed t-shirt paired with holographic leggings that clashed terribly but sort of worked. Her hair was up in bunches, revealing chunky plastic earrings in the shape of rubber ducks. But despite her vibrant appearance, it was the look in her eyes that caught Spook's attention.

"I... umm... need to speak to you," Lena told her in a pointless stage whisper.

Not now, Lena...

Spook ground her teeth together as she held the younger woman's gaze. If Lena was trying to be surreptitious, she was failing miserably. Her tech knowledge and hacking skills were exemplary, but she still had a lot to learn about the finer points of this world.

"What's this about?" Nate asked, leaning over the table. "Whatever you have to say, Lena, you can say in front of me."

Lena's eyes danced between her two colleagues, visibly bursting to spill her news. She was practically bouncing from foot to foot, weighing whether to divulge all in Nate's presence.

"It's fine," Spook said. "He needs to hear it. Say what you have to say."

"Okay, cool." Lena dropped her shoulders and shuffled closer. "I think I've found her."

Nate shot Spook a look but didn't say anything. Maybe he thought the look was enough.

"Go on," she urged.

Lena took a deep breath. "So... for the last few months, I've been monitoring a dark web forum used for all sorts of black-market dealings – you name it, drugs, weapons, human organs, even people. It's all pretty heavy, as are most of the users. But recently, the tone of the forum has changed. It's become the go-to spot for a different kind of clientele."

Nate's expression hardened. "What kind of different?"

"Wait until you hear this," Lena announced, pausing for effect. "From what I can tell, that forum is now being used by the entertainment industry." She paused again, grinning keenly at Spook and Nate. When neither of them responded, she carried on. "Obviously everyone on the forum uses aliases and heavy encryption. But I tracked some IP addresses to Hollywood. After some digging, I found they belong to movie executives and producers – industry insiders looking for extreme solutions to their problems."

"What's this got to do with us?" Nate asked. "I appreciate your hard work, Lena, but this is nothing new. People in our line of work have always had plenty of business from those in Hollywood."

"I get that," Lena said. "But I'm almost certain this forum has recently been taken over and is now part of Kancel Kulture's network."

Spook and Nate exchanged a glance. "How certain?" Spook asked.

"Very." Lena's eyes lit up. "I infiltrated the forum using an anonymised identity to slip past the initial security layers. The site runs on Tor, like most on the dark web, but as you know, no server is impenetrable. Once inside, I deployed custom-built spider bots to map out the site's structure and scrape data. They're using strong encryption like PGP and elliptic curve cryptography for messaging. Tough, but not foolproof. I set up a man-in-the-middle attack to intercept messages. By pretending to be a legitimate part of their network, I could decrypt the messages as they were sent."

Spook eyed Nate. She could tell Lena had lost him somewhere around the mention of PGP. But she understood perfectly. Lena had been clever. It was what Spook would have done.

"How do we know Kancel Kulture are behind it?" Nate asked.

"A few days ago, I created a fake listing offering mercenary services to attract higher-profile members. Someone using the alias Diablo contacted me, and through their login I traced a series of blockchain transactions. You see, cryptocurrencies like Bitcoin are pseudonymous, not anonymous, meaning with the right tools you can link online transactions to real-world locations." She flashed her eyes. "Just follow the money, baby!"

"And this won't lead back to us?" Nate asked.

"No way. I always work clean," Lena replied, serious for a moment.

"You think Diablo is Darius?" Spook asked.

"I do. I hope you don't mind, but I took the liberty of going through the messages he'd sent to Acid that were still on your laptop. The phrasing is the same, and the transaction patterns and the timing align with activities we know are connected to Kancel Kulture."

"And the upshot is...?" Nate asked, a wariness in his voice.

"I've pinpointed the server's physical location to an address in Echo Park, Los Angeles. A converted warehouse complex."

"Shit," Spook muttered, the revelation filling her with a fresh sense of resolve. She met Nate's gaze. He didn't look happy but she didn't care.

Screw trepidation. Now she was excited.

"You did good, Lena," she said, getting to her feet. "That has to be where Kancel Kulture have set up shop. And if that's the case, then Acid is there too."

Chapter Fourteen

Nate crossed his arms and relaxed his jaw, trying to appear calm as he watched the two women, their faces alive with passion as they discussed the finer details of Lena's recent efforts. He had to hand it to Lena – she was as eager as she was green, but uncovering Kancel Kulture's whereabouts was no mean feat. Yet, he'd not accounted for this eventuality and it bothered him a great deal. Spook had trained hard and she was becoming an excellent operative, but she wasn't there yet and this was a distraction they didn't need.

It was also personal, and that rubbed him the wrong way. He and Acid went back years. They were both young when they started out in the industry. But he knew – as Acid did – never to get too attached to anyone in this line of work, not if you valued your own life. Spook was still new to all this, though, and it bothered him she hadn't yet mastered the art of detachment. It could be the death of them all.

He finished his coffee and placed his mug in the sink as the two women continued trading ideas and discussing next steps. Lena was practically vibrating with excitement, her eyes bright, her hands gesturing wildly as she explained how she'd circumnavigated Kancel Kulture's security protocols and now planned to pinpoint Acid's movements. Spook, on the other hand, had gone quiet. But Nate knew her well enough by now to recognise she was fired up and eager to act on this new information.

That at least was his own fault. He'd spent the last twelve months putting her through a rigorous training regime, nurturing her tenacity and resilience. She was harder and stronger, almost unrecognisable from the nervous, uncertain woman he'd met a year earlier. If she could just get her feelings under control she'd be phenomenal.

"What do you think, Nate?" Her eyes were set with steely determination as they drifted up to meet his.

"I think we need to slow down a little," he told her. "I think we need to focus on what's important."

Spook shook her head. "How did I know you were going to say that?"

"Why ask then?" he replied. "It sounds as if it doesn't matter what I think."

Spook looked as if she was going to roll her eyes but stopped herself. "Of course it matters. You're still the boss."

"Am I?"

The truth was, Nate felt the control of their fledgling operation slipping through his fingers. Starting a new organisation had been his vision, but day by day it felt as if it was being taken away from him. It didn't help to discover Spook and Lena had been conspiring behind his back.

Possibly this was evident in his face as Spook stood and walked over to him. "Please don't be annoyed," she said. "You know how important this is to me. I just need to see her. I need to know where she stands. Either way."

"We know where she stands," he shot back. "She's with Darius."

Initially Nate had also hoped they might bring Acid back into the fold. But as time had passed, he'd let that dream go. Acid Vanilla had always been bloody-minded and unwilling to cooperate, even under Caesar's watch. It's what made her so damn good. If she'd decided she was part of Kancel Kulture there'd be no changing that, no matter how much Spook wanted to.

"We're supposed to be setting up a new operation here in the real world, not chasing ghosts on the internet," he added.

"But Kancel Kulture are our competition," Spook replied. "It's important we keep abreast of their operations."

"I know that. But that's not why you're doing this."

He glared at Spook. She glared back. She was wearing contact lenses rather than her glasses and the firmness around her eyes was unsettling. Yes, she was stronger and more confident than she'd ever been, but she was also more reckless.

"Maybe it's not entirely why I'm doing this," she said. "But it's a bonus, wouldn't you say? Kancel Kulture are making a real name for themselves right now. That's a fact. They're out there taking our business and giving a bad name to what we do."

"A bad name? Are you serious?" Nate spluttered. He was getting rather tired of Spook trying to reframe everything to give it a positive slant. "Spook, we're assassins. We kill people for money. How much worse does it get?"

He noticed both Spook and Lena flinch at his words, but he was past caring.

"I know what we are," Spook muttered. "But we have

morals, Nate. We do things differently. We're still avenging the lowly."

"You tell yourself what you need to," Nate replied, his anger simmering just below the surface.

"We have to go to LA. We have to see if she'll turn."

"No. We don't."

Spook glanced at Lena, but the younger woman averted her eyes, unwilling to get caught in the crossfire. "Come on, Nate. Please. Don't you want to take those bastards out? They're our rivals. If we remove Kancel Kulture from the equation, then we're free to build our organisation on our own terms, without worrying about the competition." Her voice softened, almost pleading. "We have to stop them, Nate. They're not like us or other organisations. They don't play fair. They're evil."

"Oh, they're evil?" Nate yelled, unable to keep a lid on his frustration any longer. "Then that means she's evil too, doesn't it? Although I'd argue it's a bit rich for you to be throwing words like that around these days, Spook."

She stepped back, her expression one of shock. Immediately he was annoyed at himself for losing control like that but he couldn't help it. She was exploiting his good nature, stomping all over his authority.

"You don't understand how this industry works," he continued, bringing his voice under some semblance of control. "I've been in this game for nearly twenty years. If we're seen planning a hit on another organisation without backing from the industry, we'll face serious consequences."

"But who says?" Lena asked, finding her voice at last. "Who actually decides these things?"

Nate gave her a hard stare. "It's just how it works," he said firmly, hoping this would end the argument. It wasn't that he was entirely unsympathetic to Spook's hopes of finding Acid and bringing her back, it's just he knew any attempt would be a fool's errand. Acid was too hot-headed, too chaotic. If she'd made her choice, she wasn't going to change her mind, even if it was the right thing to do. Okay, so maybe he didn't know Acid Vanilla as well as Spook did, but he knew her well enough. She was... an original. People in the industry still spoke of her in hushed tones.

"Let's try to concentrate on our work here," he told his colleagues. "We're still so new and there's a lot we can be doing—"

"Wait a second!" Spook yelled, cutting him off. "What did you say?"

Nate froze, confused by the look on her face. Had he misspoken? Said something to upset her? He thought back. "I said we should concentrate on our work."

"No. Not that." She stepped closer, wagging a finger at him. "You mentioned Acid. You said she was one of their top operatives *from what I hear*. Where did you hear about that, Nate? When?" Her eyes blazed with anger. "Did you know she was in LA?"

Nate stiffened, his gaze locked on Spook.

Bugger.

He hadn't even realised he'd let that slip. It was a rookie mistake. He shrugged, but it did nothing to ease Spook's death stare. "What are you talking about?"

"You know damn well what I'm talking about," Spook snarled. "Have you been keeping information from me? That's not cool, Nate."

"Fine," he said, raising his hands defensively. "I heard some rumblings a few weeks back from some contacts in the field. But it was just rumours, nothing concrete."

Spook's face turned crimson. She looked like she was

about to explode. "You didn't think to tell me this? You didn't think it was important?"

"I wanted us to focus on things here."

"But this is Kancel Kulture," she hissed. "If we have intel, we can move on them first. We can take them out before they know what hit them."

"I told you. That's not how it works—"

"Fuck how it works." She jabbed her finger into his chest. "Darius has brainwashed Acid. I know it. Or he's keeping her there under duress. We have to help her."

Nate leaned in, bristling at being scolded like a child. "I know that's what you want to believe. But it's not true. She's with Darius because she chooses to be. After all, he offered her a ready-made organisation and a new career. That's what she wanted."

"Darius killed The Dullahan," Spook countered. "You knew him. You were at his funeral. Doesn't that mean anything to you? Isn't that worse than anything else? Surely Kancel Kulture can't be respected in the industry after that."

Nate kept his expression neutral. "The Dullahan had retired. The rules aren't the same."

"That's bullshit!" Spook cried, glancing at Lena who was watching the exchange with wide, terrified eyes – like a child witnessing their parents fighting.

"Let it go, Spook," Nate whispered. "I mean it."

"How can you say that?" Spook's voice broke, her hands clenched at her sides. "We can't succeed with them out there." She turned to Lena. "Is the whole crew over in LA?"

"I'm not sure, but they've definitely got a base there. It's the closest we've come to finding them since I started working here."

"So this is something the two of you have been working

on for a while," Nate said, switching his focus between the two women. Spook didn't flinch. Lena looked at the floor.

"I wanted to test Lena's abilities," Spook muttered. "And she wanted to prove herself."

Nate rubbed his temples, feeling the pressure building. "Well, it looks as if she's done that."

"Think about it," Spook said, her voice softer but no less determined. "We need to at least check out their operations. Hell, aren't you curious? If we want to make a real go of this organisation, we need to know who we're up against."

Reluctantly, Nate nodded. He knew once Spook set her mind to something, there was no stopping her. It was a trait she and Acid shared. "Spook, I—"

"I'm going to LA, Nate. With or without you. You can't stop me."

He exhaled sharply, frustration mingling with a sense of resignation. Maybe a part of him always knew this would happen. "Why couldn't you just leave it alone?"

"Because she's my friend," Spook said. "Because we need her. I need her."

Nate looked at her, really looked at her, and saw not just the woman he'd trained but someone driven by deep, unyielding loyalty. He couldn't help but respect that, even if it complicated everything.

"Fine," he said, the weight of the decision settling on his shoulders. "I guess we're going to LA."

Chapter Fifteen

The relentless LA sun beat down on Acid as she strode down Sunset Boulevard, heading west away from her usual haunts. This was the more affluent part of the Strip, a landscape of tall palm trees and synthetic beauty. Everyone she passed looked fake, their bodies honed by surgical precision or the latest fad diet, their skin plumped and tightened with toxins and fillers. But it was Beverly Hills, after all – a place where beauty was both currency and competition.

In her black jeans and a faded t-shirt, Acid felt distinctly out of place. Her old Doc Martens scuffed against the sidewalk as she wove through the sea of beautiful people. Six months in, and LA still felt like an alien land to her. It was too pristine, too poised.

Too bloody healthy.

Side-stepping a trio of laughing middle-aged women weighed down with shopping bags, Acid couldn't hide her sneer. Everyone was so nice to each other here, but she wasn't buying it. Hollywood was a masterclass in the art of deception, a town that hid its most depraved secrets behind a veil of stunning vistas and perfect smiles. But, as Acid had always known, it was usually those who put on a facade of goodness and morality that were the most disgusting and depraved. If you wanted the truth, just ask a Catholic altar boy.

She pressed on, marching past chic cafés and designer boutiques, resisting the urge to venture inside. The dichotomy of Acid Vanilla was that she did enjoy the finer things in life. Whilst working away on assignments she stayed in exclusive hotels, spent a small fortune on make-up each month, and when she remembered to eat, she ate well.

Yet the splendour and riches she'd enjoyed, and even insisted on, in her early days at Annihilation Pest Control were no longer the be-all and end-all for her. She still enjoyed the good life and the freedom her career brought, but mostly she focused on putting one foot in front of the other, glad there'd be a few drinks coming her way at the end of the day.

Continuing her journey into the heart of LA glamour, her thoughts drifted to her life here. She'd always told herself that if she ever moved to the USA, it would be the East Coast where she'd set up home. With its rough, unapologetic spirit, she felt much more of an affinity with New York. But she had committed to making it work here in Hollywood and was determined to carve out a space among the sunshine and palm trees. For the time being at least.

Today, her destination was the Polo Lounge at the Beverly Hills Hotel, a favourite haunt of Hollywood's elite and now, apparently, her brother Darius. As she got closer the breeze shifted, carrying with it the faint notes of laughter and clinking glasses, the mating sounds of the privileged and carefree.

Reaching the entrance, Acid noticed the host eyeing her

with a blatant up-and-down, unable to hide his disdain for her appearance. Positioned under a stone archway, his posture was impeccably straight, his crisply tailored suit in stark contrast to her scruffy attire. His lips pursed as she approached, his eyes flicking from her weathered boots to meet her steady gaze. The message was clear – she didn't belong here. But screw him. The restaurant's dress code said no ripped denim, and she'd made the effort; the jeans she wore were the only pair she owned without holes.

"I'm here to meet Mr Duke," she said, dropping Darius' name like a password. Instantly the host's demeanour thawed, a wide smile replacing his earlier scrutiny. "Of course, right this way."

The cool interior of the Polo Lounge was a welcome reprieve from the harsh LA sun, its decor a tribute to a bygone era of glamour. They called it the Pink Palace and there were no prizes for guessing why, especially out on the terrace. Heads turned subtly as Acid navigated the clusters of diners, her ramshackle appearance an unusual sight in a place that prided itself on surface and style. Was she a famous actress? A rock star? Or just some bum off the street who had wandered into their haven of luxury?

Darius was sitting in his usual booth overlooking the terrace, the same booth Marilyn Monroe had favoured in the fifties. Acid was certain that sitting there, with a commanding view of the restaurant, Darius felt like he was the King of Hollywood, surveying his court. And perhaps, in some way, he was. Or at least could be, given half the chance.

He lounged with the ease of a man to whom luxury had become a way of life. His cream linen shirt, unbuttoned far too low, billowed slightly in the warm breeze, and the oily sheen on his mirrored aviator shades changed colour from blue to yellow as he tilted his head towards the sun. Observing him from a short distance for a moment as he sipped a martini, Acid wondered – not for the first time – how the hell they could be related.

But they weren't. Not really. They might share the same blood, but that was as far as it went.

Acid was a street panther who existed in the shadows. Darius, on the other hand, was a showman, the epitome of Hollywood excess. He was tanned and healthy, he ate chia seeds – whatever they were – and was fast becoming part of the scenery here in Hollywood. People respected and feared him in equal measure, and he was clearly loving life as one of Hollywood's top 'fixers'. That was how most people knew him, anyway. Those higher up, the men in the high towers who wrote the checks, knew the truth. But they respected and feared Darius just the same.

Acid pulled in a deep breath, preparing herself mentally for the conversation ahead. Darius usually summoned her here to discuss work, but there was always the possibility it was something else, something more troubling. She shook the thought away as Darius looked over, waving at her with a flourish that screamed of his newfound Hollywood affectation.

Wincing inwardly at his theatrics, she quickly sat down before he could engage in any pathetic air kissing.

"Everything good?" she asked, as he settled opposite her.

"Everything's great," he replied with a grin. "How are you?"

She shrugged. "Can't complain."

"Yet you give off the air of someone in a perpetual state of complaint." He chuckled. "Why is that?"

Another shrug. "Don't know. Must be my cheery personality and sunny disposition."

Darius leaned back into the plush leather of the booth, a smug satisfaction in his eyes that Acid found increasingly irritating. He raised an eyebrow as a server approached. "Hungry, sis? I've already ordered the McCarthy Salad. It's an absolute classic."

Acid scoffed. "Salad? No thanks." She glanced at the server, a young woman with blonde hair and a face straight out of a magazine. Most likely she'd describe herself as an actress, like every other person who worked in the service industry out here.

"I'll have a bottle of Dom Perignon, please," she said, watching Darius to see if the order would make him flinch. It didn't.

"Very good. And anything to eat?" the woman asked.

Acid puffed out her cheeks. "Oh go on then, you've twisted my arm. Bring me a portion of fries."

The server hesitated. "We have parmesan truffle fries, is that okay?"

"What?!" Acid snapped, enjoying the flicker of discomfort in Darius' face before turning to the server with a warm smile. "Yes, no problem. Thank you."

The server gathered up the extraneous cutlery before sauntering away. As always, they would wait until they were alone before continuing the conversation. Acid sat back, casting her attention around the space and soaking in the ambience. Out here on the terrace, the warm air was alive with the low hum of conversations and the subtle notes of piano jazz. Bougainvillea, vibrant with purples and pinks, spilled over the alcoves, offering a splash of natural beauty against the Pink Palace's art deco finesse. She spotted a couple of diners that looked vaguely familiar – an older woman with long strawberry-blonde hair, an overly tanned woman with a black bob – but not being au fait with popular culture, she didn't know their names.

"So, what are we doing here?" she asked, fixing Darius with a hard stare once the server had left.

"Can't a man just request his sister's presence at lunch without there being an ulterior motive?"

"He can. But that's not why you've asked me here."

Darius placed his glass down and leaned forward, his expression serious. "I've got you an audition," he said, his voice dropping to a whisper. "It's a new production, one that's going to bring in a lot of money."

Acid nodded, playing along. "What's the movie about?"

"It's a thriller," he replied, a slick salesman-like grin spreading across his face. "But *not* a slasher. Okay? I know you like that type of role, but not this time. I need you to put in a more... subtle performance than you might be used to."

"Are you saying I'm a bad actress?" Acid replied, arching an eyebrow.

Darius was about to reply when the server returned, placing a plate of diced chicken and vegetables topped with a fanned avocado in front of him and setting down Acid's bottle of champagne and bowl of fries. Acid eyed Darius' salad with a sneer. It looked like the sort of thing you fed to babies or old people, with each component cut up small for minimum effort. Maybe chewing was bad for the skin or something.

She poured herself a glass of champagne and gulped down a mouthful. It was ice cold and the bubbles fizzed on her tongue.

"But it's a good movie?" she asked.

Darius nodded. "Oh yes. But you'll need to keep a lid

on it. It's been noted you've been getting a little too... exuberant in some of the roles you've performed for me recently. It worries people."

She sniffed. *Saga.* He meant Saga. But she was glad of a new assignment. It would keep her mind occupied.

"So what's the plot of this...movie?"

Darius scooped up a forkful of chicken and tomatoes and smirked. "It's a tale as old as time, a tragic love story concerning an old guy and his wife. He's a top cinematographer, has worked on some of the biggest movies of the last ten years. She's a former dancer, now retired. They've been together for forty years but the wife has just found out her husband has been cheating on her with some young starlet. It's a bit of a cliché, but there you go. Hollywood loves a cliché. Particularly, they love movies they know will work at the box office."

Acid drank some more. "It sounds like a B-movie script, made-for-TV rather than the usual blockbusters we're involved in."

Darius laughed, unfazed. "Maybe, but there's a nice twist. The budget is huge. The wife's willing to pay top dollar to see the husband out of the picture before he can divorce her."

Acid narrowed her eyes. Somewhere along the way, Darius had lost hold of his metaphor, yet the job sounded decent enough.

"Okay, I'm in," she told him.

Finishing the glass of champagne, she got to her feet, leaving the fries untouched. "Wait," Darius hissed, grabbing for her wrist. "Where the hell are you going?"

Acid stared him out. The bats in her head had suddenly grown loud and she was eager to leave. "I want to go home and prepare," she told him.

Darius glanced around, smiling and nodding at those at nearby tables. "Fine," he whispered. "But I want you to take The Gorgon with you."

The bats grew louder. Acid focused on keeping her face neutral. "Come on, Darius. I can handle this myself. I don't need a babysitter."

"Acid!" Darius scowled. "How many times do I have to tell you? We work in teams. It's the best way." His tone said this wasn't a discussion.

"Fine. Whatever. When do we start shooting?" She grinned. Darius didn't.

"Next couple of days. The husband flies out to South Africa on location next Saturday. Get it done before then."

She picked up the bottle of Dom Perignon and filled her glass. "Have Saga send me the details."

She drank back the champagne, winking at Darius as she finished it in one gulp.

Next couple of days.

The Gorgon.

She smiled to herself as she left, the LA sun stinging her eyes as she hit the sidewalk.

A new job. It was just what she needed.

Chapter Sixteen

Nate Winters was sitting in the crowded departure lounge of Heathrow Airport, surrounded by the incessant hum of announcements and the chatter from fellow travellers. It was just after two in the afternoon, and he was still annoyed with himself for how easily Spook had persuaded him to catch the next flight to LA. Here he was now with no choice but to settle in for the ride, but he felt tired and cranky and would rather be anywhere else. Last night's sleep had been a mess of tangled bedsheets and overthinking, his mind racing with irritation at Spook and Lena for not discussing their plans with him. He'd tried to let that particular gripe go during an early morning run, but the frustration lingered.

Being so affable and rolling with the punches wasn't a new way of being for Nate, and he often worried if it was a weakness. Or if not a weakness, then unhelpful. The Dullahan himself had once told the young Nate Nitro – as he called himself back then – that he was too nice for this dark world of murder and mayhem. Nate was good at what he did, there was no denying that – he was strong and fast, with a sharp analytical mind – he just didn't believe anger was necessary to be an effective assassin. You spent your life carrying around a knot of rage, often without realising it, which sapped your life force and prevented you from moving forward. Nate understood the urge, even the desire for revenge and retaliation, but it wasn't for him. It wasn't how he operated.

Plus, he was quite capable of being cold, hard and calculating when necessary. He just didn't feel it was useful when leading a new crew still finding their feet. They needed to be encouraged and nurtured, and their confidence built. That was the main reason why he'd agreed to this trip, to keep Spook happy. Though, he had to admit – if only to himself – that he too was now harbouring hopes Spook might convince Acid to desert her new colleagues and join them. Her wealth of experience and global contacts could be the shot in the arm his new organisation needed.

Yet Nate also knew that hope alone was about as useful as being a nice guy in this industry. They needed more than hope. They needed a plan. And knowing Acid as he did, a miracle wouldn't go amiss.

A crease formed between his brows as he adjusted his position, finding it hard to get comfortable in the hard plastic chair. All around him the noise of the busy terminal buzzed with white noise, punctuated by the clatter of luggage wheels. For now, however, the worst part was over. They'd just cleared security, which was a minor triumph given they were using aliases and passports secured through a new contact.

"Nate? Do you want a drink?" Spook's voice snapped him from his thoughts.

"A coffee would be good."

"Oh, right. Because I was thinking…" She swayed her head from. side to side as if weighing her options. "No, you're right. Coffee is better. I'll get them."

Nate watched her as she headed for the Starbucks counter across the far side of the lounge. She looked good. Her body was firm and athletic, her gaze watchful as she weaved through the crowd.

He'd done a solid job with Ms Horowitz. Her progress was impressive, but she was just one operative and after a year there were still only three of them. Despite a handful of successes, things weren't going as planned. Nate closed his eyes, exhaling slowly. Establishing an international assassin network had seemed straightforward on paper, but the reality of their situation was undeniable. Who knew it would be so hard?

Kancel Kulture, on the other hand, were thriving, gaining traction every day. Their name came up frequently on forums and from his contacts in the industry. They were already major players, while he and Spook were struggling to make an impact.

Nate hadn't signed up for a life of death and danger just to become a marketeer, but that's what it felt like lately. The problem was that the murder-for-hire game relied heavily on word-of-mouth recommendations. Sure, you advertised your services in the right places, but for most of their clients it had always been about knowing a guy who knew a guy. They needed exposure, a significant assignment to put them on the map, but it had yet to materialise.

Sensing a presence nearby, Nate opened his eyes to see Spook returning with two steaming cups of coffee. She handed him one and sat down without a word. They drank in silence for a few minutes, the air between them prickly. Fine. If Spook thought he was pissed off at her, let her keep thinking it. In return, he wasn't ready to admit that she had a point about Kancel Kulture. He didn't think for a second they could or should take them out, but if they could observe them up close, and get a better feel for how they operated, it wouldn't be a wasted trip.

And if Spook could get Acid alone... who knew what might happen?

His gaze drifted, taking in the scenes playing out around them – the frazzled parents trying to keep their young children in check, the lone travellers tapping impatiently on their devices, the businessmen looking anxiously for their connecting flights. Beside him Spook appeared lost in thought, staring into the black swirl of her coffee. He knew how much she wanted Acid back in her life. For the first few months after returning from Rome she'd been lost, and hardly spoke between training sessions.

"How are you holding up?" he asked her.

"I'm okay. Just eager to get over there and see what's what, you know..." She trailed off, suddenly looking nervous.

But she had faith and Nate appreciated that. Acid Vanilla was a total wild card who'd screwed over her friends and joined forces with the man who'd slit the throat of the great Dullahan. It was no surprise to anyone who knew Acid that she'd look after number one. Yet here was Spook, still believing in her. Whether it was misplaced – and Nate was all but sure it was – time would tell, but Spook held strong to her belief. He had to admire that, even if she was on a road to nowhere.

"You know, Spook, we have to prepare ourselves for every outcome," he said. "I know you think she's going to switch sides if you can only speak with her, but... it might not work out that way."

"She's the key, Nate. If we can…" She lost her thread as her gaze fixed on something – or someone – approaching.

Nate looked past her to see Lena hurrying towards them, unmissable in a neon green jacket. She had a laptop bag slung over one shoulder and was clutching a large red slushy drink.

"What the hell?" Spook murmured.

"I thought you'd want her with us," Nate said. "She's got the tech skills we need."

Spook shot him a look that could strip paint, but quickly replaced it with a tight smile as Lena reached them, slightly out of breath.

"Hey, you guys," she gasped, grinning widely. "Are we all set?"

Spook leaned forward, her expression hard. "Lena, are you sure you want to come with us? You know it could be dangerous over there. Probably will be."

"She's part of the crew," Nate reminded her. "She should come."

"She's never worked in the field before," Spook said, sounding every bit the seasoned operative.

Nate lowered his head and gave her a stern look, but he could tell she was secretly glad of Lena's presence. If nothing else, this trip would solidify their bond.

"Don't worry, Spook," Lena piped up, her enthusiasm evident. "I'm already earning my stripes – or whatever it is you say – I've found us an awesome place on Airbnb. It's in Westlake. And it's got a pool." She said this last part in a sing-song voice, as if having a pool was a deal breaker, the least of their worries. Spook gave Nate another look.

"Airbnb?" she said. "That's risky. Too traceable."

"Relax. I used aliases and one of our multi-layered prepaid cards." Lena's smile didn't waver as she took a seat beside Nate and leaned around him to continue talking. "Trust me. It'll be fine. I've also ordered everything we might need while we're there. Drones, scrambler units, a couple of laptops."

Nate raised an eyebrow. "How much did all that cost?"

"And is it safe?" Spook added.

Lena waved a dismissive hand. "You guys need to chill. I'm not an idiot. I ordered from the same company we use for all our equipment. Delivery takes two weeks to reach the UK, but they're based in Silicon Valley so it'll take less than a day to get to Westlake. With any luck, it'll be on the porch waiting for us when we arrive."

Spook's frown deepened, a clear sign of her unease with Lena's cavalier attitude. But in Nate's eyes, she was just as bad. She'd instigated this impromptu mission without his input or say-so, and that still stung. If they were doing this, Lena's presence would be an asset rather than a liability. Hell, they'd need all the help they could get. Acid might see that coming home was the best thing to do, but from all he'd heard, she was now entrenched in Kancel Kulture, making good money for both her and Darius. Why would she give that up?

He turned his attention back to Lena, who had opened her laptop and was tapping away feverishly. "Give me a day," she said without looking up. "I'm confident I can access their networks and leapfrog their comms in real-time. After that, we'll know exactly what they're doing."

Spook watched Lena work, her expression unreadable to Nate. Was she impressed by the younger woman, or just plain nervous? Nervous about the flight, about finding Acid, about trying to reason with her. Nervous about everything. He wouldn't have blamed her.

After a moment she nodded, almost reluctantly. "Fine,"

she said. "But I need a drink. A proper drink. Whisky, anyone?"

Without waiting for a response, she was on her feet and striding towards the bar. Nate watched her go, shaking his head. There was a hardness to Spook now, a determination that was both formidable and frightening. She was more like Acid Vanilla than she realised. And much more than she'd be happy to admit. Whether that similarity was a strength or a liability, Nate couldn't yet decide.

He glanced at the departure board. Another twenty minutes until boarding. Maybe he'd join Spook for that whisky after all.

Chapter Seventeen

Spook couldn't usually sleep on airplanes. The cramped seats, the recycled air, the constant ping of the public address system, it was all too oppressive. But after downing two double whiskies in the departure lounge, exhaustion had taken over. As they climbed to cruising altitude, the gentle hum of the engines and the soft, muffled conversations around her lured her into sleep. It was eleven hours and twenty-one minutes to LAX. She spent the first seven of those asleep, a much-needed reprieve from the restless nights that had been accumulating lately. But that was understandable. Spook had a lot on her mind.

As she had done the last few times she'd managed to sleep, she dreamt of Acid. The dreams were vivid, intense and disorientating. Not quite nightmares, but far from relaxing. Spook found herself in a surreal, shifting landscape that felt familiar but wasn't anywhere she'd ever been. There were trees, buildings, roads, it was the inside of a computer, then it wasn't. Acid was there, her expression flickering between rage and compassion, telling Spook to abandon her mission, to stay the hell away from her, *sweetie*. But Spook was relentless, chasing her old friend through empty streets, never getting anywhere. One moment they were running side by side, the next they were locked in combat, Acid's hands around Spook's throat. Just as the dream tipped into violence, Acid raised a pistol at Spook's head and she awoke with a jolt, her heart racing.

Looking around, Spook saw Lena watching her from the adjacent seat, a smirk playing on her lips. "Bad dream?" she quipped, as Spook wiped the drool from her chin.

"Something like that."

Embarrassed but trying not to show it, Spook called the flight attendant and ordered a drink – a club soda this time; probably for the best. Then the food trays came around, cluttered with plastic-wrapped edibles that she picked at but didn't particularly enjoy. Over in the window seat Nate slept on, oblivious. He must have needed his sleep too. That was also understandable.

As the plane hummed on, Spook settled into the journey, adjusting her position so she could talk with Lena who was still wide awake and seemed eager to pass the time. Spook realised it was the first time they'd talked – really talked, not just the tactical back-and-forth they'd been limited to since Lena joined the team. She was surprised to find the young Londoner not just bearable, but interesting. Lena was funny, clever, and much more insightful than Spook had given her credit for.

As the conversation drifted from casual talk to more personal exchanges, Spook found herself both intrigued and slightly unsettled by how much she was warming to the younger woman. Lena explained how she was born and raised in Ealing, West London, and that she'd loved computers and technology her whole life. She also revealed that she had ADHD, which probably explained her slightly abrupt, slightly unfiltered personality. But Spook felt honoured that Lena shared these aspects of her life with her. She was a sweet person, maybe too sweet for this world. But then again, the same thing could have been said about Spook, and she'd survived.

Just about, at least.

"I found it difficult to fit in with the other kids growing up, but thinking differently helps my work," Lena continued, a flicker of pride in her eyes. "I see patterns where others see chaos. Codes, algorithms, it's like they speak to me."

"Well, it certainly doesn't hinder you," Spook agreed, and she meant it. Lena was excellent at her job, maybe even better than Spook, though she wasn't ready to admit that out loud. As Lena discussed her numerous projects, Spook felt a twinge of something close to envy. It was a rare sensation for her, one she didn't particularly enjoy. But it was clear to her that Lena was what she could have been if she'd stayed in the tech game, instead of trying to become more like… Acid.

It was a tough truth to swallow, but undeniable. Spook was proud of her skills, yet Lena had all the new tricks. Listening to her casually demystify advanced cybersecurity made Spook acutely aware of the technological advancements she'd missed while focusing her attention elsewhere.

"What are you working on at the moment?" Spook asked. "Apart from all the things I've asked of you, I mean."

Lena grinned. "Actually, I've been tweaking your facial recognition software."

"Oh. I see." Spook tried not to let that annoyance show on her face. That was her program, her baby, she'd been working on it for years.

"Your base code was brilliant," Lena continued. "Way ahead of its time. I just added some adaptive learning components and expanded the database compatibility. I've also enhanced the algorithm to learn from false positives, boosting accuracy over time without manual updates. I've already integrated it with the CCTV networks of most major European cities, and I've started linking it to LA's system. It should be up and running in the next twenty-four hours. Once synced with LA's extensive network, we'll be able to track movements across the city almost in real-time."

Spook cleared her throat. She could be upset but she chose to be flattered instead. It was clear Lena looked up to her and admired her a great deal. That was how she was choosing to read Lena's eager expression, anyway. She smiled, her defences melting away, replaced by only admiration for Lena's skills.

"That's great work," she said. "I'm very glad we hired you."

And it was true. She was impressed, really impressed, but she couldn't shake the feeling of being a relic in this new digital era that Lena navigated with ease. This world of artificial intelligence and virtual deception wasn't hers anymore. She'd gone from hacking codes to dodging bullets.

It had long been Spook's theory that Caesar had groomed Acid all those years ago – moulding and manipulating her to do his bidding. Was this what Acid had done to her? Or was it just the inevitable result of being surrounded by death and violence on a daily basis? You became so used to it that it became your new normal. You started to crave it.

As the plane began its descent, Spook clicked her seat belt on and sat back, a familiar sense of anticipation and dread knotting her stomach. Despite her doubts about the path she'd taken and the changes she'd undergone, there was no going back. Los Angeles sprawled out below them, its vast network of streets like the nerve centre of a giant computer. Whatever was coming, Spook knew it would test her to the limit both mentally and physically. But she was ready. Ready to face Acid. Ready to do what was needed. They would touch down in less than thirty minutes. Then the real work would begin.

Chapter Eighteen

Over in Echo Park, Acid had been at Kancel Kulture's headquarters since seven, putting herself through a sequence of gruelling exercises. In the main gym area, she'd attacked the punch bag with relentless fury, seeing every face that had ever wronged her on the other side of her fist. From there she moved to the kick bag, unleashing her frustration with swift, powerful kicks that made the heavy bag jerk violently on its chain.

"Stupid... mother... fucking... idiot!" she yelled between kicks, not entirely sure who her vitriol was aimed at. Although, as always, some of it was most definitely directed inwards.

After the bags, she moved on to body-weight exercises, starting with five sets of burpees that were done so fast it was tantamount to self-harm, her body hitting the floor and springing back up like her life depended on it. She was aching all over but pushed through without slowing for a second. At least if her body hurt, it took the focus off her thoughts. After the burpees she powered through a series of stomach crunches, her abs contracting painfully with each lift.

But still she wasn't done. Exhaustion clung to her like the sweat soaking her vest top but she needed more. She wanted pain. Real pain. Striding over to the wall, she slammed her fists against the rough unpainted brickwork, her knuckles cracking against the solid surface, leaving behind streaks of blood like war paint.

A smile twitched at the side of her mouth.

"There we go," she muttered to herself, finally satisfied. Pain, after all, was a sign she still felt something.

Dropping her hands to her sides, she walked over to grab her towel, her breathing heavy but controlled. Despite not cutting back on her drinking, she was stronger and fitter than she had been in a long time. Except no matter how hard she trained – or drank – she could never fully extinguish her deep inner rage.

But that was fine by her. She still needed that rage.

As if on cue, the door creaked open and her focus snapped back to the present. She didn't need to look up to know who it was – she recognised the measured way the door had opened, the stealth-like footsteps, almost ghostly.

"What do you want, Saga?" she asked, grabbing her towel and wiping the sweat from her face.

"Apologies if I'm interrupting your session."

"I've finished." She glanced over. He was standing, framed in the doorway, looking like the Slender Man, or an albino scarecrow.

He watched her, his expression unreadable as always. She knew the conversation to come wouldn't be pleasant. Saga had that effect.

"Training hard for the next job?" he asked.

"It'll be a breeze."   .

But the thought of her next assignment brought with it a fresh wave of tension. Being made to team up with The Gorgon was a good thing in the long run, but she hated how Darius still didn't trust her with solo assignments. She pictured The Gorgon's miserable face and felt the urge to slam her fist into the wall again. She could still remember the harpy's smirk as Darius had ordered Acid and Spook to fight each other back in Rome. Wicked bitch. She'd wanted them both dead.

She pushed the thought down and gave Saga the sort of flirtatious wink she knew bothered him. "Don't worry about me," she said. "I always get my mark."

"Yes, I suppose you do. One way or another." He lowered his chin, staring at her as if trying to work her out. "Are you settling in okay?"

He tried to smile but it was all teeth and no emotion. Acid had to look away.

This again.

She knew Saga was the one most wary of her in the organisation. It was him, she suspected, who was filling Darius' head with crap linking her to Nokizaru's death.

"I'm still here, aren't I?" she replied. "You need to start trusting me, Saga. I'm fully committed. I chose to be a part of this."

"Yes…" Saga paused, his eyes narrowing slightly. "I hope so. We need to be sure of everyone's full allegiance to Kancel Kulture, that's all. We're on the brink of something incredible here and—"

"I told you, I'm in!" Acid snapped. "Let it go."

Saga held her gaze for a moment longer, then nodded, though he didn't look convinced. "You have to finish up here. Darius has called a meeting."

Acid rolled up her towel and draped it around her neck. "I need a quick shower first."

"No time for a shower," he said, turning his back. "Follow me."

"Seriously?" she called after him. "I stink."

"Follow me, Acid!"

She obeyed, knowing that arguing would only cast further doubt on her loyalty. Plus, she didn't have the energy to go toe-to-toe with the lanky ghoul. She'd let Darius and the rest of them deal with her smell.

They rode the elevator to the top floor in silence, Saga's thin nose wrinkling as Acid stretched her arms and yawned. Once there, they walked down the corridor to the main meeting room. Saga opened the door and she stepped inside. Darius was sitting at the far end of a long table with The Gorgon and Grimaldi seated on either side of him. They turned to look at her as she entered.

"Sorry I'm late," she whispered, taking a seat two down from Grimaldi. On a stand opposite her, a large monitor displayed a live feed from Brazil. Frederik and Freek Kriel's gnarled, leathery faces filled the screen.

"Hallo Acid," they said in unison, flashing their metallic smiles.

She raised her hand coolly in greeting, but the bats were already gnawing at her nerve endings.

Shit. Is this bad?

Is Darius going to…?

She sat upright and rolled her shoulders back.

No. Keep it together, sweetie. Just a meeting.

Darius clapped his hands together and got to his feet. "Right then. Now we're all here I'll begin."

He was wearing a pair of white chinos that were far too tight across his crotch, and a blood-red shirt unbuttoned to the middle of his chest. To Acid, he looked more like a slimy nightclub owner or a cartoon lothario than a leader. But then, she'd worked for Beowulf Caesar for sixteen years and Darius' outfits paled in comparison to those of her old mentor.

"I've called this meeting because we've got some good news," he announced, fidgeting with the hem of his shirt as a murmur of interest swept around the table. "I've recently got off a call with the executive team at Stardust Studios. They're a new studio but already very big hitters and potentially want to work with us going forward." He paused, making eye contact with each operative in turn, almost willing them to appear excited and appreciative. When he got to Acid, she remained poker-faced. *Big hitters. Going forward.* It sounded like something you'd hear in a boardroom, not a meeting of hired killers.

"What does *potentially* mean?" she asked. "I mean in relation to this assignment, not the definition of the word."

Darius' expression fell. Yeah, he was definitely about to make that joke.

"It means, they've got a job for us, and if they like how we handle it they want to put us on a twenty-million-dollar-a-year retainer." His eyes widened as a buzz ran around the room. "This is it. This is why we relocated here. Eighteen months out of the gate and Kancel Kulture are readying themselves for the big leagues. It'll be the fastest rise of any organisation in this industry. Ever."

He glared at Acid, a cruel smirk playing on his lips. Taunting her was his new favourite pastime, a constant reminder that he was outpacing Caesar's legacy.

"What's the job?" she asked.

Darius winked, enjoying the moment. "I'm glad you asked. Titanium Media Group – a rival studio of Stardust's

– are hosting a gala event in a few days. It's primarily for the benefit of some big Japanese investors. There are three of them coming over to LA, and the client wants us to take them out. But it has to be at this event."

"No problem," Grimaldi growled. "I could do that on my own with one hand stuffed up my ass."

"I don't doubt it, my friend," Darius replied. "But as always with these things, the client wants us to create a specific narrative." He held up his hands, framing the scene in front of him like a movie director. "The deaths need to look uber-sleazy and not like a professional hit. Think drugs, hookers, rent boys – the works. The idea is to discredit Titanium Media Group to the Japanese, kill their new cash cow and tank their reputation in the eyes of future investors. It's the long game but it's what the client wants, and I've got to say, I love it. It's straight out of a Hollywood movie script. Only we're going to write it live."

"It sounds rather convoluted," The Gorgon said, in her usual monotone drawl.

"Oh, it will be," Darius agreed, leaning forward and placing both hands on the table. "But it'll also position us at the top of our game and show the studio we can deliver. I suggested making it look like a mob hit – you know, bad debts and such – but they're adamant about their idea, so that's what we're doing. I need OD deaths on all three Japanese investors and make it look like a real shitshow. Like the studio executives fucking ruined these guys." He stood up to his full height. "As it's such an important job requiring multiple disciplines, I want everyone involved."

Acid frowned. "All of us?"

Darius gave a hollow laugh, devoid of any real amusement. "Well, not me obviously, or Saga. We'll be controlling things in the background." His eyes swept across the room.

"But everyone else here. You're the stars of this show." He turned his attention to the monitor where the Blood Diamond Twins were displayed. "And that includes you two. I need you back from Brazil on the next flight."

"But we've not finished our assignment," Frederik said – or was it Freek? When the only way to distinguish the brothers was by the different metals of their teeth, it wasn't clear. "We're still staking out the Lords of the Slum gang."

Darius sniffed. "Leave that. It's got a longer timescale. This is more important."

"Okay, Boss," Freek said. "We'll be on the next flight out of here."

The crew began talking excitedly about the mission, but Acid didn't join in. Halfway through Darius' speech she'd realised just how badly she needed a shower. But more pressing than her body odour was her frustration. Disgraced movie stars, corrupt producers, and greedy exec teams – it was a far cry from the clean, straightforward assignments she'd expected. And now she was being told she had to work with not just a partner but the entire Kancel Kulture crew. This was not what she'd signed up for.

But then again, none of this was.

Chapter Nineteen

Spook stood in the centre of the rental property in Westlake, surveying what would be their home for the next week or two – maybe even longer, though she hoped not. Now that they were here in LA, it had suddenly hit her how many unknowns there were regarding this trip. Nate had been right to be cautious, but there was no point in admitting her mistake now. She needed to find Acid.

"What do you think?" Lena asked, her voice echoing slightly in the high-ceilinged room.

"It's awesome," Spook replied, taking in the bright open-plan layout. "I mean, it'll do," she added, quickly correcting herself to maintain her new tough exterior.

But the house was amazing – the way the light played across the clean surfaces, the minimalistic furniture. The living area featured two large couches, which looked brand new, either side of a glass coffee table; a massive flatscreen TV had been mounted on the wall like a picture. Spinning around, Spook was impressed by how each zone flowed smoothly into the next, from patio to lounge to kitchen, where stainless steel appliances shone against marble countertops and a large island that doubled as a breakfast bar. Adjacent to this, the dining area showcased a long, dark wood table surrounded by high-backed chairs. Four doors led off from the main space, two on each side. On the back wall, bifold glass doors framed a breathtaking view, leading out onto a wide garden where a small but perfectly formed infinity pool appeared to spill over into the scenery below, the water shimmering under the last of the California evening sun. The icing on the cake was a panoramic view of the Los Angeles skyline.

"There's an issue," Nate said, re-entering the main space. Ever the pragmatist, his focus was on security rather than aesthetics. He'd been on the move since they first arrived, doing a full recon of the building, checking light fittings, upholstery, exits and entrances. He stopped and placed his hands on his hips. "There are only two bedrooms."

Lena grimaced. "Yeah, sorry. I sort of knew that already. But I figured it was in such a good location, and look at this place – it's cool, right? And hey, there's a pool!"

Nate shot her a stern look, but she didn't seem to notice.

"It's fine," Spook said. "I'll take the couch."

"I don't mind," Nate said, pulling his shirt off over his head. "We can take it in turns. But right now I need to freshen up. I'll be in the shower if anyone needs me."

His muscular torso was highlighted under the halogen spotlights as he walked across the room and into the bathroom. Lena shot Spook a glance after he'd gone, a wry smirk on her face. Spook giggled but stopped herself almost immediately.

No. Be professional.

"Seen anything you like?" Lena asked, not letting it go.

131

"Not my type," Spook shot back, hoping her tone would put a stop to this discussion.

She walked over to the bifold doors and slid them open, stepping out onto the patio. It was still warm as hell out here, the air close and smoggy, filled with the scents of jasmine and chlorine from the pool. But it felt good to be back in the States. It had been too long.

About three hundred and fifty miles northwest of LA was Silicon Valley, where a much younger and more innocent Spook Horowitz had dreamed of working. Back then, she'd had a clear path laid out for herself. After graduating from MIT, she would move to San Mateo, close enough to the action in the tech world. She'd imagined herself working at a startup for a few years before launching her own company – founder, CEO and thought leader. It was a neat, ambitious plan, full of potential and promise.

Funny how life turned out.

Those days of dreaming about tech stardom now felt like they belonged to another version of Spook entirely. If the quantum physicist Hugh Everett's Many-Worlds theory was true, somewhere Spook Horowitz was a celebrated inventor, doing TED Talks and the like. But not here.

She walked back inside to find Lena had already set up a makeshift operations hub on the dining table. Two laptops were open in front of her, the dual-screen set-up filled with streams of data and code. She didn't look up as Spook approached, or when she yawned loudly to announce her presence. The young hacker's focus was too intense as she pored over the information, analysing network traffic and encryption protocols.

Spook busied herself making coffee, finding everything she needed in the cupboards and setting the machine to do its magic. The robust bitter aroma filled the space, arousing her senses before she'd even taken a sip. Once it was ready she poured herself a mug of the dark steaming liquid. There was no cream, but she didn't mind it black these days. Even her palate was becoming more sophisticated.

Perhaps alerted by the smell, Nate reappeared once more. He'd changed into a pair of loose-fitting canvas trousers and his hair was still damp from the shower.

"Can I get a cup?" he asked.

"Sure," Spook said, lifting a fresh mug from the cupboard and stepping aside. She watched as he poured himself a drink, quickly averting her eyes as he looked up. A slight flush crept up her neck and her pulse rose a notch, but she put that down to the caffeine.

The truth was, Spook found Nate's semi-naked presence rather confusing. Just when she thought she had her sexuality figured out, he had to start parading around topless looking like… that.

What was a girl to do?

She sipped her coffee, smirking to herself over the rim of her mug.

Jesus.

That sounded like something Acid would say. And she wasn't Acid. She had to remember that.

"Fuck yeah! I've got it!" Lena's voice cut through the quiet, snapping Spook out of her momentary distraction.

Thank God for that.

"What is it?" Nate asked, as he and Spook both walked over to where Lena was practically bouncing up and down in her seat.

"The CCTV system here is freakin' awesome. So much better than in London. They store records for a full twenty-four hours, and everything is completely up to date. And guess what? I've got a hit on my facial recognition software… on *Spook's* software," she corrected herself quickly, turning back to the screens.

"Who?" Nate asked, leaning in.

"Darius," she announced proudly, spinning one of the laptops around so he and Spook could see the screen better. "Check this out."

The image displayed was a grainy still from a CCTV camera, showing a man with black and blond streaked hair outside a large warehouse.

"That's him," Lena said. "And that's his building, I'm sure of it. Kancel Kulture's headquarters. I've tracked him there three times in the last twenty-four hours. He goes in and out multiple times."

"Can you find the address?" Nate asked.

"Already on it. I've uncovered the IP address, which wasn't easy. Now I'm working on hacking into their system. I'm confident we'll be able to intercept their comms."

"How long?" Spook asked, placing her hand on Lena's shoulder.

"Depends on when the next call comes in," Lena replied. "Could be hours, could be minutes."

"Okay. Keep monitoring it," Spook said. "I'm going to get a shower and then I'll do a stint so you can rest."

"Nah, I'm fine," Lena said. "I want to be here for any updates."

"Only if you're sure," Spook told her. But as she walked away she couldn't help smiling to herself. Lena's dedication was reassuring but rest was important also. Despite sleeping on the plane, the jetlag was already dragging at Spook's soul, leaving her antsy and unsettled. She needed to be sharp and fully prepared for when she faced Acid again. Experience told her it was going to be far from a walk in the park.

Chapter Twenty

Acid was already semi-conscious, festering in her bedsheets as she fought through the haze of a crushing hangover, when the shrill ring of her phone jolted her fully awake.

"Get lost," she mumbled, burying her face in the pillow. "I'm not here…"

But the phone kept on ringing. Whoever it was, they weren't giving up. Groaning, she rolled out of bed, the remnants of last night's drinking session throbbing at the edges of her skull. She squinted at the caller ID. Saga. Of course it was bloody Saga. Just what she needed. She also noticed it was nearly lunchtime.

She stretched her mouth and opened her eyes as wide as they'd go in an attempt to rouse herself. Then, with a resigned sigh, she swiped to answer.

"Hello?"

"Ms Vanilla. Have I woken you?"

Damn it.

She'd put on her best phone voice, too. How could he

tell? She glanced around her bedroom, suddenly apprehensive that she was being monitored.

"I've been up hours," she lied. "Just got back from a run."

"We're moving up the timeline on your next gig," Saga said, his tone allowing no argument. "The cinematographer job. His location shoot date has changed, so our window has diminished somewhat."

Acid dragged herself out of bed, catching sight of her reflection in the mirrored door of the wardrobe. She looked a real a state – her hair was a tangled mess; she had yesterday's make-up smeared under her eyes.

"When?" she asked, freeing her twisted knickers from her butt crack.

"Today."

Bugger.

She stretched, her back popping as she moved.

"Details are on their way," Saga continued. "I've just spoken with The Gorgon. She'll call you to arrange everything. Get ready, Acid. It's time to go to work."

He hung up. Acid flung the phone onto the bed and trudged into the bathroom to get ready. She splashed cold water on her face at the sink, then attacked her grimy mouth, flossing and brushing vigorously before rinsing with mouthwash. It helped, but not much. Next, she washed her face thoroughly with soap, trying to ignore her sallow skin and the dark shadows under her eyes. Brushing her wild, knotted hair was a battle, but she managed to tame it into a somewhat presentable ponytail. Just as she switched on the shower, her phone buzzed again from the other room.

"For God's sake!"

Leaving the water to run hot, she returned to her bedroom. Saga had sent over an image file – a flyer for an art exhibit at Hammer Museum in Westwood Village. She forwarded the flyer to her laptop on the nightstand and ran the image file through a metadata extraction program. Hidden beneath layers of digital noise, she found an encrypted packet which she fed through a decryption module. Inputting a one-time keycode – the date of the art exhibition – she was able to open the contained document.

It was a detailed dossier on Lou Jefferson, the cinematographer and her latest mark. The document included basic personal data, known associates, and recent financial transactions. More importantly, it linked to a real-time surveillance app that Saga had installed on Jefferson's phone following a successful phishing attack. A live map showed Jefferson's current location – a pulsing dot moving slowly across a map of Los Angeles. Below the map, a panel displayed his recent messages, call logs, and app usage data. Each message could be expanded to reveal its full content, and the call logs showed timestamps, durations, and caller identities where available.

Modern technology.

It almost made this job too easy.

Acid was memorising the critical information when another call came through. The caller ID flashed as KK3. The Gorgon.

"You ready to hit this Jefferson guy?" she said as Acid picked up.

"And hello to you too, sweetie."

The Gorgon was silent.

"Yes. All set," Acid said.

"You have the details? You can see he's got a dinner reservation for 7 p.m."

Acid scanned the screen. "Yep. Got it."

"Good. I'll meet you at HQ just before eight. Don't be

late. We'll park up opposite the restaurant and tail him when he leaves."

The Gorgon continued laying out her plan, but after a few more seconds Acid left the phone on the bed and went for a shower. She'd always preferred crafting strategy on the fly rather than sticking to a rigid plan. Most of the time things didn't go the way you wanted them to, and if you were too stuck in your approach you were screwed. Acid worked best with a little chaos; it was where her instincts came alive. But she was pleased with the timeline. It gave her a chance to freshen up and get her head together.

Eight hours later, dressed and focused, Acid met The Gorgon as arranged and they drove to Beverly Hills in one of the company cars Darius had recently bought. Without any discussion, The Gorgon took the driver's seat, which was fine by Acid. The car, a black Maserati with garish, shiny gold trim and alloys, wasn't her style at all, but it blended perfectly as they cruised along Sunset towards the Hills. That was LA for you.

Acid opened the window as they drove, enjoying the early evening breeze on her skin. She felt better than she had done on waking, that was for sure. She'd even indulged in some yoga that afternoon. Not that she'd ever admit it, but she found doing the poses and stretches rather helpful. Of course, being Acid, it wasn't the crystals-and-chakras type of yoga that most LA residents favoured. Instead, she'd discovered a YouTube channel called *Punk Rock Yoga*, and bending and stretching to the sounds of Black Flag and Bikini Kill worked for her just fine.

It seemed the adage was true – if you could imagine it, then it existed somewhere on the internet.

The Gorgon parked in a side street opposite El Flamingo Restaurant in Beverly Hills. "There he is," she said, pointing to a man and a woman at a corner table visible through the large windows.

Acid squinted. The man was a little chunkier and had less hair than in the picture she'd seen, but it was Jefferson all right. They would have already been there an hour and were onto dessert, Jefferson spoon-feeding his mistress something sweet from a tall glass on the table between them.

"The nerve on this guy," she muttered as they watched. "Sitting at the front of the restaurant with his twink for everyone to see. No wonder his wife wants him gone."

But she could see why Jefferson's head had been turned. The woman with him was the real deal – blonde, slim, with a mischievous smile and a pair of impressive assets that had to be fake. She eyed Jefferson over her wine glass, her dark blue slip dress clinging just right, not revealing too much, but perfectly showcasing her long, tanned legs. She could have been a model; more likely, she was an aspiring actress. No doubt Jefferson had dangled promises of stardom, just as long as she didn't mind choking on his old saggy balls now and again.

Six months in LA had stripped away any of Acid's remaining illusions about Hollywood's glamour. Despite the noise of the Me Too movement, it was still a male-dominated circus and predators like Jefferson were the ringmasters. Sharks in a sea of hopeful minnows. The rule, not the exception. From Saga's file, Acid knew Jefferson was a total shit. His wife claimed he had illegitimate kids scattered across the city and that he'd come home on more than one occasion with blood under his fingernails, refusing to explain why. Whatever he'd been up to he was a bad guy and that was all Acid needed to know. Sometimes you did the job for the money; sometimes the pleasure of taking down a creep like Jefferson was its own reward.

"We'll wait until he goes to his apartment and it's just the two of them," The Gorgon continued. "Then we break in, spike him, and make it look like an overdose. If we have to take out the girl too, we will."

Acid frowned at that. Collateral damage wasn't her thing. Never had been. "Maybe we'll all get lucky and he'll have a heart attack screwing her before we get there," Acid replied. "She looks like the sort of girl who could do that to an old guy like Jefferson."

The Gorgon raised her head but didn't even crack a smile as she stared at the mark. But that wasn't a shock. The woman was devoid of humour. But then, so were the rest of them at Kancel Kulture – Grimaldi, Saga, the whole damned crew. It was becoming a real drag for Acid. In her line of work, you needed a bit of gallows humour to stay sane, but they were all so fucking serious. Even Darius. When she first met him he was a twisted bastard, but he was also nervous and awkward at times. Now, infamy had gone to his head in the worst possible way and turned him into a full-blown prick – self-obsessed, humourless, like some hustle-culture bro who thought hating women and shouting was a personality.

But he was her brother. And he provided her with steady work. That's what she wanted, wasn't it? Working in a field where she could thrive. Doing the only thing she'd ever been truly good at. And when the time came, she'd—

"Whoa! Here we go." Her thoughts snapped back to the present as Jefferson and his date stood to leave. She nudged The Gorgon. "Time to roll, Chuckles. The mark's on the move."

Chapter Twenty-One

Planet Fitness in Downtown LA buzzed with overly motivated energy that was almost obscene for a Tuesday evening. It was well past nine and the gym was crammed with the night crowd. It was individuals mainly, each plugged into their own world via their EarPods, eyes locked on their reflections in the floor-to-ceiling mirrors. Anyone walking in now looking for a free machine or weight bench would have a wait. Every treadmill, every exercise bike and elliptical was occupied by tense, harried people eager to shed the day's stress along with their calories. The air was thick with the smell of sweat and rubber. Fluorescent lights cast a harsh glow over the rows of machines and their dedicated users. Fast electronic music blasted from the overhead speakers, keeping the energy high and the pace relentless, underscored by the rhythmic thud of treadmills and the clanking of weights.

On a treadmill in the back corner of the gym, Abi Sandoval was starting to hit her stride, sweating out the issues of the day and chasing some much-needed endorphins. She pulled in deep breaths as she ran, moving at a steady pace, but not so fast she couldn't enjoy the old episode of Seinfeld playing on her phone, propped up on the machine in front of her.

Abi had been a fan of Seinfeld all her life, or more accurately her mom had been, and so she'd inherited the appreciation by proxy. The sitcom's familiar humour provided a welcome distraction from the monotony of her workout, keeping her mind from drifting back to the complexities of her day.

As a new episode began, the iconic slap bass introduction resounding in her EarPods, her gaze wandered across the gym. In one corner, a pair of muscle-bound body-builders struck exaggerated poses, grimacing at their reflections as if trying to intimidate their muscles into growing. Nearby, two women walked in synchronised steps on angled treadmills, punctuating their exercise with laughter and the occasional gasp of disbelief as they exchanged gossip.

By this point Abi had been running for half an hour, which was ten minutes longer than usual. Maybe she was trying to outrun the day's irritations, pushing herself further than she normally would.

She didn't hate her job or her life here in LA. But to say it was what she'd dreamed of for herself would be a stretch. Unlike many moderately ambitious, moderately attractive young women who flocked to LA with visions of becoming famous actresses, Abi had come to study film. She dreamt of success not in front of the camera, but behind it. Originally from Thousand Oaks, she'd been a huge movie fan her entire life, and while she appreciated a dramatic monologue, her true obsession was with camera angles, focus pulls, and how lighting, texture and colour could transform the mood of a scene. Since discovering at thirteen that cinematography was an actual career, she'd been determined to pursue it. And where better to learn than the LA Film School?

Continuing to scope out the room, Abi's eyes locked with those of a creepy-looking guy wearing a tank top and shorts a few metres away. He was only lifting a pair of tens but making a show of it. He also didn't look away when their eyes met.

"Fucking weirdo," she muttered, averting her gaze. In doing so, she caught her reflection in the mirrored wall in front of her. She'd been avoiding that – hence the distraction of Jerry and co – and she really wished she hadn't looked.

Jesus, some guys will perv on anything.

Abi knew her mixed heritage – African American and Costa Rican – gave her features a distinctive edge, and she could look pretty good when she put in the effort. Medium height, slim but with curves in the right places, she'd recently cut and chemically straightened her hair, and when styled properly it framed her oval face perfectly. But not today. Today she looked like a sweaty mess. Her hair clung to her forehead, and under the harsh lights her skin appeared pale and unhealthy.

But she looked like her mother, she realised, and that wasn't a bad thing. Her mom had died four years ago when Abi was just twenty-two, and it still hurt. Her mom, her best friend and biggest fan, had moved to California at eighteen, disillusioned by Costa Rica's misleading moniker as the 'rich coast'. Once here, she'd hooked up with the first guy she met with prospects and got pregnant with Abi. The rest, as they say, was history.

Only it wasn't. Not really.

Abi's father, a hotshot lawyer, was no longer in her life.

He'd pushed her to study law at university, so when she told him she was going to the LA film school to study cinematography he practically disowned her. But screw him. He'd been looking for an excuse to distance himself since his divorce from her mom when Abi was ten. He hadn't even attended her mother's funeral – too busy with his new family in Los Altos. To claw back some semblance of payback, Abi had dropped her father's name, Martin, in favour of her mom's maiden name, Sandoval, when she started in the industry. It sounded cooler anyway, more exotic. Tobias Martin was now just another name on Abi's list of men who'd let her down.

The treadmill hummed beneath her feet and she upped the pace, trying to outrun the familiar sense of loneliness on the outskirts of her consciousness. On her phone, Kramer had just thrown a bowl of cereal mixed with tomato juice against Jerry's wall. Abi wished she had friends like Jerry and Kramer, even if they were a bit nuts. But most days her social interactions were limited to work contacts and her demanding boss who… Would you look at that?

Think of the devil and he shall appear.

Her employer's name flashed on the screen, interrupting Seinfeld. Call waiting.

Bastard.

She slammed her hand against the treadmill's red emergency stop button, grabbing the sides as the machine came to a sudden halt, almost throwing her forward. Composing herself, she answered the call.

"Good evening, Mr Jefferson, sir. Everything okay?" She emphasised the word 'evening', but he didn't pick up on it.

"Abigail, thank God." He sounded stressed. "I need you to do something for me."

Abi had been working for Lou Jefferson for nearly a

year, initially enticed by a job listing that promised a stepping stone into the industry as an assistant cinematographer. Jefferson, a member of the American Society of Cinematographers, had an impressive résumé with major films like *Death of a Saint* and the recent *Sharks! Sharks! Sharks!* under his belt. At the interview they'd hit it off, and Abi had high hopes for her new role. But, like many things in her life, reality soon diverged from her expectations. Jefferson was a real obsessive, rarely allowing Abi near any actual cinematography tasks, and preferring instead to delegate jobs that were decidedly less creative and more clerical. Forget assistant cinematographer; she was more like the old bastard's personal assistant.

Yet she was sticking it out, for the time being at least. Working for Jefferson would look impressive on her résumé and would hopefully springboard her into more legitimate and fulfilling roles when she was ready. She'd made a deal with herself to endure Jefferson's bullshit for another year, all in pursuit of her larger goal.

"What is it, Mr Jefferson?" she asked, putting a professional sheen on her voice as her breath returned.

"I've forgotten my wallet," he said. "I need it tonight."

Fucksake...

She could hear the muffled sound of traffic in the background. If he was driving somewhere and needed to pay for gas, why not use his iPhone like everyone else?

"I left it in the studio," he continued. "I need you to get it and bring it over."

Abi suppressed a groan. This wasn't the first time she'd been tasked with something mundane and time-consuming.

"Fine," she said, already admitting defeat. He was her boss, after all, and she'd recently discovered he paid her slightly above industry standards. Plus, he always got so pissy if she mentioned it was after hours or played her union card. It wasn't worth the hassle. "I'll bring it over to the house in the next hour."

She pictured Jefferson's huge mansion over in Beverly Crest, with its high walls and gold-plated gates that always seemed to take forever to open for her. Despite living in LA for so long, the mansion's grandeur still amazed her every time she had to run errands there.

"God, no," Jefferson spluttered. "Don't go to the house. I'm heading to my apartment. Bring the wallet there. You have your set of keys?"

"Ah, I see. Yes, I have keys."

Abi had been to Jefferson's apartment in West Holly-wood a few times. The one his wife, Laura, knew nothing about – or at least pretended to know nothing about.

That explained the anxious phone call, then.

Jefferson didn't need his wallet for the credit cards it contained, but for the packet of little blue pills he kept in there.

"Bring it here ASAP," he insisted. "I'll reimburse you for any cab fare you accrue."

Abi puffed out her cheeks. Clearly he didn't give a shit if she had plans this evening, but why didn't he have a stash of pills stored somewhere? All he used that apartment for was entertaining his latest pretty young thing.

She wondered if he was testing her loyalty. Or maybe he was just a sick bastard and wanted her to know he was still getting laid even at his age.

"No problem, sir," Abi said, forcing a big grin he couldn't see but might sense. "I'll be there as soon as I can."

"You'll find it okay?"

"Yes. No problem."

She hung up and shook her head. Would she find it

okay? Yes, she reckoned so. She'd been at Jefferson's love nest only a few months earlier, having been ordered to clean up for the randy old bastard after a hooker had ingested stupid amounts of liquor and barbiturates and was feared dead. Luckily, Abi had managed to revive the poor girl, but there was still a hell of a lot of vomit to clean up and a very rattled boss to calm down. Some days, she felt as if she wasn't even Jefferson's PA but his fixer – hired to keep his misdemeanours and mistakes from reaching the press. But as a casting agent had once warned her, all assistants are fixers in Hollywood.

Grabbing her towel and phone, she headed for the changing rooms. Seinfeld would have to wait. She had a job to do.

Chapter Twenty-Two

Over in Westlake, Spook and Lena were seated in front of their laptops, pretending not to listen as Nate paced up and down on the patio outside, phone pressed to his ear.

"I know it goes against the code," Spook heard him say. "But humour me... Just hypothetically, where would you stand *if* someone made a move on them?"

Spook exchanged a glance with Lena, both straining to catch every word. A pause followed, then a muffled response that Spook couldn't quite decipher.

"Yeah, I get that." Nate sighed. "Okay. Thanks anyway." He ended the call and stared off into the distance for a long time.

"Is he okay?" Lena whispered.

Spook didn't reply. She had no answer for Lena, but she felt a fresh twinge of respect for Nate. He didn't like this idea but was putting the effort in all the same, feeling out his contacts, gauging their stance on Kancel Kulture.

Both women snapped their attention back to the screens as Nate stepped into the room.

"It's not good news," he said, rubbing the bridge of his nose. "I've not spoken to all my contacts yet, but so far no one wants to commit to anything. They're scared to rock the boat with Kancel Kulture. The consensus is they're already industry leaders, with far too much influence. Macademeus just told me that if we were to try anything against them it'd be suicide. They're too powerful."

"That should be us," Spook said. "We should be the industry leaders."

"We will be," Nate replied. "But it's going to take time."

"Not if we take them out," insisted Spook, looking to Lena for support but getting nothing.

"You sound bloody ridiculous," Nate snapped. "And quite frankly I'm getting a little sick of it, Spook. I'm doing what I can, but Macademeus is right. It's reckless and it's against the industry code. We should focus on building our own organisation, not destroying others."

"Fine. Sure." Spook's voice rose unexpectedly as she got to her feet. "And when we do get going, really making a name for ourselves, how do you think Darius will react? Do you honestly think he's going to respect some dubious code of ethics?"

Nate turned to face her, not backing down for a second. "Everyone in this industry follows the same rules."

"Bullshit!" Spook shot back, her frustration mounting. "If Darius even suspects we're a threat to his organisation, he'll take us out without blinking. You don't know him the way I do, Nate. I've stared into his eyes. He's a psycho. He'd kill us all without a second thought."

"Perhaps you're forgetting there's only three of us," Nate replied, his voice rising as well. "Only two if we don't count Lena. Plus, this is Kancel Kulture's home turf now." He stepped closer, eyes narrowing. "Besides, that's not the real reason we're here, is it, Spook? It's not why you forced our hand. You're still on some pointless crusade to save Acid Vanilla's soul."

Nate's words hit hard, but Spook maintained eye contact. She knew he had a point; deep down part of her agreed, but admitting it was another matter. Out of the corner of her eye, she saw Lena shifting uncomfortably in her seat.

Taking a moment to compose herself, Spook's voice was low and steady when she spoke again. "All I'm saying is, while we're here we might as well check out the landscape."

"No," Nate snapped. "It's too dangerous. I still have a few contacts to call. Maybe we can set up some meetings while we're here. These are experienced operatives who might be interested in joining our ranks."

"But we're wasting an opportunity," Spook insisted. "Not observing Kancel Kulture's operations up close while we're here is dumb."

Nate groaned, about to reply when Lena yelled, "Wait!", prompting Spook and Nate to turn.

"What is it?" Spook asked.

"I've done it!" Lena's eyes were wide as she stared at her screen. "I'm in."

Spook moved closer. "Seriously?"

"Yeah. And it looks like we got lucky."

Spook glanced at Nate, and they each took a seat beside Lena, leaning in as she continued.

"Kancel Kulture's operations are centralised through a control centre monitored from their headquarters, but that set-up has a backdoor I've managed to exploit," Lena explained. "Using some network intrusion tools I designed for such a purpose, I injected a line of spyware into their system framework that can log calls, read texts and track phone locations." She paused to catch her breath, her eyes gleaming with excitement, reflecting the light from her laptop. "A message just came through. It's coded, but the gist is clear enough – there's an active job happening right now in Beverly Hills and… Oh, shit! I'm getting real-time alerts! There's a phone call coming in. I can't tap into the audio, but I've got the number."

"Can you triangulate the call?" Spook asked.

"Doing it now," Lena replied, her fingers flying over the keyboard. "It's a burner phone, bought from Walmart. It's only ever dialled a few numbers but I can see its location. Burners are hard to link to an ID, but their cheap tech is riddled with vulnerabilities. The burner is in Beverly Hills too. Looks like it's our guys."

"Can you get a precise reading?" Spook asked.

"Sure."

"Send the location to my phone," Spook said, getting up. "I can track it on the move."

"What are you doing?" Nate asked.

"I'm going to see what's going on."

Nate slapped the table. "I thought we'd just agreed to lie low. I need to talk to more contacts, and get a better read on the Kancel Kulture situation. We don't want every fucker in the industry gunning for us."

"But it could be Acid."

"Forget Acid!"

"I can't!" Spook grabbed her jacket and backpack. Decision made. "I have to see it through, once and for all." She headed for the door.

"Don't be so bloody reckless," Nate yelled after her. "You're not her, Spook. Stop acting like her. You haven't yet got the skills, for one thing."

Ouch. That stung.

But Spook brushed it off. Maybe she was being reckless. Foolish, even. But she had to try.

"Get back here, Spook," Nate snarled, but she already had the door open, she was already stepping through.

"Be careful," Lena called after her.

Spook paused. "I'm always…" she started, before catching herself. She swallowed. "I will be," she said. Then she left, letting the door slam shut behind her.

Chapter Twenty-Three

Acid and The Gorgon sat in tense silence inside the black and gold Maserati, parked in the shadows across from Jefferson's apartment. Half an hour earlier, they'd watched Jefferson park in the adjacent lot and enter the building with his date through a small entrance on the roadside.

"Give it a few more minutes," The Gorgon murmured, picking up on Acid's growing impatience. "Once he's done what he came here for, he'll likely fall asleep. Makes our job easier."

Acid leaned closer to the windscreen to get a better view of Jefferson's building. It was more low-rent than she'd expected, the sort of place you'd walk passed without a second glance. But if this was the eminent cinematographer's sordid little sex den, maybe he got off on living like a bum for a few nights a month. Or maybe it was actually the perfect hideaway for someone leading a double life, a place his wife and colleagues would never think to look.

She leaned back. Beside her The Gorgon, always the

consummate professional, was methodically inspecting the contents of a black duffel bag. She extracted a small leather pouch, unzipping it to reveal the two syringes prepped for their task tonight. Each was loaded with a lethal blend of heroin and cocaine – a speedball strong enough to kill anyone, regardless of their tolerance. The duffel also contained wraps of cocaine and heroin powder, cotton balls, plastic baggies, a silver cigarette lighter and burnt spoons, the props needed to stage an apparent overdose. Darius had insisted on a clean execution – in fact, 'graceful' was the exact term he'd used – and despite her misgivings about Kancel Kulture's operations, Acid had to admit there was an artistry to crafting a narrative this way. Caesar often had his operatives execute such meticulous set-ups, especially for clients willing to pay top dollar. His mantra, that 'accidents happen, for the right price', was always a source of amusement for him. But this cloak-and-dagger play-acting left Acid cold, never quieting the bats the way splattering someone in front of a truck or slicing open their arteries in a bathtub did.

"We've waited long enough," she said. "Let's go."

The Gorgon glanced at the clock on the dashboard and nodded. They waited for a shirtless young man in jean shorts to wander past, then exited the car. The streetlights cast long shadows as they crossed the road and approached Jefferson's building. Skirting past the main entrance, they moved around the corner to hide in the shadows while keeping an eye on the door.

"There are two floors and he's on the second level," The Gorgon whispered. "Apartment number nineteen."

Who did this wizened cow think she was dealing with?

"Yes, Saga briefed me too," Acid told her. "I have all the details committed to memory."

"Did Saga also tell you to stick to the plan?" The Gorgon asked.

Acid sighed. She was sick of trying to prove herself to these people. "He didn't need to. I'm a professional."

Their conversation was cut short as the door to the main entrance swung open, and a small man wearing a bucket hat exited the building. The moment the coast was clear, Acid moved swiftly to the door, her hand darting out to catch it before it closed completely. She managed to wedge two fingers into the narrow opening, gripping the edge of the door just enough to pull it back. With a flick of her head, Acid gestured for The Gorgon to follow. They slipped inside the building, letting the door close silently behind them.

The building was a typical sixties LA apartment complex, two storeys wrapped around a central courtyard with a rectangular pool that mirrored the moonlight. From the outside it had seemed unremarkable to Acid, but up close it had a certain hipster charm. Plus, no doorman, and no security cameras either. It was likely that most of these apartments were owned by men like Jefferson – rich guys needing a secluded place to fuck their mistresses or engage in drug benders with local hookers.

They ascended the narrow staircase to the second floor, moving down the landing towards number nineteen. Acid got there first and paused outside, listening for any sounds from within. She heard nothing. No muffled conversations, no grunts or sighs of satisfaction. Jefferson and his date must already be asleep.

Satisfied, she stepped aside, allowing The Gorgon to move in. Pulling a quad comb set from her pocket, the older woman knelt in front of the lock and set to work. Moments later, the mechanism gave a soft, almost inaudible click.

"We're in," she whispered, glancing up at Acid and easing the door open.

Acid slipped inside, entering a dimly lit kitchen, quickly followed by The Gorgon who closed the door behind them, plunging the room into darkness. They paused, allowing their eyes to adjust to the gloom.

Beyond a high breakfast bar lay a sparse lounge area with two couches, a coffee table, and not much else. The trappings of a man uninterested in the aesthetics of his sordid little love nest. As long as it had a bed, right?

They moved through the space with practised stealth, Acid leading the way down the hallway towards the bedroom at the far end where they expected to find Jefferson, worn out and snoring. As they neared, she noticed the door was slightly ajar and there was a light on. Closer still, she could hear the low murmur of voices from within.

Shit.

Jefferson and his companion were still awake.

This was not what they were expecting. Before Acid could reassess the situation, The Gorgon stormed past her and into the room. Jefferson and the woman were seated side by side on the edge of the bed, both undressed down to their underwear but no further. They looked dismayed and awkward for the split second before their attention was captured by The Gorgon's abrupt entrance.

Jefferson leapt up. "What the fuck?"

The woman screamed, covering herself with her arms and making for the door. In one swift motion The Gorgon grabbed her by the head and slammed her against the wall, leaving a hole in the plaster. The woman slumped onto the carpet with a dull thud, unconscious.

"Hey!" Acid yelled.

"Get the hell out of here!" Jefferson shouted, louder.

Not missing a beat, The Gorgon drew a pistol and pointed it directly at Jefferson's head. "Be quiet," she hissed.

"Whoa there," Acid said, her eyes fixed on the Beretta in her colleague's grip. "Who's going off script now?"

The Gorgon ignored her. "On your knees," she snarled at Jefferson, who was engaged in a pathetic on-the-spot dance, unsure what to do. "Now!"

Jefferson immediately dropped to his knees. It looked as if it hurt him, but hell, the guy wouldn't be suffering long. He was wearing white boxers and long black socks – a really sexy combination and no mistake. His stomach bulged over the waistband and his skin glistened with sweat. A poorly chosen tattoo – a shooting star that had gone green and blurry on his upper arm – was the icing on a very unattractive cake.

"I can give you money. As much as you want," he stammered, his voice desperate.

"It's not about money," Acid said, walking over to him. She grabbed a handful of his sweaty, thinning hair, yanked him to his feet and shoved him onto the bed. The Gorgon moved quickly, pinning him down and shoving the Beretta's barrel into his mouth to stifle his screams.

With the bats screeching for blood, Acid unzipped the duffel bag strapped to The Gorgon's back and retrieved the leather pouch. She slid out one of the syringes and held it up to the light. The liquid inside was cloudy and brown, resembling murky river water.

"Keep him still," she ordered The Gorgon, clambering onto the bed beside Jefferson. He was struggling and whining, making for a difficult target, but by placing her knee on his biceps she was able to still him long enough to stab the needle into his vein and release the lethal mixture with a steady hand. "Okay. Clear."

"Give her the other syringe," The Gorgon said, nodding towards the unconscious woman slumped against the wall.

Acid hesitated. "No. We don't need to."

"Yes. We do. She has to die." The Gorgon's voice was cold, her bony hands still gripping Jefferson's shoulders as she waited for the drugs to take effect.

"She didn't see anything," Acid replied.

The Gorgon glared at her. "She knows there was a break-in. If she speaks to the cops, it won't fit the narrative. This way it looks like he got rough with her. Maybe he couldn't perform and took his frustration out on her. Then he took some more drugs. Too many. Maybe she did too. Or you can strangle her. Either way, she has to die."

Acid held The Gorgon's gaze, a silent battle of wills playing out between them. The Gorgon was challenging her. This was a test. Jefferson made a low groaning noise as if he was having the best sex of his life. Acid scratched at her neck. She knew The Gorgon's logic was sound from a twisted, criminal perspective. The scene had to look legitimate for the CSI team. Done right, her narrative made sense. The poor woman would need to be high to endure sex with this slimy prick.

She lifted out the second syringe, but as she looked down at the woman crumpled in the corner, naked but for her panties and bra, something held her back.

"Get a move on," The Gorgon hissed. "This one's nearly gone."

"Give me a chance."

But The Gorgon, impatient, clambered off Jefferson. She grabbed the syringe from Acid and shoved her against the wall. "I'll do it myself."

She was advancing toward the fallen woman when a sudden knock on the front door echoed through the apartment. Both women froze, staring at each other wide-eyed as the knocking came again, shattering the tension like a rock through a window.

Buggering shit.

"Who the hell is that?" Acid whispered.

The Gorgon shushed her. They remained still, bracing for more complications. Acid counted back from ten, trying to focus her attention away from the sensation of tiny bat teeth gnawing at her synapses.

Whoever it was stopped knocking. Acid relaxed her shoulders as The Gorgon knelt beside the woman. She was about to administer the fatal dose when the unmistakable sound of a key turning in a lock redirected their attention to the door.

"Mr Jefferson? Are you there?" a woman's voice called out. "I've got your wallet. Sorry if I woke you, but you did say it was important."

Acid looked up just as a young woman appeared in the doorway. Her ethnicity was ambiguous but her bobbed hair gave her a sharp, put-together look despite the late hour. She was wearing yoga pants and a large hoodie. She saw Acid. She saw the syringe in The Gorgon's hand.

"What the fuck?"

Her gaze darted from the syringe to Jefferson's lifeless form sprawled across the bed. She got it immediately; Acid could see it in her eyes. As the realisation spread, she screamed and grabbed the doorframe, propelling herself back the way she came.

"Damn it!" The Gorgon cursed, tossing the syringe onto the bed. "Take care of this," she told Acid. "I'll handle her."

Acid nodded, unable to come up with a response before The Gorgon sprinted out of the apartment after the woman. She could hear her footsteps as she raced along the landing outside.

"Well, Mr Jefferson," she said, sitting down on the bed next to his corpse. "This is all we bloody need."

Chapter Twenty-Four

Abi's heartbeat thundered in her ears as she sprinted along the landing, running as fast as she could, running for her life. Her head spun, struggling to process what she'd just witnessed. Despite working behind the scenes in Hollywood for a relatively short time, she'd already seen a lot of sordid shit, but nothing like this.

She could still see an image of the room imprinted on her mind's eye. The menacing stare of the woman in black with dark hair and thick bangs, and the sheer contempt from the other woman with pale skin and sunken cheeks – the one now chasing her. She'd been holding a syringe, poised to stab it into the young woman huddled in the corner. Jefferson's mistress, no doubt. Poor bitch. She only looked to be in her early twenties, not much younger than Abi.

But it was the image of her boss she couldn't shake from her mind as she raced towards the stairwell. Jefferson, sprawled in his underwear with white foam leaking from his mouth. Dead. Or if not dead, definitely on his way out. The same as his girlfriend. The same as Abi, too, if she didn't get away.

Because witness was the operative word here. Abi was young and relatively inexperienced, but she knew how these things worked. The fact she'd seen the women's faces made her a problem for them.

A problem that had to be eliminated.

Reaching the end of the landing she practically threw herself down the stairs, taking them two at a time, a rush of adrenaline fuelling her. She leapt the last few steps, stumbling as she hit the hard concrete below.

Get up. Get moving.

Scrambling to her feet she sprinted for the exit, the echo of footsteps above spurring her on. Her pursuer was close behind.

Who the hell were these people?

Clearly, Jefferson had pissed someone off. Her mind raced. Who had a motive, and more importantly who had the means and motivation to have the poor bastard killed? Jefferson wasn't a good boss or a good man, but he was a damn good cinematographer and he didn't deserve to die. Did he?

Regardless, it didn't matter now. Someone had sent those women to kill him, and Abi had disturbed their plans. There was no way they'd let her just walk away.

Reaching the entrance she slammed her open palm against the door release button.

Come on. Open up, damn you!

The lock mechanism clicked and Abi flung herself at the door, bursting out onto the street. The cool night air hit her face as she stumbled out of the building, her heart pounding in her chest. She looked around frantically, shivering in her sweat-soaked shirt. The street was empty, the buildings dark. She needed to find help and fast. The adrenaline was beginning to wane, leaving a gnawing fear in its place.

Think, Abi. Think.

She sprinted away from the building towards downtown, the voice in her head screaming at her to keep moving. Glancing back over her shoulder, she saw the woman was still chasing her. In the pale moonlight she looked like a ghoul from a horror movie.

Abi turned back and quickened her pace, all those nights on the treadmill now paying off more than she ever imagined. Her eyes darted left and right, scanning her surroundings for any sign of help or a place to hide. Turning sharply into an alley, her sneakers skidded on loose gravel, nearly sending her sprawling to the ground again. Cursing herself, she regained her balance and pushed forward, her arms pumping, each stride fuelled by raw fear.

Another glance over her shoulder revealed only the dark alleyway. But she was almost certain her ghostly pursuer wouldn't give up so easily. Reaching the end of the alley, she burst onto a narrow back street cluttered with overflowing dumpsters. She veered right and ducked down another side street. Lactic acid seared through her sides and her muscles screamed in protest, but fear kept her moving, pushing her body beyond its limits.

Rounding another corner, a chain-link fence loomed suddenly in the dim light. She almost collided with it but managed to stop herself. With no time to lose, she scrambled up, her fingers clutching the cold metal, her feet desperately finding purchase in the diamond-shaped links. She hoisted herself over the top and dropped down on the other side, a jolt of pain shooting up her leg as she landed badly.

Ignoring the pain, she pushed off, limping now but determined not to stop. She ran to the end of the street and into another alleyway. The back streets of west LA were a labyrinth at night, shadows morphing into shapes that played tricks on the eyes. As she hurried onwards, she tried to figure out where she might come out. The alley was long and winding but she could see lights at the far end. With any luck it would open into a busier area, perhaps with traffic, maybe even taxis, if she was lucky.

Risking another glance back, Abi saw no sign of her pursuer. She was almost clear. Her mind spun wildly with scenarios for when she reached her apartment. Should she call the police? Would they even believe her?

Her whirlwind thoughts came to a stuttering halt as a figure stepped into the light at the end of the alley.

"No! Fuck!"

It was her. The killer.

Time slowed to a crawl as Abi scrambled to reverse direction. But the uneven ground betrayed her once more and her already damaged ankle buckled, sending searing pain up her leg.

"Please… no!"

She stumbled forward, gravel tearing at her palms as she tried to break her fall. The pain in her ankle was excruciating, throbbing in sync with her pounding heartbeat.

Get up! Move!

She struggled to stand but the agony was too much, and she stumbled over once more.

The woman began walking towards her, her ghostly silhouette framed by the lights at the end of the alley. Her hand moved out from her side, revealing the unmistakable shape of a knife.

Abi clutched her ankle as panic and dread spiked

through her system. This wasn't fair. She had nothing to do with her boss. She was just in the wrong place at the wrong time. With a desperate effort, she dragged herself along the ground, her anxious mind turning over as she cycled through her options. But each one led to the same grim conclusion.

Screw that prick Jefferson.

Screw whoever sent these people.

Tears streamed down Abi's cheeks as she pleaded for her life. But she knew it was useless. She was going to die here, alone in this alleyway. She screwed her eyes shut, then snapped them open again, unsure which was best. Possibly because the answer was neither. Whether she saw the fatal strike coming or not, it was on its way.

Cold dread settled over her as the woman raised the knife. But just as the blade was about to descend, Abi became aware of a new presence in the alley – a figure, moving fast, darting through the shadows. For a split second Abi thought it was the dark-haired woman from the apartment. But then the newcomer slammed into the ghost woman with a sudden burst of energy, knocking her to the wall and sending the knife clattering to the concrete.

Abi was left gasping for breath. She could hardly believe what was happening.

Was this someone come to help her? Was she actually going to survive this nightmare?

Or was this just another cruel twist in what was fast becoming the worst night of her life?

Chapter Twenty-Five

Spook had taken a cab to a spot two blocks from the address Lena's tracking system told her was the current location of two Kancel Kulture operatives, choosing to walk the rest of the way to avoid drawing attention. She'd been crouched in the alley opposite, eyes fixed on the entrance, when a young woman had entered the building. At first Spook had thought nothing of it. The woman was young and seemed unremarkable except for the haste in her movements, but it was late at night and she was probably eager to get indoors.

But within minutes, the same woman had burst back through the doors, pursued by the woman Spook knew as The Gorgon. Spook had trailed them through a maze of side streets, leading to this dark alleyway.

"You!" The Gorgon snarled, regaining her footing and squaring up to Spook. Up close, she was taller than Spook remembered. Her gaunt, pale features seemed ever more wraithlike under the flickering streetlight. Her eyes burned with fierce anger.

"That's right," Spook responded, her voice steady despite the knot of tension in her stomach. "Me!"

She quickly assessed her surroundings as Nate had taught her, keeping her focus on her opponent. The Gorgon's eyes darted to a knife lying on the ground at the same moment Spook noticed it. But Spook was closer. She didn't have time to grab it but managed to kick it away just as The Gorgon lunged for it, sending the blade skittering into the shadows.

"What the hell are you doing here?" The Gorgon demanded, falling into a defensive stance.

"I'm here to stop you from hurting her," Spook said, glancing over at the young woman who was still struggling to stand on what appeared to be a twisted ankle. "After that... well... you don't need to know."

"Why's that?" The Gorgon's voice dropped to a venomous hiss as she inched closer.

Spook raised her fists as she ran through possible scenarios – everything that might happen in the next few seconds. "Because you'll be dead," she replied.

Without giving The Gorgon a chance to react, Spook lunged. It was a calculated risk, designed to unbalance her more experienced opponent. She landed a solid blow to the taller woman's jaw, immediately followed by an elbow to the abdomen. The Gorgon, caught off guard, swung her fists wildly, but Spook ducked under each blow then kicked out, sweeping the woman's legs and sending her crashing to the concrete with a heavy thud. It was a satisfying move, played out almost exactly as Spook had envisioned, but she knew better than to gloat. She stepped back, ready for what came next.

The Gorgon recovered quicker than Spook anticipated. Rolling onto her side, she pushed herself up with a grunt, her features twisted in fury. She lunged forward, her movements now swifter and more calculated. Spook side-stepped her advance but The Gorgon grabbed her wrist, twisting her arm behind her back and forcing Spook to bend forward.

"Now we see what you're made of," The Gorgon snarled, using her free hand to deliver a series of hard punches to Spook's side, driving the air from her lungs. Whilst Spook fought to breathe, the taller woman leaned forward, leveraging Spook's weight against her and propelling her towards the alley wall.

Shiiiiit.

Spook braced for impact but at the last second managed to twist away so it was just her shoulder, rather than her head, that smashed into the rough stone. Painful, but not deadly. As they broke apart, the air was filled with their heavy gasps.

"You're out of your league," The Gorgon hissed, wiping blood from her split lip. "I'm going to kill you here in this alleyway. The both of you."

Spook, her chest heaving, glanced at the young woman now huddled against the wall, her eyes wide and unblinking as she took it all in.

"No. Not happening," Spook shot back, Acid's face flashing in her mind. "I've got bigger issues to deal with than the likes of you, *Gorgonzola.*"

She knew it was a lame put-down the second it left her lips – not even close to Acid at her most cutting – but it was the best she could do in the situation.

With a banshee scream The Gorgon flew at her again. Spook feinted left, then spun around with a textbook roundhouse kick that The Gorgon blocked with ease.

Not what she needed.

Jumping back, Spook adjusted her stance but The Gorgon wasn't giving her a moment's rest. They clashed close range, their fists and feet a blur as they exchanged blow after blow. A heavy punch to Spook's cheekbone sent a shockwave through her skull. She tasted blood, but it only spurred her on. She countered with a solid kick to the knee, as Acid had taught her. The Gorgon cried out and staggered back. Seizing the moment, Spook launched a series of rapid punches, driving her opponent against the wall.

But The Gorgon was a trained killer and no pushover. She dodged two punches and countered with one of her own before karate-chopping Spook across the chest and kicking her away. Spook stumbled but stayed upright, drawing deep breaths as she fought through the pain. The fight was less about technique now and more about endurance, each woman trying to outlast the other in a grim test of will. Spook dodged a wild swing and countered with a sharp elbow to the ribs. The Gorgon cried out, losing her balance as she collapsed to one knee with a pained grunt.

"Okay, okay, you got me," she gasped, her hand clutching her side where Spook had struck her. Her head was bowed. She was weakened. Vulnerable, even.

Spook lowered her guard a little, breathing heavily from the exertion. "Get up," she said, not taking her eyes off the cold-blooded assassin.

The Gorgon chuckled, her teeth bloody, her weary expression suddenly sinister. More sinister.

Spook's instincts flared in the second before The Gorgon surged upwards with a swift violent motion, a glint of metal catching in the moonlight.

Shit! The knife!

Spook barely had time to react as The Gorgon lunged, slashing wildly with the blade. Cursing her lapse in vigilance she backpedalled frantically, searching for an escape route, but the narrow alley confined her movements. Ducking low, The Gorgon kicked out, her boot connecting with Spook's Achilles tendon, knocking her feet out from under her. The world spun as she hit concrete, the impact knocking the air from her lungs. Winded and dazed, she didn't even register The Gorgon straddling her until the cold, sharp edge of the knife pressed against her throat. Her hands shot up instinctively, gripping The Gorgon's wrists, desperately holding her back.

"You're done," The Gorgon hissed, leaning in so close her sour breath mingled with Spook's. Shifting her weight, she pressed down on the blade, the point biting into the thin skin of Spook's neck. Her heart hammered in her chest, her options dwindling rapidly.

"You were stupid to mess with me. To mess with Kancel Kulture," The Gorgon continued.

Spook held onto the sinewy wrists with everything she had left, keeping the blade from her throat.

This was it. She'd imagined this moment so many times over the last few years, but she wasn't ready to die. Not here, not at the hands of this monster. But maybe that was the problem all along – she wasn't ready for this life of murder and mayhem, period. Nate had told her as much. Acid said it all the time. Now here she was, seconds from death, only realising fully. It wasn't right. She was—

: A dull thud reverberated around the alleyway. Above her The Gorgon's eyes widened in shock before her body went limp and she collapsed in a heavy, lifeless heap. Spook just managed to move out of the way in time as the knife clattered to the ground beside her.

Blinking against the pain and surprise, Spook looked up to see the young woman she'd saved standing over them, a heavy-bottomed glass bottle clutched in her trembling hands. The young woman tossed the bottle aside and helped Spook haul The Gorgon's lifeless body off her, then helped Spook to her feet.

"Thank you," she gasped.

"No. Thank you," the young woman replied.

But The Gorgon was already stirring, making a strange gurgling noise as she struggled to regain consciousness. Without hesitation Spook snatched the fallen knife and plunged it deep into The Gorgon's throat. The girl yelped, and The Gorgon made one final gurgling noise then went still. As a pool of dark crimson spread out around her, Spook stepped over her and looked the young woman in the eyes.

"Come with me," she said. "We need to get out of here. Now."

Chapter Twenty-Six

Spook knelt and inspected her new ally's ankle. It was hard to tell in the gloom of the alleyway but it didn't seem broken. A few hours of elevation and an ice pack should sort it, but they had to get out of here first.

"Wh-Who are you?" The woman's breathing was shallow, her eyes wide as they flicked between Spook and The Gorgon's bloodied corpse.

"I'm no one," Spook said.

"You don't act like no one. You some kind of street vigilante or something?"

Spook gave a half-smile. "I wish. I just saw you were in trouble."

"Right. Well, you got that right." The woman still hadn't blinked. She was in shock.

"What's your name?" Spook asked her.

The woman hesitated as if she was reluctant to say. A glance at The Gorgon's dead body seemed to change her mind. "It's Abi. Abi Sandoval."

"Well listen, Abi. My name's Spook and I want to help you. If you let me."

Abi shook her head. "Spook? Your name's Spook?"

"Don't get hung up on it. You're safe now but we need to move." Spook edged closer, gently taking Abi's arm and guiding her forward. "Come on, let's get you to safety."

Abi was limping quite badly and Spook knew once the adrenaline wore off the pain would only intensify. Although, saying that, it was seven years since she'd met Acid and she wasn't sure her adrenaline levels had ever returned to what they'd once been.

At the end of the alleyway Spook paused, scanning the dimly lit street for threats. Under the streetlight she realised she had blood all over her top. She also had nothing but her bra underneath. Either option made her too conspicuous.

"Have you got anything on under that?" she asked, gesturing at the hoodie Abi was wearing.

"A t-shirt, that's all."

"Okay, take off the hoodie for me."

Abi crossed her hands across her chest. "What? No way." She seemed to be moving past the initial shock and resistance was a good sign, but Spook did need to cover up.

"Please, Abi," she urged. "We need to get away from here. Her associates may be close by."

"Shit, yeah," Abi whispered. "There was another woman."

Spook nodded. She'd suspected as much. "I can't walk around like this," she said, waving her hand at the blood-stained shirt. "It draws too much attention. I promise I'll give you the hoodie back and pay for the dry cleaning."

Abi reluctantly took off the hoodie and passed it to Spook, who gave it a quick shake and put it on. It fit perfectly and smelt faintly of oranges.

"You know you've got a cut over your eye, right?" Abi said.

"I can deal with that." Spook loosened her hair tie and let her hair fall forward to mask the injury. "Come on, we need to get going."

Seeing Abi still in pain, Spook slid an arm under her shoulder and helped her walk out of the alley. If her sense of direction was right, they were heading north toward the relative safety of Santa Monica Boulevard, which would still be bustling at this hour.

"That woman knew you," Abi said. "Who was she?"

Spook cleared her throat, considering how to respond, but Abi wasn't done.

"She was in my boss's apartment. I think she killed him. Her and the other woman."

Spook gritted her teeth. "Yeah, you mentioned that. What did this other woman look like?"

"Medium build, dark hair, heavy bangs," Abi replied. "Kind of a rock chic vibe but really intense."

Spook's stomach tightened. The description was unmistakably Acid Vanilla.

"Did she see you?" she asked, as they approached a crossroads.

"Yeah," Abi said, all the life gone from her voice suddenly. "I'm pretty sure she did."

"That settles it then. You definitely need to come back with me."

Abi recoiled. "Not a chance. What I need to do is get home and call the cops."

Spook stopped and faced Abi with a hard stare, the kind Acid used to give her back in the day. "Listen to me, this is serious. You're not safe right now and the cops can't help you." It was only a minor lie, she told herself, and necessary.

She couldn't involve the police. Not only was it against every code in this industry she was now a part of, but she couldn't endanger Acid before having a chance to talk to her. She stepped closer and softened her expression. "I'm going to help you, Abi. But we need to figure some things out."

"What the hell is going on?" Abi cried, throwing her head up to the heavens. "I can't deal with this. What is going on? Who the hell are you – *Spook*?"

Spook hesitated, but she saw no other option. Nate always said it was important to create connections with people who could help you.

"My real name is actually Spook," she began. "Spook Horowitz. I work for a special… organisation, and we can help you better than the LAPD can. In fact, right now we're the only ones who can keep you safe from the people who killed your boss."

Abi nodded and looked to be processing this information, but she still didn't move forward.

"If it needs saying," Spook continued, "those are dangerous people, and they're going to be coming for you. They won't leave any witnesses."

Abi bit her lip. "Yeah, that's what I figured."

"Good. So come with me," Spook urged, spotting the lights of a main street in the distance. "I swear I won't let anything happen to you."

Abi sighed. "I guess I've got no other choice," she said, raising her arm so Spook could help her walk. "Let's get the hell out of here."

Chapter Twenty-Seven

Acid stood under the scalding spray of the shower, hot water cascading over her like it was some kind of purifying torrent. She always showered after a job these days. It had become sort of a ritual for her, a way to cleanse herself of the day's grime. She would turn the water up as hot as she could bear and stay under as long as possible, stepping out bright pink but refreshed. Tonight, however, she noticed her hands were trembling as she twisted the temperature dial – a rare show of nerves that she wasn't accustomed to.

She shut off the water and grabbed a towel, wrapping it around herself as she strode across the cool tiles to her bedroom. The digital clock on her nightstand told her it was coming up to midnight. She picked up the glass of Chivas Regal she'd poured herself before stepping into the shower, the amber liquid catching the light as she swirled the glass. She took a long sip. It tasted like home, spicy and floral, and it burned all the way down just the way she liked.

Walking into the main living area she headed for the stereo system. She was still wide awake and needed music to drown out the buzz in her skull. She opted for L.A.M.F by Johnny Thunders and The Heartbreakers, and as the opening guitar riff of *Born to Lose* filled the room, she collapsed into an armchair. Another large gulp of her drink helped things along, the potent combination of alcohol and classic punk rock replenishing her soul as her tight muscles began to relax. She was home, she was alone, and for the time being she could switch off.

It had been one hell of a night, but she was satisfied with how the assignment had gone. Back at Jefferson's apartment she'd taken great care to set up the bedroom so it told a convincing tale of excess and tragedy. That was LA for you. That was the movie industry for you.

Acid's only potential issue was Jefferson's date. Despite already being on Saga's watchlist, and The Gorgon explicitly instructing her otherwise, she couldn't bring herself to kill the young woman.

So while the woman was still sleeping off her head injury in the corner, Acid had improvised. She found an old shirt in Jefferson's wardrobe and wrapped it completely around her head, shielding her eyes with a pair of sunglasses found on a dresser. As the young woman regained consciousness, Acid had manoeuvred her onto the bed and told her in no uncertain terms – and her best LA accent – that she was to go home and not breathe a word of what she'd experienced to anyone.

"Listen to me, Mirabelle Shaffer," she'd said, having found the woman's ID in her purse. "If you tell anyone what you saw, I will know, I will find you, and I will kill you. Do you understand?"

Mirabelle, still groggy and confused, had seemed more than happy with that deal, and after Acid helped her get dressed, she'd stumbled out of the apartment without another word. She was still concussed as hell, so with any luck she wouldn't remember much of the evening.

Back in her apartment, Acid was snapped back to the present by a loud banging on the wall, her neighbours complaining about the noise.

"Sod off!" she yelled back. "I'm trying to relax here!"

The walls echoed with another thump but she ignored it. On the stereo, Johnny Thunders was wailing about defeat and disaster, and being a glorious fuck-up.

Born to Lose.

You said it, baby.

She closed her eyes and nodded along, attempting to lose herself in the music. But Johnny had now started singing about wanting to be loved, which cut even closer to the bone than the first track. She groaned; the music was no longer doing the trick. Downing the Chivas in one gulp, she abandoned the glass on the coffee table and went over to the window. It was already open a touch and she pushed it out further, letting the cool breeze wash over her skin. The city lights below were a jumbled mess, too bright and too distant.

"What the hell am I doing?" she asked them regardless.

The LA streets had no answer for her. The truth was, she felt more lost than ever here. The bats were a constant presence on the edge of her psyche, but even they seemed disoriented.

She stretched her arms above her head, ignoring the towel as it dropped to the floor. At this time there was no one around to see and she didn't care if they did.

She had to remain optimistic, she told herself. It was important. Positive mental attitude and all that crap. Everything would work itself out as long as she stayed focused.

You chose to join Kancel Kulture and they're a good team.

And whilst Darius isn't perfect, he is your brother.
He's giving you the life you wanted.

These phrases had become her mantra lately, and they helped. Most of the time.

She closed the window and picked up the towel, about to pour herself another whisky when her phone vibrated from where she'd left it next to the door. She knew it was Darius before she even looked at the screen.

"What do you want now?" she said on answering. She'd already spoken to him once, to confirm the Jefferson job was complete.

"Tell me again what happened earlier with The Gorgon," he said, without any preamble.

She sighed. "Some young woman appeared who seemed to know the mark. The Gorgon chased after her whilst I made up the crime scene. I did a circuit of the area before I left, and she wasn't in sight so I went home." This last part was a lie. Acid hadn't done a sweep of the area at all. She'd assumed The Gorgon would deal with the young woman, and not wanting to know the gory details, she'd finished her task and walked back to Sunset to hail a cab. "There were no issues," she told Darius. "You said you were fine with what happened."

The line went quiet for a moment. "Yes, well, now I'm not."

Acid glanced at herself in the mirror across the room above the stereo. Standing here naked whilst talking on the phone, she felt more ridiculous than rebellious all of a sudden.

"What is it?" she asked.

"I need you to come into HQ."

"What? Now?"

There was another long pause. She walked closer to the mirror, scowling at her reflection.

"No, not now," Darius replied. "I need some rest. So do you. But come in first thing in the morning. Before nine."

Acid curled her lip. She didn't like the sound of this. "What's wrong, Darius?"

"The Gorgon hasn't checked in with me or Saga. Have you heard from her?"

She told him she hadn't. She'd assumed The Gorgon had taken out the young woman and gone straight home. Being so caught up in her own chaotic mission, she hadn't given it much thought until now.

"Well, you'd better hope she shows," Darius said. "You were the last to see her, after all."

He ended the call without saying goodbye. Acid stared at the phone in her hand for a moment before throwing it as hard as she could against the wall.

"Bloody buggering shit!"

Chapter Twenty-Eight

Abi's legs were unsteady as she stepped out of the cab into the unfamiliar quiet of Westlake, but at least her ankle wasn't hurting quite so much. Whether that was due to the panic in her system suppressing the pain she wasn't sure, but for now she'd take it.

It was a dark starless night, the kind her mom used to say foretold a gloomy day ahead. But that figured. Abi had a feeling it might be a long time before she enjoyed the warm, carefree ease of a summer's day again.

"Follow me," Spook whispered, ushering her towards a sprawling single-level property, half-hidden by a lush garden of trees and shrubs.

Abi trailed behind and they circled to the rear of the property, where an underlit pool and expansive patio came into view.

"Keep it down," Spook instructed, inserting a key into a set of bifold doors that dominated the back wall of the house. She slid one door open with a soft click.

Inside, the house was shrouded in darkness, but the

moonlight revealed an open-plan layout, stylish and comfortable, twice the size of Abi's tiny apartment and the kind of place she could happily set up home in if she had the cash.

"It's late and we both need sleep," Spook whispered, closing and locking the door behind them. "We'll talk properly in the morning. You can crash on the couch for now. I'll take the floor. It'll be fine."

Before Abi could respond, lights flooded the room, making her squint. She blinked rapidly, her vision adjusting to see a man striding out from one of the rooms.

"Spook? Is that you?"

He was wearing dark grey linen pants, the top half of his impressive physique naked. He was tall, with boulder-like shoulders and pecs that would make most Hollywood A-listers envious. His dark blond hair was slightly wavy and tousled, probably from having just woken up. Despite the tension in the room and the precariousness of her situation, Abi couldn't help but notice he was undeniably attractive, even with his face twisted in anger.

Thankfully, most of that anger was directed at Spook, not her.

"What the hell is going on?" His voice was rough from sleep and his accent difficult to place. Scottish, maybe? "Who is this?"

Abi shrank back, letting Spook handle the introductions. "Nate, this is Abi Sandoval. She's cool, I swear it. I had to bring her back here. There was nowhere else for her to go. The Gorgon was going to kill her."

"Whoa, slow down for a second." The man – Nate – held his hand up to her whilst simultaneously rubbing his eyes with the thumb and forefinger of his other hand. "Start again."

Spook took a deep breath. "Okay, so… Abi here is the assistant of some guy Kancel Kulture were lined up to take out this evening. Lena's tracking system led me to the address, and while I was scoping the place I saw Abi running away, with The Gorgon chasing her. Abi had interrupted her and another operative in the act."

Abi winced as Nate let out a heavy sigh. He clearly didn't like the sound of the story, and she couldn't blame him. While Spook relayed the events of the last couple of hours, Abi edged into the kitchen area. It felt like stepping into the future, with its polished surfaces and gleaming chrome appliances. She leaned against the counter, pretending to examine a high-tech coffee machine.

"The second woman was Acid," Spook was saying. "Abi's description of her leaves no doubt in my mind."

Abi straightened, watching Nate as he paced the living room. "What do you want me to do with this information?" he asked.

"Well, The Gorgon's dead. I killed her," Spook said, sounding more triumphant than Abi was comfortable with. "So that's five of them left. Three if the Blood Diamond Twins are still in Brazil, like Lena thinks." Her eyes widened, her voice gaining a harder edge. "Three isn't a big number, Nate."

Abi continued to watch as Nate turned and fixed Spook with an intense stare. If he'd been an actor, and she was his agent, she might have described it as 'smouldering'.

"You're crazy," he said. "You want us to hit them, now, unprepared and impulsively? Just me, you and Lena?"

"Three of us against three of them?" Spook replied, showing no sign of backing down. "We can do it."

"It's not three of them, though, is it?" Nate said, holding up his hand and counting off his splayed fingers. "Darius,

Stig Saga, Grimaldi and… oh, who's this last one? Oh yes. Acid Vanilla!" He jutted his chin at Spook as if daring her to respond.

"She'll come back to us," she said, almost to herself.

Nate slammed his fist down on the table, making Abi jump. "Enough, Spook," he growled. "This is fantasy."

Spook frowned in frustration and looked away. Nate rubbed at his stubble for a few seconds before turning to Abi.

Shoot.

She tensed as he wandered over. Was he going to throw her out? If he asked her to leave right now, it was probably the best she could hope for. "So she saw Acid taking someone out?" he asked, addressing Spook while pointing at Abi. "And now what?"

"We can't let her leave," Spook said.

"Yes, you really can," Abi interjected. "I can call an Uber and be out of your hair in no time…"

She trailed off as Nate held his finger up to her, signalling for silence. He smiled, his manner softening a little as he looked her in the eyes. "I'm sorry you got caught up in this mess," he said. "And I apologise for getting angry. I'm Nate Winters, by the way."

Abi raised her hand and grinned awkwardly. "Abi," she said, feeling dumb even as she was saying it.

"But Spook shouldn't have brought you here," he continued.

"Darius will want to tie up loose ends. You know he will." Spook moved in front of Nate to stand between him and Abi. "She's in danger. She saw too much."

"Yes, and now she's seen our faces too," Nate countered. "It's bad form, Spook, bringing a civilian here."

Abi's mind spun as she processed his words. *Civilian.*

What were these people – Feds? Spooks? Some kind of British secret service team?

Shit.

Panic gripped her. Were these people going to kill her? Though feeling overwhelmed, a part of her – the part that always looked for an angle, a way out – began to stir. She might be out of her depth, but she wasn't helpless.

"Don't worry. I know what's going on. I get it," she said, her voice steadier than she felt. She looked at Nate, forcing herself to maintain eye contact despite feeling like she might pee herself. "I work behind the scenes in the movie industry, so I'm already a part of this seedy world. I understand how these things work. People like you, and those women tonight, are hired by studios and the like to fix problems no one else can handle. My job isn't a million miles away from yours. Maybe not to that extreme, but I'm not stupid. I know what happens. I don't like it, but I'm a part of it."

She swallowed, ensuring she had their full attention before continuing. This was her one chance to sell it, and she had to do it right. One thing she knew for certain in this life – if you wanted to save your ass you had to make yourself useful. If you could make yourself indispensable, even better.

"I can help you," she said, glancing at Spook. "If you want to get at the crew who killed Jefferson, and it sounds as if you do, then I can help you with that. Not because I give a shit about my boss or what happened to him. But because they know I was there, and you both showed me tonight that's not a good situation for me to be in."

Her resolve hardened as she spoke, her tone growing more serious and professional. "I know the game in Hollywood. You keep me safe and I'll work with you. I'm a good player. I know people. I've got contacts all over the industry.

I can give you the inside story, get you into places you need to go, anything you need. Help me, and I'll help you."

Nate and Spook exchanged a look. Spook grinned, eager and expectant. "Come on, Nate," she urged. "This is our best chance. Three of them against five of us if we can turn Acid. That puts us at a real advantage. We could wipe out the competition in one easy step."

Nate's eyes narrowed as he considered her proposal. Abi was convinced he was going to say no, but then he let out a sort of half-laugh, shaking his head as if he couldn't believe what he was up against.

"All right, fine. I'm in," he said, glancing between the two women. "So where do we go from here?"

Abi caught Spook's eye, allowing herself a small triumphant grin. She was safe. For now.

Best negotiation she ever did.

Chapter Twenty-Nine

Acid awoke drenched in cold sweat, her sheets clinging to her skin. It had been another rough night, her sleep plagued with vivid and fitful dreams – though she couldn't remember now what any of them were about. Probably for the best.

Untangling herself from her cotton tomb, she swung her legs out of bed. She felt like total crap, but for a few seconds there was just the dull throb of a headache to deal with. Then, like a boot to the gut, the memories of last night hit her.

The Gorgon...

"Bloody hell."

She trudged toward the bathroom, hoping a shower would cleanse both the stickiness from her skin and the lingering dread from her mind. Under the hot jets, the night's events replayed in her head – sharp, disjointed images that she tried to rinse away with water that never seemed hot enough.

Once showered, she blow-dried her hair and dressed in

a pair of black leggings and an old Motörhead t-shirt. After checking her reflection in the mirror and sneering at what she saw, she grabbed her wallet and phone and left the house.

She'd already had two missed calls and a voicemail from Darius while she was getting ready. As she walked down to Sunset, she listened to his angry ramblings with the same sneer twisting at her mouth. He was climbing the walls, demanding she come in and see him.

"Yeah, yeah. I'm on my way."

On the Strip she hailed a cab, and as they set off she closed her eyes, attempting to clear her mind of worry and ignoring the potential confrontation that awaited her at HQ.

Once there, she let herself in and rode the elevator up to the top level, striding along the silent corridor towards Darius' office. She knocked once and, after waiting all of five seconds without a response, eased the door open.

Stepping inside, her heightened senses immediately picked up on the shift in atmosphere – from the calm stillness of the corridor to a room charged with nervous energy. Darius didn't notice her enter. He was too busy pacing in front of his desk, muttering to himself like he often did when he was stressed. Every so often he'd stop and wave his hands in the air, telling himself, "It's okay! It's all going to be okay!"

But it wasn't okay. At all. Darius liked to present a veneer of control, but the tightness in his shoulders and his jerky movements told a different story.

Acid stepped forward. "Darius. I'm here."

"Ah, good." He stopped pacing and glared at her. "Well? What the hell happened last night?"

She moved closer, working on keeping her voice steady

as she once again laid out the events of the previous night – her version of it, at least. When she finished, Darius was quiet for a few moments, nodding to himself as he allowed her explanation to sink in.

"So apart from this girl appearing, there were no other mistakes, none of your little missteps or *improvisations*?"

"Not from me," Acid said, choosing to ignore the snide comment. "As I told you, The Gorgon went after the intruder. She was just a young woman and would have posed no trouble at all for a trained operative. I finished up inside and did a sweep of the building. Then I went home. I assumed she'd done the same."

"The Gorgon never checked in," Darius said, his voice flat. "And early this morning, local cops found a body matching her description. Saga is trying to get confirmation, but *I'm* going to *assume* it's her. She'd been stabbed in the neck."

Acid nodded, keeping her face neutral.

Shiiiiiit!

Darius walked right up to her, leaving only a few centimetres between them. She could smell the coffee on his breath and the cologne on his neck. "Was it you?" he asked, his eyes searching hers.

"No!" She recoiled instinctively, her voice rising a few octaves. "Of course it wasn't!" She shook her head and looked away, pushing down the indignation spreading through her chest. "You need to stop accusing me of being involved in every little problem."

"You think the death of one of our operatives is a *little problem*?"

She puffed out a breath. "Bad choice of words. But come on, you know the risks we take. Shit like this happens in this industry. Operatives die."

Darius made a fist and brought it to his mouth. "Who was it then?"

"I don't know. I doubt it was the woman who disturbed us," Acid replied. "But if The Gorgon walked home it could have been anyone. A woman alone, maybe someone jumped her, some rotten junkie or a gangbanger. This is LA, Darius. There's a lot of bad people out there. Even worse than the likes of me and you."

He closed the distance again, their nearly identical noses almost touching. He narrowed his eyes.

"I'm legit, Darius," Acid said, her voice as serious as it ever got. "How many more times do I have to prove myself? Hell, I've passed thirty bloody lie detector tests for you." She leaned back. "I'm here because I want to be. You're my brother, the only family I have left. Beyond that, I want to be part of Kancel Kulture. You're building something amazing here."

Darius paused, his scowl softening as he considered her words.

"Let me in, Darius," she continued. "I mean really in. I want to be a part of the inner circle with you. Trust me. Please. I don't want to just take orders. I want to be right there with you, at the forefront, leading. That's what you promised me."

He sighed. "There's just too much weird shit going on. Everything feels off balance. I'm on edge."

Acid reached out, placing her hand on his shoulder. "I understand. But that's why you need to trust me. We're in this together."

He hesitated, then smiled. But before he could respond there was a loud knock on the door. It swung open to reveal Stig Saga. They both turned as he came towards them with wide, purposeful strides. He looked even paler and more abnormal than usual, his watery blue eyes flickering from her to Darius.

"Can we speak, sir?" he said. "In private."

Acid stiffened. "If it's about the organisation, you can speak freely in front of me."

"In private," Saga repeated, giving her a stern look.

Darius nodded, shooting Acid a look that said, *We're done here.*

"Fine. Whatever."

She didn't like it. But what could she do? Giving Darius a curt nod, she turned and headed for the door. She didn't want to be part of any pathetic boy's club anyway. She had better things to do with her day.

Chapter Thirty

Darius turned to his right-hand man, gesturing for him to continue. But Saga held up a finger and hesitated, his eyes fixed on the door until it clicked shut behind Acid. Only then did he face Darius.

"What is it?" Darius asked. "What do you have for me?"

Saga lowered his head before meeting Darius' gaze. "The Gorgon is dead, sir."

Darius sucked air through his teeth. "Fuck!"

This was horrific. Not because he had any affection for the morose cow – he'd always found her difficult to relate to – but The Gorgon had been a valuable member of his team and her loss was another unwanted stain on his leadership. Losing two of his top operatives in such a short time looked bad. In fact, it looked bloody amateurish.

"We can't let the new client know about this," he said, his mind racing through the implications. "Or anyone else, for that matter."

"Of course," Saga said. "I'll manage the optics."

Darius returned to his desk and leaned back in his chair,

putting on a good impression of a man in control, pondering his options. "I suppose you're going to tell me you think my sister had something to do with this?"

Saga shook his head. "No, I don't. Not this time."

Darius sat up. "Oh? And why are you so sure?"

Saga took a seat across from Darius, his face sombre. "Because someone has been infiltrating our comms," he said.

"What?!" Darius shot up from his chair, the anger rising up his neck. "How?"

"I'm sorry, sir." Saga looked away. "The security protocols I implemented were robust, but it appears someone exploited a zero-day vulnerability in our firewall. They were... highly skilled. However, I managed to trace their activity through advanced packet analysis and cross-referenced their IP address with known networks on the dark web."

Darius rubbed at his cheek, his anger morphing into focused attention. "And...?"

"They're part of a new outfit based in London. They're active on some of the same forums we use, advertising their services as a 'clean-up crew'."

"Shit." Darius began to pace the room, unsure how to channel the heightened energy bristling through his system. His eyes fell on the paperweight on his desk, and he had a sudden urge to grab it and chuck it through the window. Pushing that thought down he continued pacing, eyes wide and unblinking, chewing on his bottom lip. "Go on then," he yelled finally. "Continue."

Saga cleared his throat. "Initially I thought they were just a rival organisation aiming to jeopardise our operations. But they aren't. Or at least, I don't believe that's their primary objective. That's not why I wanted to speak with you in private."

Darius stopped pacing. "What do you mean?"

Saga stood and joined him at the window. LA was waking up, and the early morning light painted the city in a blanket of gold.

"I tapped into the city's surveillance network and pulled all CCTV footage of The Gorgon's last known movements," Saga explained, as they looked out on the scene. "I then hacked into the municipal servers and wiped the footage from their records, as per our protocol."

Darius nodded. "Good work. But you didn't answer my question." He leaned in. "What are you finding so difficult to tell me, Saga? You're making me nervous."

Saga continued to stare out the window. "In her last moments, The Gorgon is seen chasing a young woman, presumably the one Acid mentioned. I've also seen footage of the same woman entering the mark's building a few minutes after our team. Her name is Abigail Sandoval. She's the mark's assistant."

"Do we know if The Gorgon finished off the girl before she was killed?" Darius asked.

Saga shook his head. "The LAPD network reports only one body found at the scene. They haven't discovered the mark yet. So…"

Darius clenched his fists. "So… we have a civilian out there who's seen two of our operatives in action. This is awful. This is really fucking awful."

"Yes, it is," Saga agreed, turning from the window, his expression grim. "The last footage I have shows them entering an alley. The same alley where The Gorgon's body was found."

"So this young assistant killed one of our top operatives?"

Saga lifted his head, the tendons in his neck going rigid. "I don't think it was her, sir."

"Why not? How can you be so sure?"

"Because…" Saga said slowly, "thirty seconds after The Gorgon enters the alley, someone else follows her in. Another woman."

Darius screwed up his face. "So she killed The Gorgon?"

"I believe so."

"Okay, and do we know who this is? Do we have an ID?"

Saga looked grave. "Yes, sir," he replied. "I recognised her immediately. It was Spook Horowitz."

Chapter Thirty-One

Darius stared at Saga, searching his gaunt, angular face for any sign this was some misplaced joke.

"Spook Horowitz? As in, my sister's pathetic lapdog? Are you sure?"

Saga's expression remained sombre. "Yes, sir. I'm certain."

"Bloody hell," Darius yelled. His initial shock turned to incredulity and then to amusement as he burst out laughing. "What a world, hey?"

"I couldn't believe it myself," Saga said. "But I ran the images through two separate facial recognition programs. It's her. After further cross-checking, it appears she's part of a three-person team that arrived in LA Monday evening."

Darius stopped laughing. "Do we know why they're here? For me? For her? For us?" He coughed, composing himself.

"That's what I want to find out," Saga replied.

"Okay. Good. Keep digging," Darius instructed. "Find out where they're holed up. Do we need to worry about anything coming back to us regarding The Gorgon's body? I don't want any loose ends."

"All taken care of."

"What about the assistant?"

"I believe she's with Spook Horowitz," Saga said. "We find Spook, we find her."

Darius nodded slowly, though his mind was spinning. "Tell me truthfully, Saga. Do you think they're going to hit us?"

Saga's lip twitched. "I've been putting some feelers out and the industry is tense right now. Their leader, a man called Nate Winters, has been asking questions about us. But there's nothing concrete to suggest they're planning an attack."

"Let them try. We'd wipe the floor with them in seconds," Darius scoffed. "Okay. Let's keep an eye on the situation but focus on maintaining our momentum."

"My thoughts exactly," Saga replied, almost managing a smile. "We've got the big assignment coming up. Once we prove ourselves to the client, nothing can stop us. We'll be Hollywood's most in-demand clean-up operation."

"Good," Darius said. "Keep me up to date with information as it comes in."

Saga bowed his head. "Of course."

Satisfied, Darius got up and saw Saga out. But as the door clicked shut behind his right-hand man, a sudden wave of loneliness and vulnerability washed over him. His office, once a sanctuary of control, now felt both vast and claustrophobic. He walked to the window and looked out over the city, seeking solace in the view, but finding none.

He sat at his desk and ran his fingers through his hair before standing again with restless energy. Leaving his office, he marched down the corridor and summoned the elevator, riding it down to the second floor.

The gym was quiet, the only sound the muffled thud of fists against leather. On the far side of the room, Acid was punching the hell out of one of the heavy bags hanging from the ceiling. Darius leaned against the doorway, watching her. There was a real ferocity in her movements and a controlled aggression that he couldn't help but envy. She looked fierce and deadly and a lot fitter than she had been when they'd first met. Her face was twisted in a cruel snarl and she grunted as she slammed her fists and feet against the heavy bag. It looked as if she was battling her own inner demons, exorcising them one blow at a time.

He strode over to her, arms folded, head held high, exuding an air of unshakeable authority. She noticed him approaching and halted, regarding him with a look of surprise.

"Don't stop on my account," he said, though he was ready to grab one of the free weights from off the rack and beat her with it if she continued hitting that damn bag.

Acid stared at him, sweat running down her face, her eyes wide and wild. "What do you want?" she gasped.

"I thought you might want to know – your friend is in town."

She wiped her forehead with the back of her hand. "What are you talking about?"

"Spook Horowitz."

Acid sneered. "She's here? In Los Angeles?"

"Indeed."

He watched her intently, searching for any hint of a reaction. But her face remained neutral. She turned back to the bag but lowered her fists. There was a flicker of something in her eyes – confusion, perhaps – but nothing more.

For a moment there was silence, save for the sound of their breathing. Then she shook her head, and Darius thought he saw a flash of anger behind her eyes.

Darius had always felt himself skilled at reading human behaviour, catching those blink-and-you-miss-it moments that revealed true feelings. Anger was good. Maybe it was time to trust her more, and bring her into the fold.

"How do we know this?" she asked.

Darius relayed everything he knew, as Saga had told him – about the CCTV footage, the alleyway, the near certainty that Spook had taken out The Gorgon. As he mentioned The Gorgon he lowered his chin, watching Acid even more intently; he knew she and The Gorgon didn't get along. But apart from a slight shrug of indifference, there was nothing.

When he was finished she was quiet once more, but he didn't take his eyes off her. He studied her, searching for any sign of hesitation, of weakness.

Finally, she looked up. "I'll deal with Spook if she becomes an issue," she said.

"You'll do better than that," he replied, his mouth slowly forming into a wide grin. "This is how you prove yourself, Sis. You're going to bring her here, to me. And then I'm going to watch you execute the meddling bitch."

Acid held his gaze for a moment, her face hard, her eyes cold. Then she gave a single nod. "Okay," she said. "I'm on it."

Chapter Thirty-Two

Darius marched from the room, the door to the gym slamming shut behind him and Acid turned back to the heavy bag.

"Stupid. Fucking. Idiot!" she spat, the words punctuating her actions as she lashed out, punching and kicking the bag until her knuckles and feet were raw.

Why couldn't that stupid woman just leave her the hell alone?

Ignoring the pain she carried on, the sound of her assault on the bag drowned out only by the chattering fury of the bats. With one final powerful kick, she ended her attack, leaving the bag swinging wildly and her chest heaving from the exertion.

"Damn it, Spook," she whispered. "This is all I need."

Dripping with sweat, she placed her hands on her hips, staring at the bag as it slowly came to a stop. She grabbed her towel, drying her face and armpits as she marched out of the room. The bats in her head were incessant, her mind a chaotic whirl of anger and confusion. She walked down towards the elevator on the balls of her feet and with her fists clenched as if ready to kill someone. Maybe because she was.

She couldn't think straight. Should she go home and try to get some rest? Go for a run? Or maybe drown her sorrows at the Rainbow for a few hours? Instead, she found herself calling the elevator and pressing the button for the third floor.

She emerged into Kancel Kulture's surveillance and security hub ten seconds later, a cavernous open-plan space bathed in the soft glow of computer terminals. Rows of processors and banks of servers hummed with activity, a symphony of beeps and clicks filling the air, mingling with the faint scent of electricity and the cool air pumped from vents. Acid's likeness flickered across several monitors as she walked deeper into the room, spotting Stig Saga in front of a bank of screens.

She'd hoped to find him here.

Stopping, she observed him for a moment, ensuring he wasn't planning her imminent demise, then coughed.

Saga spun around in his chair. "Oh, it's you." His smirk was unsettling. It wasn't the first time Acid had seen him crack a smile, but it was rare. "Not often you come up here, Acid. To what do I owe the pleasure?"

She squared her shoulders, her eyes scanning the complex web of interconnected systems around her. "I need your help," she told him. "I want to set a trap."

Saga's smirk widened. "A trap? For whom?"

"Spook Horowitz," she said quickly. "I'm sure you're aware she's in LA. If she's here, she'll be looking for me. I'm certain of it. Darius wants me to bring her in."

"Very well," Saga said, a glint of interest in his eyes. "Then I can help. What do you need?"

"What can you tell me about the situation so far?" she asked, assuming he knew the full story and had been the one to tell Darius – probably why his smirk was making the rounds. "How did they track us to the job last night?"

Saga looked away. "They"re clever. She exploited a flaw in our communication channels." He turned back to his keyboard. "It's been a learning experience, one I intend to fix."

Acid moved closer, standing beside him. "Can you help them locate me but make them think they did it themselves?"

He nodded. "Easy. They're already monitoring our comms. I was going to block them, but if we keep the network open and play dumb, all you need to do is message HQ and identify yourself. Then just keep your phone switched on. They'll link its ID and track you down eventually. If that's what you want."

Acid stared at the screens. "It is."

Saga looked up, a serious glint in his eyes replacing the smirk. "And you're going to bring her in?"

"That's what Darius wants."

"Very well," he said. "But be ready, Acid. Whatever comes next is on you."

She nodded, the bats screaming for blood. "Don't worry, I'll deal with Spook. Just make sure she finds me."

Chapter Thirty-Three

Spook raised her head off the floor and groaned at the early afternoon sun creeping into the room under the blackout curtains. After the chaos of last night, she'd hoped for a few hours of rest, but there was something about knowing the day was going on without her that kept her from settling. She sat up and looked around. The ticking of a clock somewhere was the only proof time was moving at all. Behind her on the couch, Abi lay with her back to her, snuggled into the cushions and snoring softly.

Good for her. But Spook was more wired than tired.

Resigning herself to the situation, she stood and moved quietly over to the kitchen where she filled a glass with water. She drank it down in one go and refilled it, sipping as she tried to get her head around everything that had happened. She might have finished off The Gorgon last night, but she'd have been the one bleeding out in that alley if it hadn't been for Abi.

She decided not to tell Nate that part and would try not

to dwell on it herself. Despite being stronger and tougher than ever, she was still that same nervous tech-geek inside, vulnerable and uncertain. If she was honest with herself – and she always seemed to be in these still, solitary moments – she had doubts about the path she'd chosen.

Maybe it was because she hadn't really chosen it at all but had it thrust upon her by need and circumstance.

It was human nature. No one liked to think their autonomy had been compromised. But it happened. It happened all the time.

Shaking away these unhelpful thoughts she leaned against the counter, watching Abi as she turned over in her sleep. The poor thing looked so young and innocent, yet from what she'd said, it sounded as if she'd already dealt with a lot of scary shit in her short life.

That made two of them.

Footsteps across the room caught Spook's attention and she looked up to see Nate shuffling towards her.

"You couldn't sleep?" she whispered.

He shook his head, giving her a wonky grin. "No."

Spook set down her glass. "Same here. There's a lot to think about, huh?"

Nate moved past her, took a glass from the unit next to the sink and filled it with water. He drank, staring off into the middle distance. "Yeah. This all got very messy very quickly," he muttered.

He didn't look at Spook, but she offered him a thin-lipped smile all the same. "I guess it did, but… we're here now…"

"How do you want to play this?" he asked, still not looking at her.

"You're the boss."

"Oh, you remembered?" He turned, the skin around his eyes tight as he considered her.

Spook held his stare, ignoring the comment. "I'd bet everything I own that Darius knows we're here," she said, speaking fast. "That means we've got two options. One: we stay, we fight. We take these bastards down and show the industry that we're the true heirs to Caesar's reign."

Nate nodded, unmoved. "Or...?"

Spook frowned. "Or... what?"

"You said we have two options. What's the second one?"

She shrugged. "We give in. We go home. We admit Kancel Kulture are the winners and that we'll always be playing catch-up. We scrape a living on the lower tiers, taking out mid-level drug dealers and adulterers for mid-level fees."

Nate let out a bitter-sounding laugh. "You make it sound so glamorous."

"I'm being serious, Nate," Spook replied, an unexpected surge of anger lifting her spirits. "Is that what you want? Really?"

He studied her for a moment, the weight of their situation evident in his grim expression. She hoped he was going to tell her no, of course he didn't want that, but before he had a chance, Lena entered the room carrying an open laptop.

"Hey guys," she said, her eager, well-rested demeanour so at odds with theirs. "We've got some action."

She was wearing a pair of Batman Bermuda shorts and a white tank top that Spook couldn't help but notice was slightly see-through under the light from the laptop screen.

"I'm not sure why, but their comms have just lit up like a Christmas tree," she continued, placing the laptop on the table as Spook and Nate walked over to join her.

"Probably because one of their operatives is dead and they're calling everyone in," Nate said.

"Or maybe they know we're in town and are worried," Spook added.

Lena looked between the two of them, giving a confused look that said, *Tell me more*. But then her eyes fell on Abi, still asleep on the couch.

"Whoa, who the hell is that?"

Nate and Spook exchanged a look. "That's Abi," Spook replied. "There's a few things you need to know."

She sat down beside the younger woman, relaying to her the events of the previous night.

"Wow. A lot happens while you're asleep," Lena said once Spook was finished. "That's heavy as shit. And you... killed The Gorgon?"

Spook glanced at Abi, making sure she was still asleep. She nodded. "It had to happen. But now we've got the upper hand."

"We haven't yet," Nate added, ever the pessimist.

"Maybe not, but things are on a knife edge," Spook said. "And I reckon if I can get Acid alone and talk with her, we could tip the balance."

"But why, Spook?" Nate asked, turning to face her head-on. "You keep saying this – once you talk to her, you'll make her come back to us. But why would she? What are you going to say to change her mind? Is it even possible to change Acid Vanilla's mind?"

Spook tensed. It was a tough question to answer. But she had faith in her plan. Hell, she had to – it was the only thing keeping her going right now.

She drew in a deep breath, her gaze unwavering as she met Nate's probing eyes. "If anyone can get through to Acid, it's me," she said. Then turning to Lena, she nodded at the screen showing the live feeds from Kancel Kulture's intercepted communications hub. "Can you identify who's who by the phones linked to that network?"

"Not directly," Lena replied. "But I can tell you the location of each phone."

Spook rubbed at her chin. She figured as much. "Okay, where are they all?" she asked, leaning closer.

Lena brought up a map with a series of red pointers that seemed to blink in time with Spook's harried breath. "I've got two in Brazil, four in LA," she reported.

"Where in LA?"

"Give me a second." Lena enhanced the granularity of her search and brought up a map of the city. Beside her Nate sighed, shaking his head as Spook met his eye.

"You're not going to let this go, are you?" he said.

"Not until me or Darius are dead," she replied, the abrupt statement surprising even herself. But it was true, and Nate seemed to get that because he turned back to the screen without another word.

"Cool. Here we go." Lena pointed to the blinking dots on the map. "I've got two of them at the HQ we've already identified. Plus one here in Koreatown and one moving slowly along Sunset Boulevard. Oh, they appear to have just stopped."

"Can you tell where?" Spook asked.

"It's not a hundred percent accurate, but there are a few bars in this area. The Rainbow, for instance."

Spook leaned back. "The Rainbow? Why have I heard of that place?"

"It's a famous venue," Nate said, sounding resigned. "It was a hangout for all the bands in the seventies and eighties."

Spook looked up. "That's Acid! Has to be."

She began to gather herself together. She needed a shower but there was no time. She moved around the room, looking for her phone and jacket. "If she's alone I can talk to her," she said. "I'm going there now." Before Nate could respond, she located her phone and handed it to Lena. "Can you check if the tracking software is still working now that we're in the States?"

As Lena set up the phone, Spook slid on her leather jacket. It was probably too hot outside to wear it, but that wasn't the point. She turned back to Lena when Abi stirred, making a grunting sound as she sat up and looked around.

"Ah, shit…" she mumbled. "I hoped it was a bad dream." Spook moved over to sit beside her on the couch. "What time is it?" Abi asked.

"Almost one in the afternoon," Spook replied. "You're safe. But I need to go out for a few hours."

Abi came instantly alert. "Can I come with you?"

"No. It's too dangerous."

"More dangerous than hanging out here?" she hit back, lowering her voice as she glanced at Nate. "I'm not sure about him."

"His bark is worse than his bite," Spook assured her. "Well, as long as you're on our side at least."

"But I know LA like the back of my hand," Abi said. "And I know danger. I'll be a good person to have with you if you're heading into new territory."

Spook sucked in a breath. She made a good point. "Do you know the Rainbow Bar?" she asked.

Abi snorted. "Who doesn't know the Rainbow?" She lowered her chin, fixing Spook with her big brown eyes. "Please, let me come with. I don't really know what you guys are up to, but you saved my life, and you've got to trust someone in this world, right? Plus, I sort of saved your life too, remember? You might need me again. Come on, Spook, I need to do something. I'll go crazy just sitting here."

Spook glanced at Nate, who shrugged as if he knew any input from him was pointless. "Okay," she said. "Let's do this."

Chapter Thirty-Four

Spook stared up at the huge, tattooed barman looming over her. "Come on, what'll it be?" he asked, in a gruff voice.

Spook grimaced. Abi had ordered a club soda, but that didn't appeal to her. "Erm… give me a Jack Daniels," she spluttered. "One chunk of ice. Thanks."

The barman nodded but didn't smile. Spook puffed out her cheeks as he moved away to prepare their drinks. She didn't even like Jack Daniels – it was too harsh and spicy for her taste – but it fit the persona she was trying to project. Plus, if Acid was here, she needed the Dutch courage. A glass of neat Jack also matched the ambience of the Rainbow Bar and Grill. It was not yet two in the afternoon, yet the place exuded the vibe of a bar that never truly closed.

The walls were plastered with rock memorabilia – guitars and gold records, along with framed photographs of musicians who had played or drunk here. The air was heavy with a mixture of contrasting aromas – citrus from freshly sliced lemons, the yeasty stench of stale beer, plus the lingering ghosts of a hundred thousand cigarettes. A familiar guitar riff played over the PA system, but Spook couldn't name the song or the band.

When the barman returned, Spook paid for the drinks and they carried them over to one of the red leather booths. The seat released a soft sigh as Spook slid around to the far side, allowing Abi to sit opposite. They sipped their drinks in silence for a few moments as Spook scanned the room for Acid. It had only taken them twenty minutes to get here by taxi, maybe she was around a corner or in a back room. From this spot, Spook had a clear view of the bar and would see her if she surfaced.

"So... "Abi said, tracing the rim of her glass with a finger. "Here we are..." Spook had filled her in during the cab ride – as best she could with the driver listening – but it seemed Abi wasn't entirely satisfied with the brief rundown.

"Do you honestly think this Acid woman is going to be cool with me after... you know, what I saw her doing?" she asked.

Spook forced herself to take another sip of her bourbon as she contemplated a suitable response. "Acid is... complicated," she said. "She can be very volatile, but she has a heart under all that cynicism and chaos. We were close. Once. And I don't believe she's as deep into Kancel Kulture as Nate does. I think I can bring her back."

Abi chuckled. "You know you sound like Luke Skywalker talking about his old man."

Spook couldn't help but wince. Yeah, she'd realised that herself as she was speaking. She shrugged. "It is what it is."

Abi's expression straightened as she toyed with the straw in her soda. "Tell me more about her. About you. How did you... you know... end up here?"

Spook exhaled. "I was an analyst, working for Cerberix

Inc., if you remember those guys. I saw something I shouldn't and they tried to take me out. One moment I'm minding my own business, the next I'm caught in a global conspiracy with a price on my head. It was Acid and me who exposed Cerberix."

"Whoa!" Abi's eyes lit up. "You mean at the keynote, with the videos and shit?"

Spook nodded. It felt like a lifetime ago now. "Yep. But getting there was a nightmare. I was just an innocent civilian, and out of nowhere I'm dodging bullets with people trying to kill me at every turn. Acid saved my life. On more than one occasion. And she did so by putting her own life on the line." She paused, her eyes drifting to the memorabilia on the walls. "It's funny, in the thick of it you don't grasp how insane it all is. It's only afterwards, looking back, that you realise the madness you've lived through."

"Crazy shit," Abi agreed. "What sort of name is Acid Vanilla anyway?"

"It was a codename. Her handle, I suppose," Spook explained. "I tried to get her to go back to it once everything settled down, but she prefers being called Acid. It's how I know her, I guess."

"O-kay," Abi said. "Well, good luck bringing her back from the dark side, Luke."

Spook smiled and then raised her head as someone approached the bar. But it was a young man wearing a black and white striped sweater. "What about you?" she asked. "How did you end up in the seedy underbelly of Hollywood?"

"Ah, you know, I was just lucky to get the breaks, I guess. Or maybe unlucky enough to not have anyone to warn me against my career choice." She swirled the ice in her soda before taking a sip. "My mom died four years ago. It hit hard, you know? She was my best friend, my biggest cheer-leader. My dad was – is – a lawyer. He wanted me to follow in his footsteps, so when I got into film school instead, he practically cut all ties." She scoffed, a bitter edge to her laughter.

"I'm sorry," Spook said.

"Nah, to hell with him," Abi replied, a look of defiance in her eyes. "I don't need that sort of shit in my life."

Spook smiled. She liked Abi. She was ballsy but with a good soul. Leaning back she scanned the room again. More customers had entered the bar since they'd sat down, but there was still no sign of Acid.

Damn it.

She must have left already. But if the Rainbow was one of her regular haunts – and Spook's instincts told her it was – then she could come back another time. Maybe she'd even pluck up the courage to ask the barman if he knew her.

"It's not looking good," Abi said, picking up on Spook's mood.

"No. She's not here." She stretched her neck to one side as a wave of tiredness washed over her. "I'm going to use the restroom," she said, hoping a splash of cold water might clear her head and steady her nerves. "Then I suggest we head back to the house and see if Lena has any new leads."

Leaving Abi to finish her drink, Spook slid out of the booth and weaved her way through the bar to the restrooms. The women's room was in stark contrast to the lively bar, brightly lit and clinically clean, with white tiles reflecting the harsh fluorescent lights.

Spook bent over the sink and splashed cold water on her face, trying to wash away the fatigue. Water dripped off her chin as she straightened up, meeting herself in the mirror. She looked as drained as she felt.

"Nice jacket," a voice said from one of the stalls. The tone was low and mocking.

And unmistakable.

"Acid!"

Before Spook could react, Acid's forearm slammed against her throat, pinning her against the wall with enough force to make her teeth rattle.

"Get... off me!"

Spook's hands shot up, gripping Acid's wrist and twisting it away to ease the pressure. Acid gritted her teeth and retaliated, punching Spook in the stomach.

"Idiot!" Acid snarled as Spook doubled over, coughing through the pain. "You're a bloody idiot coming here."

The blow had knocked the air out of Spook, but she didn't buckle entirely. As Acid stepped back, she launched herself forward, grabbing her old friend around the waist and using her momentum to flip her over. They went down as one, Acid hitting the tiles with a thud, Spook on top.

"I'm here to save you," she spat, holding onto Acid's flailing arms.

"Don't be fucking stupid." Acid bucked her hips, shoving Spook off and twisting away. She booted Spook in the side as she scrambled to her feet. "Do you think I'm some tortured, brainwashed loser?"

Spook grabbed hold of one of the sinks and hauled herself up. She had to admit, that was kind of what she had thought. Maybe because the alternative was too much to deal with. She and Acid circled each other like caged animals, eyes locked on one another. In Spook's head, this reunion had been a lot more tearful, and with more hugs.

Acid was right. She was a bloody idiot.

"I had to come," she said, raising her fists. "I had to know."

"You don't get it, do you?" Acid snapped, dodging as Spook grabbed for her. She shoved Spook away and they squared up again. "There's nothing you can do."

"I had to try."

"I knew you were tracking me," Acid shot back, raising her fists. "Darius knows, too. He wants me to bring you in and slaughter you in front of him."

Spook's eyes narrowed. "Go on then. Do it. Take me in. Kill me."

Acid glared at her with that intense stare – almost like she was trying to turn her to stone. Spook remembered it well. She'd almost missed it.

Strengthening her stance, she readied herself for another attack, but Acid just let out a derisive snort and shook her head.

"You're going to mess the whole thing up," she snarled.

"What?" Spook said, lowering her hands slightly. "Mess what up?"

"You need to leave. Now," Acid told her, dropping her fists and straightening. She walked towards the door. "Go back to London, Spook. I mean it."

"How the hell do you do it?" Spook called after her. "Working for Darius, after… everything."

Acid stopped and turned around. "I've put up with worse, sweetie," she said. "And besides, it won't be forever."

"What do you mean?" Spook's body was still tense, but now for answers rather than a fight.

Acid looked troubled suddenly. Desperate, even.

"You know the old adage about cutting off the head and the body dying?" she said. "It's bullshit. Killing Darius would only make things worse. If I do that, his crew will come after me. They're loyal as hell and they won't stop. I don't want to spend the next five years constantly looking over my shoulder or hunting them down one by one like I did with my old colleagues."

Spook stared at her open-mouthed. This was not how she'd expected this to go. "So... you want Darius dead?"

Acid curled her lip. "Of course I want him dead," she hissed. "He killed The Dullahan. He was going to kill both of us."

"But he's your—"

"This is personal," Acid cut in. "But not in that way. Maybe he and I share the same DNA, but that's where it starts and stops as far as I'm concerned. It's also the DNA of a wicked, hateful man who almost killed my mother. I feel nothing towards Darius Duke but hatred."

Spook blinked. "Right... good... yes!"

"But I need to deal with Kancel Kulture first," Acid continued. "It's the only way to finish this, except I have to be clever about it. Two are already dead. That leaves four more before I deal with Darius. Then it's over. Then I'm done."

"But the Blood Diamond Twins are in Brazil," Spook said. "That means there are only two left here."

"Never discount Frederik and Freek Kriel," Acid replied, raising an eyebrow. "They're absolute thugs and merciless killers. They'll be the trickiest to take out. But I'll do it. I have to."

"Let me help you," Spook said. "I've been training all year and—"

"No!" Acid's hand was on the door now, her back to Spook. "You can't help me. At best, you'll mess up my plans. At worst, you'll get yourself, Nate, and all your new little friends killed." She glanced back, her face hard. "Go back to London. Forget about me."

"But you might die," Spook said.

Acid smirked. "I'm already dead, sweetie."

She held Spook's gaze for a moment longer, then yanked open the door and was gone, leaving Spook alone once more.

Chapter Thirty-Five

Acid marched out of the Rainbow Bar and hit the street, walking fast, not caring who she barged into or where she was going. She kept her head down, clenching and unclenching her fists, silently daring someone to take her on. The late afternoon air was thick with the usual smells of West Hollywood – car exhausts, street food, and the occasional waft of someone wearing far too much cologne. As she approached a dive bar, she ignored the catcalls and lewd comments from a couple of guys smoking outside. But as she got closer one of them reached out to grab her arm.

"Hey baby, I'm talking to you…"

"Go to hell!" she snarled, shoving him with such ferocity he backed off instantly. His scruffy friend laughed, loud and fake, as she strode away, but she didn't care.

She headed south, escaping the bustle of the Strip. She needed to walk, to think, to find some clarity. Spook showing up had thrown everything into chaos. Acid had been so careful, so patient. She had her reasons for staying with Darius, for biding her time. But Spook's arrival threatened to unravel it all, jeopardising her meticulous planning and hard work. It was bloody infuriating. She could sense the bats under her skin, screeching at her, tearing at her nerve endings. Her jaw ached from tension; her muscles were coiled tight, ready to snap. She needed to release this pressure before it consumed her.

She zigzagged through the back streets, her mind racing. She was so close. She hadn't outwitted thirty of Darius' bleeding polygraph tests only to fail now.

That stupid bloody… kid!

The thing about lie detectors – they weren't actually too hard to fool if you knew how. The first time Acid faced one she was nervous, but she quickly learned the tricks. The initial questions The Scientist asked were always simple stuff: her name, her location, who the president was. The answers to these questions were meant to establish a baseline, and so to throw it off she'd bite her tongue or the inside of her mouth – just enough to create a small spike in the readings. This set a higher baseline, making any deviations less noticeable. It was a simple trick, but effective, manipulating her responses to create a false normal and a baseline that gave her the leeway she needed.

When The Scientist asked a critical question – like "Did you kill your colleague Nokizaru?" – she'd counter it with her own question in her head; something irrelevant like, "Do I have blonde hair?" The answer was always no, always truthful, blocking out the real question and keeping her responses steady. With this simple misdirection, she was able to fool the machine and The Scientist.

Another method involved clenching and unclenching her pelvic floor muscles. It was all about control. Clenching at the right moment, releasing when necessary. She practised until it became automatic. The lie detector picked up on the physical response but it was always the wrong one; a subtle shift in tension that skewed the results just enough to throw off the reading. It took practice, but once she'd mastered it, it was like a switch she could flip at will.

Because, ultimately, the polygraph was just a machine, and machines could be beaten. To Acid it was like going to a bar with a fake ID. Confidence was key. If you acted like you belonged, no one questioned you. In front of The Scientist, her body language, her tone – everything about her – screamed honesty, even when she was lying through her teeth. It was all about playing a role, and Acid had mastered that art a long time ago.

Approaching the crossroads at the corner of Fountain and Laurel Avenue, she stopped, unsure which direction to take. The irony of the moment wasn't lost on her, but she was too frustrated to find it amusing. Nothing about her situation was funny. She stood there, fists clenched, scanning left and right, uncertain of where to go next.

Damn you, Spook.

She forced herself to move, heading up Laurel Avenue. Since joining Kancel Kulture, memories of Caesar and Annihilation Pest Control often haunted her thoughts, and as she walked, those memories returned and overwhelmed her. She couldn't afford to repeat the same mistakes. Her vendetta against her old crew had too many loose ends and had dragged her across the globe for months. It had also been damn dangerous, putting both her and Spook at risk time and again.

Acid was getting too old for this lifestyle. Each day she felt herself running out of time and patience, the burden of a life that was becoming too much to bear. She had to work smart, eliminating Kancel Kulture one by one whilst ensuring each death looked like an accident or human error.

It was how she'd taken down Nokizaru. It was how she would have dealt with The Gorgon if she hadn't got herself killed first—

Bloody hell.

The realisation hit her like a claw hammer to the gut. Spook had killed The Gorgon. She shook her head, feeling an unexpected surge of pride welling up before she pushed it down. She was still furious at that bloody woman.

But the fact remained: Acid wanted Darius dead. Brother or not, he'd tried to kill her and Spook, and she wasn't going to let that slide. Despite what Spook might think, she wasn't the callous killer she once was. Spook had changed her, she accepted that now. She'd helped her find her conscience again and maybe that was what she'd needed all along. But having a conscience didn't mean letting bad people get away with things. In fact, it meant the exact opposite.

Even Caesar had morals, twisted as they were. She remembered him saying once how being an elite killer didn't mean you couldn't justify your actions – as long as you positioned yourself correctly in the industry and were in control of the situation. His reasoning might not stand up to scrutiny in a room full of ethics scholars, but it was good enough for Acid.

But working for Darius? No. He was a sick, egotistical man, who had surrounded himself with an equally sadistic and deadly crew. For Darius it was all about money and fame, at any cost. It was all about him.

Plus, he'd killed The Dullahan. He'd killed her friend. Caesar would never have stood for that and neither would she.

Passing a liquor store, she ducked inside almost without thinking and bought herself a bottle of white wine. It wasn't the good stuff, but it was cold and alcoholic, and that's all she cared about right now.

After crossing the street she entered Laurel Park, relieved to find it all but deserted. The late afternoon air was cooler here, the canopy of leaves providing a welcome respite from the city's heat. She found a spot under a tall tree, the raised concrete surround making a reasonable enough seat. She twisted the top off the wine and took a long drink. The tranquillity of the park felt almost surreal compared to the havoc swirling in her head. But the birds chirping softly in the trees, and the rustle of leaves in the gentle breeze, did nothing to subdue the bats screeching across her soul.

She took another swig of wine. She was near the edge, teetering on the brink of a decision that could change everything, and she didn't like it. Maybe she had been going about this wrong? As always, she was battling her inner demons along with those she worked with at Kancel Kulture. On any given day she felt sad, angry, hateful. But now she was starting to second-guess herself, and that was a death knell in the field. Confidence was as crucial in this world as it was with the polygraphs. She'd been half-joking with Spook earlier, masking her doubt with cynicism as usual. But if she didn't trust herself, she really was a dead woman walking.

She despised Darius for what he'd done and for his lineage. She had no doubt she wanted him dead. But maybe it was time to admit she couldn't do this alone. She took another drink, feeling the alcohol warming her from the inside out. Despite herself, she even found a smile forming.

Spook being here in LA had thrown a massive spanner in the works.

But wasn't that just like the kid?

Chapter Thirty-Six

On the opposite side of the Strip, Spook marched down the sidewalk with uncommon haste and determination. Abi trailed behind, struggling to keep up. They hadn't spoken since leaving the Rainbow, and Spook preferred it that way. The silence allowed her space to think, to process the whirlwind of emotions and decisions she had to deal with. They crossed North Gardner Street, Abi almost jogging to stay close.

"You going to tell me what the hell just happened?" Abi asked. "Or at least tell me where the hell we're going?"

Spook glanced around. She hadn't considered a destination. They appeared to be heading toward the rental in Westlake, but it would take hours on foot.

"Spook, please talk to me," Abi tried again. "Did you see her? Is that it?"

Spook stopped, her eyes on the street ahead. "Yes. Briefly."

"Shit, seriously? Where?"

Spook turned around. "I don't want to talk about it."

They resumed walking, the silence growing heavier with each step. But Abi wasn't one to give up easily. "Come on, you can tell me. I mean... I know what you are, and I'm still here, right? You're still my best chance at staying alive this week. If you do want to take out that clean-up crew, I'll help in any way I can."

"You can't help," Spook replied. "The situation has got very... complicated."

A part of Spook had always questioned if Acid had some devious strategy up her sleeve, a plan to dismantle Darius' operation from within. It was the only explanation keeping her optimistic. She hadn't shared her theory with Nate – maybe out of fear of jinxing it – but it was a key reason for her eagerness to confront Acid face to face. Now that she knew the truth, her anxiety only deepened.

Was Acid up to the task?

Was *she*?

"People like that don't just stop," Abi said. "My only choice is to try and get rid of them. Or go to the cops."

"You can't do that," Spook snapped. "Not whilst Acid is still linked to them."

"Exactly. I knew you'd say that," Abi replied. "And I'd be worried anyway. I know too much about some of the people in Jefferson's circle. They'd panic. I reckon it wouldn't take much for me to end up dead in police custody. A freak accident, you know? The kind you guys are good at making happen." She grabbed Spook's arm, her eyes wide and pleading. "Let me in. Let me help you. If you kill them all, it puts me in the clear and saves your friend."

Spook sighed, feeling the weight of the decision pressing down on her once more. She was starting to regret ever wanting more autonomy. What could she say? Abi's courage was inspiring, but this was a dangerous game. Still, the tough young woman had a point – if they could pull this off, it would solve a lot of problems.

"Fine," she muttered. "But first, we need a cab."

They hailed one and rode in relative silence over to Westlake. Spook paid the driver, and they walked down Wilshire Boulevard into MacArthur Park, finding a secluded bench overlooking the lake. It was a hot afternoon, but being near water seemed to shave a couple of degrees off. Ducks floated lazily on the lake's surface in front of them, and on the other side of the water an older woman in bright orange yoga pants played fetch with her dog.

After ensuring no one was within earshot, Spook gave Abi a thorough rundown of everything that had transpired over the past seven years. She began with the first time she learned that someone named Acid Vanilla was coming to kill her, and recounted every twist and turn up to the present. It took almost forty-five minutes, and when she finished, Abi was silent for a long time.

"Jesus," she said, finally. "That could be a Hollywood film script."

"I know."

"Do you think it has a happy ending?" Abi asked. "I mean… it rarely happens that way outside of the movies, right?"

Spook stared out over the water. "Yeah, that's what I'm afraid of." She leaned back, thinking hard for a moment, then jumped to her feet. "Listen, can you find your way back to the rental from here?"

"Yeah… sure." Abi looked confused. "But why?"

Spook glanced at the path leading out of the park. "Go

there now. Tell Nate and Lena I had something to deal with. Tell them not to worry and that I'll be back soon."

Abi nodded. "Okay, fine. But if you're going back to find your friend, be careful, okay?"

Spook managed a small smile. "I'm always careful," she said.

Chapter Thirty-Seven

Darius Duke lay sprawled across his silk sheets, a smug grin plastered on his face. The hot LA sun filtered through the heavy drapes, spears of gold lighting up the master bedroom of his new three-storey Beverly Hills mansion. He guessed it was somewhere around late morning or lunchtime, but he'd only woken a few minutes earlier, having not got to bed until around 6 a.m.

This was the life Darius had always dreamed of.

King of Hollywood.

Next stop, the world.

He closed his eyes and grinned. It might be a tired, clichéd statement used mainly by jumped-up idiots, but in his case it was the truth. Another two years and Kancel Kulture would have the world at their feet. A truly global operation – elite, unreachable, unstoppable.

He opened his eyes and glanced around his palatial bedroom, groaning slightly at the remnants of last night's indulgences. Empty champagne bottles, a couple of half-filled glasses, piles of clothes, as well as discarded condom wrappers and sex toys. It was hot and airless in his room, the smell of perfume and sweat lingering. He could still taste the faint chemical tang of grade-A narcotics in his throat.

He glanced left and right at Sydney and Sara, the two wannabe movie stars he'd met the previous evening in the VIP area at Bootsy Bellows. They'd believed he was a successful casting director – mainly because he'd told them so – and had been all over him from that point on. They'd arrived back at Darius' place around five. So while he did go to bed around six, he probably didn't fall asleep until sometime after nine.

What a night.

He reclined, ignoring the mess for now, and considered whether he should invest in a mirrored ceiling. It would be costly, and some might think it a little cheesy, but he liked the idea. Besides, no one would dare say anything to his face about it.

He sneered, wishing he had one right now. What a sight this would be. Sydney was still fast asleep, her blonde hair splayed across the pillow, and he was delighted to see the cocaine residue still visible on her pert buttocks. On the other side of him, Sara was half-awake, her slim arm draped across his torso, her fingers playing with his chest hair.

Yes. This was the life all right. But he knew he couldn't stay here all day. He was, after all, the head of the most significant organisation the murder-for-hire industry had ever known.

As if on cue, his phone began to vibrate on the dresser across the far side of the room. Lifting Sara's arm off him, he got up to answer it.

"Hello, Darius Duke speaking."

"Mr Duke… It's Brian here."

Darius cricked his neck and put on a big smile, adopting his poshest English accent. "Good afternoon, Brian. How lovely to speak with you."

Brian cleared his throat. "Yes indeed." Brian was Darius' contact at the studio – the one he hoped would soon become a top client. "Are you okay to talk?"

"Hang on one second." Darius muted the call and walked over to the bed, clapping his hands loudly. "Up! Get up! Time to go."

The two women stirred, confused and groggy. Sydney blinked her eyes open, a pout forming on her bright red lips. "What's going on?" she asked, in her nasal Cali-girl drawl.

"Get your clothes and get out," Darius barked, snatching underwear off the floor and flinging it at them. "I mean it! You need to leave. Now!"

Slowly, begrudgingly, the two women climbed out of bed. Darius watched their naked flesh shivering as they gathered up their clothes. Why were they taking so damn long? Grabbing them each by the arm, he hustled them to the door. "You change out there and see yourselves out."

He yanked the door open and shoved them through it, ignoring their whiney protests as he slammed the door behind them. "Sluts," he snarled, striding back to the dresser to retrieve his phone.

"So sorry about that, Brian," he said after unmuting the call. "Where were we?"

Brian sighed. "We need an update, and we need a guarantee that you can deliver what we've asked for."

Darius forced a smile, fighting the urge to tell Brian to go to hell. Who did this prick think he was? Darius was eager to sign the contract and secure the retainer the studio execs were offering, but he wasn't going to jump through hoops for these saps.

"Haven't we already discussed this?" he asked, keeping his voice steady. "I have the best people working on it. We'll create the narrative exactly as arranged."

"The Japanese are arriving soon," Brian said. "The welcome gala is in three days. Will you be ready?"

"Relax, Brian. We're professionals. This is what we do. Tell your paymasters everything will be taken care of."

Brian started to say something else but Darius hung up. "Next time, have the organ grinder call me," he yelled at the phone. "I don't deal with fucking monkeys."

Composing himself, he walked over to the large gold-framed mirror hanging on the wall next to the bathroom. He was stark naked and hungover, but he liked what he saw. His time in the gym and under the California sun had done wonders for his skin and physique. His hair was wild, and lipstick smears around his mouth gave him a Joker-like appearance, but he didn't mind that one bit. Lifting an arm he sniffed at himself. He smelled of wet animals and sex, but he kind of liked that and decided against having a shower. Instead, he grabbed a bottle of cologne and sprayed himself liberally, the strong scent only slightly masking his feral depravity.

He moved to his closet and dressed quickly, choosing a bright red silk shirt, unbuttoned to mid-chest as always, paired with black leather trousers – no underwear – and black heeled boots. To finish the ensemble, he slid on a pair of oversized sunglasses, smirking at his reflection. Very cool. Very Jim Morrison. Perfect.

Downstairs, he was relieved to find Sydney and Sara gone. He grabbed a coconut water from the refrigerator and headed for the door.

Outside, his driver Aslan – a burly defector from the Russian Bratva – stood waiting by Darius' gunmetal grey

Mercedes-Benz G-Class SUV. Aslan opened the door without a word, and Darius slid into the back seat, the leather cool against his skin.

"HQ," he ordered.

With a nod, Aslan climbed into the driver's seat and started the engine. Almost as big as Grimaldi and looking every bit the Russian bodyguard, Aslan never spoke or asked questions, which Darius appreciated. They drove to Echo Park in silence, the city a blur of motion outside the tinted windows.

Upon arriving at Kancel Kulture's headquarters, Darius left Aslan outside and made his way up to the control room. Stig Saga was right where he expected him, hunched over a bank of monitors, his long slender fingers tapping furiously at a keyboard. The screens cast an eerie green glow over his pale face.

"There you are," Darius called out to get his attention. "Hard at it, I see."

Saga looked up. His eyes were bloodshot as if he'd been staring at screens for most of the day. "Rest is for the weak," he said.

"Yeah, totally," Darius replied, running his fingers through his hair. "I've just had that muppet Brian from the studio on the phone, checking up on us. He rang with some pretence, but he was just double-checking we can deliver on time."

"I'm working on our approach right now," Saga said. "But with The Gorgon dead, we'll need more men on the ground."

"No worries." Darius placed his hands on his hips. "The twins will be touching down at LAX in the morning."

Saga made a guttural noise. "I worry we won't have

enough operatives for the plan to run smoothly. We might have to get involved in this one."

Darius hesitated. "You mean... as in you and I?" he clarified, waving a finger between himself and Saga, who nodded in response. "Won't it be risky?"

"Not if we do it right."

Darius thought about it. He didn't like the idea of getting his hands dirty or endangering his own life. But, hell. Why not? The excessive amounts of dopamine in his brain, courtesy of last night's cocaine binge, told him it'd be fun, that he'd be fine.

Saga turned back to his monitors.

"Any news on Acid?" Darius asked.

"She's gone off-grid. Like she always does when she knows we're concerned," Saga said, as ever unable to hide his distaste whilst talking about Acid. "Her old friends are still monitoring our comms, but I'm allowing it in the knowledge we can feed them what we want. But that woman still worries me."

"I know," Darius said.

Saga looked up again. "Do you ever regret not killing her and that Spook idiot?"

"She's my sister."

"I know that. But that doesn't answer my question." Saga held Darius' stare until it was clear he would get no response, then turned back to his screens. "I only ask, because we've had a new assignment come through."

That perked Darius up. "What is it?"

"The client is APD Pictures. It's a standard hit. But they want it done soon. Tomorrow."

"Not an issue. What's the story?"

"It seems APD have a senior producer with a predilection for young actors. Very young actors. Apparently, he's been at it for years. He doesn't care about the gender of these kids as long as they're sweet and innocent-looking. The studio has been managing it with threats and NDAs, but with the current climate they're getting antsy. They can't fire him because he has too much dirt on the executive team. But he's become a liability."

With a few keystrokes, Saga brought up the file on the screen. Darius recognised the guy from a party he attended a while back up in the Hills. "There's also a former victim – some Z-list actor – who's become a bit too vocal about what happened to him," Saga continued. "He's in his early twenties now and has a massive drug problem, been blabbing to anyone who'll listen. Yet that actually works in our favour, and the studio's."

Darius leaned over the back of Saga's chair to examine the screen. "Go on... what's the plan?"

"The idea is we hit the producer and frame the actor for his murder," Saga replied. "That way we take down two birds with one stone."

Darius straightened up. "Sounds fiendish but it'll need a lot of planning. Can you handle this one along with Grimaldi? It needs brains as well as brawn."

Saga held up a hand. "I was thinking of sending Acid with the big man."

"Oh? Why?"

Saga chuckled, an odd sound that grated on Darius' nerves. "I have an idea of how we might test your sister's allegiance once and for all," Saga said. "I've already briefed Grimaldi, and he's more than happy to go along with the plan."

Darius stuck out his bottom lip. "But it won't interfere with the job?"

"Oh no. It's just an added... bonus."

Darius lowered his head, thinking a moment. He rubbed at his stubble; he scratched his neck. "Fine," he said. "Do it. Whatever you think. I trust your judgement."

"Excellent," Saga replied. "Mark my words. If things go as planned, this will expose Acid Vanilla's true intentions better than any polygraph machine ever could."

Chapter Thirty-Eight

Acid was not happy. It was yet another hot day, and she'd planned to spend it indoors, plotting her next move. So when Saga called her three hours ago and informed her she was to accompany Grimaldi on a new mission, she'd been rather put out. She'd agreed, of course – one of Kancel Kulture's policies was that operatives took the jobs they were assigned without question – but it wasn't what she needed today.

When her Uber arrived, she climbed in the passenger seat and watched out of the window as the car weaved its way up Mulholland Drive, the roads becoming narrower and more winding as the houses grew larger. She had the driver drop her at the end of Palo Vista Drive and walked the rest of the way up to Woodrow Wilson Drive where the hit was to take place. The relentless LA sun beat down on her as she walked, the air up here like a thick, oppressive blanket.

Saga had been his usual morose self on the call and hadn't provided any details about the job, only that she was to meet Grimaldi at the specified time. Acid didn't like not knowing what she was stepping into, but at least it was work. She was a little surprised that Darius' orders about bringing in Spook hadn't been mentioned, but if they weren't on her back about it, that suited her fine. There was no recompense in killing her old friend, and that was of utmost importance for Kancel Kulture. Darius enjoyed vanquishing his enemies, but he enjoyed money even more. Money always came first.

Pushing thoughts of Spook aside, Acid rolled her shoulders and continued down the leafy street.

One step at a time.

As she rounded the corner, she saw Grimaldi leaning against a white-rendered wall. He was a huge beast of a man, built of dense fat rather than muscle, but today he looked even bigger, bloated and grotesque under the hot sun. He was wearing beige shorts that exposed his thick, pale legs, and a terrible Hawaiian shirt emblazoned with a pattern of hot dogs and already soaked in sweat. His thinning, greasy black hair clung to his forehead like fat spider legs.

He didn't look at her as she approached, his gaze fixed on the winding driveway opposite and the white gates keeping them from the grandiose property beyond.

"That the place?" Acid said, getting closer.

"Hello to you too, Ms Vanilla," he grunted, wiping sweat from his brow. "The mark's already inside. I've been here a few hours, watching."

Acid glanced at the house. It was a typical LA mansion, secluded and opulent. "You need to give me the details. Saga was rather brief on the call."

"It's some producer called Mike Henris. We're to make it look messy and unprofessional – almost as if it was a

236

crime of passion. I thought you'd be good at that."
Grimaldi grinned, showing yellowed teeth.

Acid stiffened and looked away, but she couldn't help
but smile. She liked the sound of this job. Plus, getting out
of her thoughts for an hour or two could only be a good
thing. She needed clarity and that was almost impossible
amidst the chattering frenzy of the bats.

"So... what are we thinking?" she asked.

Grimaldi turned and lifted the back of his shirt to reveal
a Glock 17 stuffed into his waistband. "You want to do the
honours?"

Acid saw where the gun muzzle was tucked, the sweat
soaking through the cotton of Grimaldi's shorts. "No. It's
fine. It's your gun, you can do it."

"You're too kind." Grimaldi turned back to the house.

"That's it?" Acid said. "We just shoot him?"

Grimaldi sighed. "Didn't Saga or Darius fill you in?"

"No. He just told me to meet you."

"Typical," Grimaldi muttered. "Okay, this Henris guy is
a big producer in the movie biz, but he's also known to run
a classic 'casting couch' situation with the young actors he
encounters, some of them underage. He's a real piece of
shit, from what Saga told me. We kill him, then call Saga.
He's gathering DNA evidence to frame some pissy little
actor that Henris took a liking to ten years ago. The actor's
readying himself to do a tell-all to the media, so this way we
take out the mark and get the actor sent down for the
murder. Apparently, the client considered having the actor
killed as well, but decided this approach was better for
them. They want to come clean about Henris – reckon it'll
be good for their brand if they're seen publicly disowning
him – but also want to control the narrative with the actor
out of the picture. They say they can 'open up a conversa-

tion', and that it will position them as 'a safe, forward-thinking and transparent company where young actors can flourish' – all that woke shit people say these days."

Acid narrowed her eyes at the building. "Where's the mark currently?"

"I did a circuit a few minutes before you got here," Grimaldi replied, waving his hand down the street. "There's a clear line of sight into his front room further down. He's in there with headphones on. Probably meditating or some shit. Looked like he'd be there a while."

"Got it." Acid observed the building, a thought hitting her. "And how old is this guy?"

"Mid-sixties," Grimaldi said.

"Any security? Bodyguards?"

Grimaldi grinned. "No."

Acid nodded. She was wondering if she could eliminate Grimaldi and pin it on the producer's security team, but if there was none, it was too risky. "Fine," she said. "Let's do this."

With Grimaldi taking the lead, they moved a little further up the street and then veered into a thicket of lush evergreens.

"There's an entrance to the garden through here," Grimaldi whispered.

Acid had assumed as much, but held her tongue. Instead, she pulled a pair of latex gloves out of her back pocket and slipped them on. In front of her, Grimaldi was doing the same. Not an easy task in this humidity.

They ducked under a series of low-hanging branches and approached a small side gate in the walled garden. Grimaldi shot Acid a grin and pushed the gate open with a triumphant smirk.

"Paid off the gardener yesterday evening," he said. "Gave him two hundred bucks to leave the gate unlocked."

Acid raised her chin. "I see," she said, wondering why Grimaldi had known about this hit since yesterday while she was only told hours ago.

Bloody Saga!

"Don't worry, it won't come back on us." He chuckled. "I followed him home and smothered him with a pillow while he slept. Can't have loose ends, and I don't like giving money away."

"As long as you were careful," Acid replied.

They stepped onto a well-manicured lawn at the back of the property, surrounded by exotic plants. In front of the house was a large patio with expensive outdoor furniture, and beyond that, a gleaming pool reflected the bright sun. The air smelled of freshly cut grass and chlorine.

Acid's eyes darted around as they crept up to the house, taking in the expansive windows and French doors. On the nearest side of the property, she noticed a single door with a glass panel halfway up, likely the staff entrance. That was her way in.

Pulling her lock-picking kit from her pocket, she knelt by the door and went to work, inserting the first rake into the lock and feeling for the pins.

"Come on," Grimaldi huffed behind her. "Hurry up."

Acid ignored him, concentrating on freeing the lock. She felt the last pin give way and the mechanism turned just as a large rock smashed through the glass pane above her. She recoiled, twisting around to see Grimaldi standing beside her and grinning.

"You bloody thug," she hissed.

"He's got headphones on."

"Yeah?" she said, getting to her feet. "And what about his neighbours?"

"It has to look like the actor broke in and killed him," Grimaldi said, pushing past her into the house. "Remember, girly – messy is good for this one."

Biting her tongue, she followed him inside and down a dim corridor that opened into the main part of the house. The interior was as lavish as the exterior – high ceilings, modern art on the walls, designer furniture. A crystal chandelier hung above the grand foyer. Silently, they moved into the next room, Acid's senses on high alert.

They entered a plush dining area with a table big enough to have hosted the Last Supper. This room fed into the front of the house, a vast lounge with a grand piano standing in one corner. The wall to Acid's left was lined with bookshelves filled with hundreds of books – most of them movie-star biographies – along with bound scripts and photographic collections. A plush, cream-coloured sofa dominated the centre of the room and an enormous abstract painting hung above a modern fireplace.

As Grimaldi had mentioned, the mark was reclining on the couch, facing away from them. From her position Acid could only see the top of his head – bald, tanned and shiny – but he was indeed wearing a ridiculously large pair of headphones and humming softly to himself.

She gestured to Grimaldi to split up, and they moved silently around the couch to approach in a pincer movement. Up close, Henris looked younger than she'd expected, but that was LA for you, with the best plastic surgeons money could buy. His eyes were closed, but he must have sensed a shift in the atmosphere because they were only waiting a few seconds before they shot open.

"What the fuck!?" Henris yelled, yanking the head-phones from his head. "Who the hell are you?"

His eyes widened in panic as he stood, but before he could say more, Grimaldi drew his pistol and shot him twice in the chest. Henris staggered for a moment, looked as if he was trying to solve an impossible maths problem, then collapsed back onto the couch.

Acid watched as the light left his eyes. She felt nothing.

"Fire two more rounds," she told Grimaldi. "One into the couch over to one side, and another higher up in the wall behind him." When the big man frowned, she added, "It has to look amateurish, remember?"

Grimaldi obliged, then stuffed the pistol back into his waistband and pulled a phone from his pocket. Moving over to the fireplace, he made the call.

"Hey Saga… it's me…" He wandered over and examined Henris' body. "It's done… Yeah, no problem, I'll tell her…"

He hung up. "Saga's on his way with the evidence we need to plant. We have to wait here until he arrives."

Acid shot him a look. "Is that wise? What if the door you just smashed is linked to some kind of off-site security?"

"Relax. It isn't. The gardener assured me the back door was safe. He was allowed to let himself in and out to get tools and things if Henris wasn't in. But he hated Henris, so was glad to share information when he thought I was going to rob the place."

Acid ran her fingers through her hair. "So why didn't you get the gardener's keys when you killed him?"

"Oh yeah, I didn't think of that."

Talk about bloody amateurs…

She walked away, shaking her head, unwilling to stand too close to Grimaldi's sweaty form while they waited for

Saga. She wandered into the dining room and through another door, leading her into a kitchen that was so white it hurt her eyes. Pulling open a few drawers, she rifled through the producer's possessions in the hope she might discover something useful for the narrative.

In a drawer near the window, she found a bunch of Polaroids of young actors. Knowing Henris' history, she found them unsettling, but there was nothing incriminating.

"Sick bastard," she muttered, tossing the photographs back in the drawer.

She was heading back towards the lounge when she heard a noise and froze. It came from the corridor leading to the back door. Moving silently, she crab-walked over to the kitchen island, and was reaching for a knife when a man appeared in the doorway holding a gun.

"Don't even fucking think about it," he snarled.

His eyes were wild, his expression one of grim determination. He was wearing a white t-shirt and jeans, but with his shaved head and mean expression he had the look of a former soldier; perhaps turned actor or stuntman considering where he lived. His biceps bulged as he moved forward, his aim trained on Acid's head.

She raised her hands in response. "Let's keep calm," she told him. "Who are you?"

"I live next door. Where's Henris?"

Stupid bloody Grimaldi.

"Henris is fine," she lied. "Put the gun down and we can go see him. I'm a friend of his. Just visiting."

"I don't think so, lady." His eyes were bloodshot and a vein throbbed at his temple. "You're breaking and entering. And I have the right to use extreme force to take you down."

Shit.

Maybe he wasn't a soldier. Just some pumped-up meat-head who thought he was Rambo. The kind of guy who'd been waiting for this moment his entire life. Her mind raced, searching for a way out. The rage in the man's eyes was worrying, his finger tightening on the trigger. She could smell the sweat and adrenaline coming off him, could see the intent in his eyes, his body twitching with pent-up aggression.

"Please," she said, softening her voice, smiling. "Don't hurt me. I'll leave... This was a mistake. I promise I haven't—"

She winced as blood splattered across the kitchen, the side of the man's head opening up in a shower of bone and brain matter. Grimaldi stood in the doorway, grinning as Rambo crumpled to the floor.

Acid met his leer. "Thanks for that."

"Don't mention it. Stupid bastard." He stepped over the bloody corpse to inspect his handiwork. "Saga will have someone clean that up," he said, tucking his gun back into his waistband.

Acid sucked in a deep breath as Grimaldi turned and walked back the way he'd come. Stepping over the body she followed him into the dining room, where he stood on the far side of the room, looking out over the lounge with his back to her.

She paused, glancing around as an idea hit her – a golden opportunity – but she had to act fast. With the bats screeching their encouragement, a new narrative formed quickly in her mind. The neighbour had burst in after hearing a commotion and killed Grimaldi, after which she had killed the neighbour. It was terrible bad luck, she'd say, really awful news about the big man, but at least they'd got their mark, right? And that's what happened in this shadowy world.

It would put her under the spotlight once more with Saga and Darius, but there'd only be four of Kancel Kulture left.

She stepped forward, knowing that if Grimaldi moved much further away from Rambo's fallen body it would cast doubt on her story. It had to be now. Letting her instincts take over, she grabbed the gun from his waistband and jumped back.

"What the fuck?"

Grimaldi spun around and she shot him twice in the chest. It was risky this way, not guaranteeing an instant death, but a head shot would look professional and put too much heat on her. Aim for the centre mass – that's what people are told, that's what an amateur would do when taking down a hostile intruder.

"Fucking bitch."

She stepped away as Grimaldi staggered forward, a look of shock and betrayal flashing across his face. Then he collapsed to the ground with a heavy thud. She fired three more rounds into the walls to emphasise the chaos of the situation and slid the Glock down into the waistband at her back. For the story to be cast iron she should have used Rambo's gun but it was too late for that, and Saga wouldn't have chance to run ballistics.

Grimaldi lay on his side, motionless, but she knew he wasn't dead yet. Even if she'd got him in both ventricles and shredded his heart, it would take him a minute or two to die. Thankfully, the shock and trauma had incapacitated him.

She approached him cautiously, her heart pounding.
What the…?

She paused, scanning his body. There were no exit wounds. No blood. She moved around and rolled him onto his back. Still no blood. Just three holes in his shirt.

No...

Shit...

She ripped open his shirt and her heart dropped into her stomach. Grimaldi was wearing a military-grade ballistic vest.

Before she could move, his eyes sprang open. "Surprise!" he snarled.

Chapter Thirty-Nine

Grimaldi's eyes gleamed with a smugness that made Acid's skin crawl.

"That wasn't very nice," he growled.

She hesitated, confusion clouding her mind. What the hell was going on? Had he orchestrated this? Was this his plan all along?

Before she could gather her thoughts, a heavy fist slammed into the side of her head, knocking her into the wall. The impact rattled her senses, sharp pain exploding through her skull. She managed to stay on her feet, but her vision blurred, and her ears rang, disorienting her further.

She barely had time to react before Grimaldi grabbed her and threw her across the dining room table. She slid across its surface and landed on a chair, which tipped over, sending her sprawling onto the floor. Pain shot through her ribs, stealing her breath momentarily, but she forced herself up, gasping for air as Grimaldi advanced, his massive frame dominating the room. He was relentless, his fists raining down on her like sledgehammers.

He lifted her again, dragging her into the front room and slamming her into the bookshelf. Books and trinkets rained down, a heavy tome striking her temple and adding to the dizzying pain. She crumpled to the floor, dazed and bleeding.

Come on, Acid. Get up.

Fight back.

She rolled away just as Grimaldi's boot crashed down on the spot where her head had been. Grabbing a heavy-bottomed vase from the fallen shelves, she smashed it across his knee. He grunted in pain, but it was like trying to fell a tree with a penknife.

He kicked the vase from her hand before lifting her off the floor and hurling her against a glass cabinet. It shattered around her, shards embedding in her arms and back, but the pain also jogged her memory. Stumbling forward, she pulled the Glock from her waistband and fired off three rounds as Grimaldi leapt behind a wall, the bullets missing him by inches and embedding in the plaster with dull thuds. She was shaky and her vision was off. She adjusted her aim, firing two more shots, but Grimaldi ducked out of the way, grabbing a dining room chair and hurling it at her. One of the legs hit her arm with a bone-jarring force, knocking the gun from her grip and sending it skittering across the floor.

Shit.

She chased after it but Grimaldi got to her first, slamming his knee into her stomach with the force of a battering ram, sending her sprawling. The blow left her dazed, barely able to keep her eyes open, her breath coming in shallow gasps. As she pushed herself up, she saw a sadistic smile playing on Grimaldi's lips, his eyes alight with cruel amusement. She braced herself for another assault, but instead he waved mockingly at her before retreating through the dining area and down the corridor to the outside.

No. She couldn't let him escape.

If he got away and told Darius what had happened, she was a dead woman. She scrambled for the Glock, her hands slick with blood and trembling from adrenaline. Rolling onto her side she fired after him, but after two unsuccessful shots the slide locked back.

Out of ammo.

Bugger.

She threw the gun in frustration and pushed herself to her feet. Every muscle screamed in protest but she was determined not to lose him. Grimaldi was surprisingly fast and agile for such a massive brute. Pushing through the pain, she sprinted after him out of the house, the bats screeching at her as she went. The garden became a blur of green as she burst through the door, spotting Grimaldi disappearing through the gate. She gritted her teeth and pressed on. She couldn't let him get away. Not now, not ever.

She chased him out of Henris' grounds and down Mulholland Drive. Her ribs ached with every step, but she clenched her fists, refusing to let the pain slow her down. Grimaldi was not only fast for his size, but the downhill slope gave him an advantage. If he got back to Darius, it was over. There'd be a hit out on her within the hour. She pumped her arms, willing her legs to move faster as Grimaldi darted into a side street and vaulted over a low wall, crashing through someone's meticulously tended flower garden. Acid leapt over after him, barely registering her surroundings. Her focus was solely on Grimaldi's retreating figure as he cut through the next garden, heading for the avenue beyond.

They raced through the vacant twisting streets of Hollywood Hills, Grimaldi ducking into driveways and cutting through the landscaped yards of luxurious homes with Acid never far behind. As he ran, he knocked over trash cans and garden furniture, creating obstacles in her path that Acid hurdled, her injuries numbed by adrenaline. The chase was relentless, driven by desperation on both sides.

Finally she cornered him in a narrow cul-de-sac, the high walls of gated estates on either side leaving him nowhere to go. Or maybe he'd stopped on purpose, realising he had the advantage.

Acid slowed to a stop, suddenly aware of how outmatched she was in size, weight and power. But this was her last chance. She had to stop him.

Grimaldi faced her, his expression distorted with malice. "Well, here we are," he snarled. "You should have known better, girl."

She squared her shoulders but didn't reply. As Grimaldi took a step closer she lunged, aiming a swift kick at his knees. But the big man anticipated the move and grabbed her leg, twisting her off balance. She hit the ground hard, the impact jarring her already bruised ribs.

"You're finished," he growled. "Don't you see?"

"Never." She scrambled to her feet and ducked under the arc of a heavy punch, putting all her weight behind her elbow as she smashed into his ribs.

Grimaldi grunted but barely staggered. He swung again, a brutal backhand that she narrowly avoided. Acid knew she couldn't match his strength head-on. She needed to be quicker, smarter. Feinting left, she drove her knee into his gut, aiming for a vulnerable spot. He doubled over and she followed up with a sharp uppercut to his jaw, feeling the impact through her arm. Grimaldi's head snapped back, but he cried out in anger rather than pain.

As she spun around for another attack he wrapped his arms around her, squeezing against her damaged ribs. She yelled but managed to reach back and claw at his face, her nails raking across his skin. Grimaldi roared, dropping her and clutching his bleeding cheek. Summoning all her strength, Acid leapt up and caught him on the jaw with her elbow. The blow rattled him but he recovered almost instantly and knocked her away with another vicious back-hand. She staggered, her vision blurring as he came at her again.

He grabbed her by the throat and lifted her off her feet as if she was a rag doll. She kicked and struggled, her fingers scrabbling at his hands, but his grip was like a vice around her throat. She felt her strength fading, the edges of her vision turning black.

"Fucking traitor," he snarled, his hot breath in her face. "You were never going to get away with it."

Acid fought to stay conscious. She really was getting too old for this game. And it looked as if she wasn't going to get any older.

Dark fog seeped across her eyes. She was going. She was—

A dull crack echoed around her. Grimaldi's grip loosened.

What?

He let go of her and she fell to the ground, scrambling away in time to see the big man drop to his knees, a neat red hole between his eyes. He stared wide-eyed into the middle distance for a moment, perhaps seeing his God, before pitching forward and hitting the ground.

Acid blinked, trying to clear her head. Looking over she

saw Spook standing a few metres away, a pistol with a silencer in her hand. She looked different, older, there was a hardness around her eyes Acid hadn't noticed previously.

Spook lowered the gun and rushed over. "Are you okay, can you walk?"

Acid nodded, still trying to catch her breath "Yeah... thanks... I didn't... How did you find me?"

Spook helped her to her feet. "I've been tracking you since you left your apartment. Figured you might need backup."

Acid leaned against the wall, feeling the adrenaline ebbing away. "I guess I did."

"I'd say so," Spook said coldly. She fixed Acid with a hard stare. "Now... are you going to let me damn well help you?"

Acid glanced up the street, too exhausted to argue. "Yes, Spook," she said. "I'm going to let you damn well help me."

Chapter Forty

Spook could practically feel the tension radiating out of Acid as they trudged along North Curson Avenue, heading back to Westlake. They'd been walking for over an hour, sticking to back streets whenever possible. It was late afternoon, and the streets were relatively quiet, but Acid looked like she'd just emerged from a bar fight, and it was best not to draw undue attention.

The air between them crackled with unspoken words and unresolved emotions. They hadn't exchanged more than a few sentences during the entire walk, and now the silence was becoming suffocating for Spook. She kept stealing glances at Acid, trying to work out what she was thinking and offering her the occasional smile. She got nothing in return. Acid was holding her side, her jaw clenched tight as if dealing with a lot of pain, but other than that her expression was unreadable. What Spook wouldn't give right now for a shrug or one of Acid's infamous eye-rolls. At least it would show she was still in there somewhere.

Spook knew she should focus on what was going to happen next in regard to Kancel Kulture, but right now she was consumed with finding something to say to snap Acid out of her funk. The two women hadn't spoken properly in a year. Spook had a hell of a lot she needed to get off her chest, and she imagined Acid did too.

Instead they carried on walking in grim silence, the late afternoon sun casting long shadows as they veered left onto West 3rd Street.

"Are you going to keep quiet the whole way?" Spook finally asked. "I thought there'd at least be some snide comments or sarcastic asides by now."

Acid sneered, not bothering to look at her. "What do you want me to say, Spook? That you've ruined everything?"

"Excuse me?" Spook stopped walking and turned to face her, heart pounding in her chest. "I've ruined everything? What the hell are you talking about? I just saved your life."

Acid paused. "I had it all planned out," she muttered, still not meeting her eye. "It was going well."

"Was it?" Spook snapped. "So, was being strangled in the street by some goon part of your plan?"

Acid sighed and looked to the heavens. Not for the first time, she reminded Spook of a petulant teenager. "I was playing the long game. Taking them out one by one, making their deaths look like accidents or the result of unforeseen events," she continued, her voice cold, monotonous. "Darius and Stig Saga are both suspicious of me, but I can talk my way around Darius and he's all that matters. Plus, they need me too much, especially if they're losing all their operatives."

Spook's eyes widened. "And you were prepared to take out Darius too?"

"Absolutely. He wouldn't see it coming until it was too late. By then I'd have dismantled his entire network."

"What happens if they decide all these deaths are too much of a coincidence?" Spook asked.

Acid shrugged, wincing as the movement pulled at her injuries. "By that point I'd be ready to finish the job. But it would have been on my timescale. You just fucked everything up."

"I sped it up, that's all," Spook retaliated. "You should be thanking me. I came all this way because I was worried about you."

Acid stared at her. For a moment she looked as if she was about to laugh. Or cry. But she just tutted and set off walking again.

Spook sighed as loud as she could and followed after her. "Why didn't you contact me and let me in on this?" she asked. "You could have got a message out somehow."

"It was too risky and I didn't want you involved," Acid replied. "You and I were done. After Rome, you should have forgotten about me."

"Do you really think that's possible?"

"I'd forgotten about you."

"Go to hell," Spook snapped. "You should have got in touch."

"I couldn't, you idiot," Acid snapped. "I wanted to protect you. Back in that room in Rome, all I was thinking about was how we both got to live. Me joining Kancel Kulture and convincing Darius to free you was the only way I saw that happening. But then, as time went on I realised I could also get free and avenge The Dullahan in the process. It *was* working out great."

Spook looked around, scanning the quiet residential street for any signs of movement. "Yeah, really great. That guy was about to kill you."

"I'd have figured something out."

"Really?"

Acid went quiet again, and they marched on, their steps falling in sync with one another as they moved along West 6th Street. After a few more minutes of uncomfortable silence, Spook glanced over, hoping to ease the tension. Acid appeared to be brooding, but not in her usual chaotic, manic way. Not in any way that Spook found comforting. The muscles around her eyes were tight and she seemed introspective, almost dour. It was a rare look for her.

"Are you sure you're not injured?" Spook asked.

"I'm fine. Leave it."

"I'm sorry for caring."

Acid released a bitter laugh, as if to say, *This again.*

"And I'm sorry for saving your life," Spook added, and in that moment she almost meant it.

"I didn't need saving."

"Is that so?"

"Yes! You should have left me to it," Acid said. "You always do things like this. You're too impulsive."

"I am not," Spook hit back, her fists clenching at her sides. "I've changed."

"Have you?" Acid looked her up and down, a cruel smile tugging at her lips.

Spook stopped, prompting Acid to do the same. "Yes. I have."

They faced off. The tension between them was electric. Acid's eyes bore into Spook's, challenging her like she always used to, expecting her to back down. But this time Spook held her ground, refusing to look away or withdraw.

"You don't get to do this," Spook said, keeping her voice steady. "You need my help. You admitted it yourself back there. So let's do this. Together. Like old times."

Acid's eyes flickered with something unreadable. She was the one who looked away first.

"Like old times?" She scoffed and shook her head. "The good old days, hey?"

"Yes," Spook replied, refusing to let Acid's cynicism win out. "Something like that."

Acid took a deep breath, her expression serious. "We need to take them down all at once now. It's the only way. But we have to be smart about it."

Spook nodded. "Agreed. *We* do."

Acid looked at her, and for a moment Spook thought she was going to smile. Instead she puffed out her cheeks and gave her a curt but approving nod.

But that was enough.

For Spook – from Acid – that was enough.

Chapter Forty-One

Abi Sandoval sat on the patio at Spook's rental property, taking long drags on her vape, the minty flavour doing nothing to soothe her frayed nerves. Across the pool, Nate Winters was pacing, his movements erratic, his face rigid with tension. Abi exhaled a large plume of vapour, her eyes never leaving him as he clenched and unclenched his fists, muttering under his breath. He looked like a caged animal, ready to strike.

Spook had been gone for forty-eight hours now, and if not for Lena being able to track her location and check in with her, they would probably have assumed she was dead. So Abi got why Nate was furious, and she understood the gravity of the situation. But he didn't have to act like such a dick.

Twenty minutes earlier, she'd been watching Seinfeld on her phone by the pool when he had snatched the phone from her, saying it was distracting him.

Yeah, well, fella, one person's distraction is another's safe space.

Seinfeld had been her mom's favourite show. Watching

it all these years later, Abi felt a closeness to her mom she rarely found in photographs. All those nights on the couch together, snuggled in a shared blanket, laughing at the exploits of Jerry, George, Elaine and Kramer – it was an escape from the void left by Abi's father. They were good times. Innocent times. At least they were for Abi. Looking back, she imagined her mom had been going through some serious shit.

From the patio she didn't take her eyes off Nate. His pacing remained agitated, anger evident in the stiffness across his shoulders and the deep scowl furrowing his brow. She felt like he was going to snap at any moment.

Not cool, man...

Leaning back in her chair she assessed the situation, noting the layout of the patio and everyone's positions. Lena was inside, still glued to her laptop as she had been the entire time. She seemed like a decent kid, but a total nerd, completely absorbed in whatever she was working on. Abi started to wonder; if Nate went berserk, could she hold him off? Her gaze landed on a heavy ceramic ashtray sitting on the edge of the low wall bordering the patio. It might do the job.

But what then?

She was still considering her options when she heard voices from inside the house. A second later, Spook stepped out onto the patio, accompanied by a woman with thick black hair. The woman from Jefferson's house.

Shit.

Abi jumped up as her fight-or-flight hormones went into overdrive. Did she run for it? Where would she go?

Spook walked straight over to her and raised her hand. "Don't worry. It's fine. I already told you. Acid is one of us. She's not going to hurt you."

"Oh yeah?" Abi hissed, her voice rising unexpectedly. "Because she was doing pretty bad shit the last time I saw her..."

Abi watched, unblinking, as this Acid chick walked over to speak with Nate. A moment later Lena appeared, laptop in hand, and sat on a chair beside the one Abi had just vacated.

"Don't mind me," she said, returning to her screen.

But this was all getting too much for Abi. She gasped for air as if forgetting to breathe suddenly.

"Hey, it's fine," Spook whispered, placing her hand on Abi's arm and making eye contact. "I promise."

Abi peered cautiously around her. On the other side of the pool, Acid was speaking with Nate in hushed tones, their conversation intense and animated.

"She's not going to kill me?"

Spook shook her head. "No. Never. I swear."

Abi tensed as Acid glanced her way. She said something else to Nate, then came over, her eyes locked on Abi as she approached.

Yeah, thanks, Spook.

It was pretty hard to believe this crazy woman wasn't after blood whilst caught in her death stare.

Up close, she was striking. She was about Abi's height and build, wearing black spray-on jeans, motorcycle boots, and a faded black t-shirt. Her thick black hair framed her face, the heavy bangs only accentuating her intense eyes. She had good bone structure, too – high, sharp cheekbones, and full lips set in a perpetual pout. Her presence dominated the space, filling it with a sense of danger but also a certain charisma.

"You're the assistant, right?" Her voice was husky, but

more refined than Abi had imagined, with a crisp British accent.

Abi nodded, unable to look away from those eyes. She'd just spotted that the irises were different colours – one brown, the other a startling blue. The whole look only added to Acid's otherworldly appearance. She could be a movie star, especially if the movie was about punk rock vampires.

Abi raised her chin, trying to project an air of confidence she didn't feel. "Yeah, I was the assistant," she replied. "Until… you know…"

Acid's lips curled into a knowing smile. "Until I killed your boss."

"Yep. That. Are you going to kill me too?"

Acid's grin widened. "Not right now."

"Not *ever*," Spook added firmly, stepping between them.

Acid shrugged and winked at Abi. "But you did witness me taking out your boss, right?"

"Yeah, but he was a piece of shit. I'm not going to lose any sleep over the guy." Her heart was still pounding, but it was calming down a little.

"Can you keep it to yourself?" Acid asked.

Abi scoffed. "Are you kidding me? I work in Hollywood, in the movie industry. Of course I can keep it to myself." She paused, searching Acid's eyes for any sign of doubt. "That's what we do here, keep secrets. For someone like me it's the most important part of the job. You think your line of work is dangerous, you have no fucking idea. Sleazy is putting it mildly."

Acid smirked, clearly enjoying this display of defiance. She took a step back, giving Abi a little more space. "Good," she said, turning to Lena who'd been listening to the exchange. "And you must be the new Spook?"

Lena swallowed. "Umm… If you mean, am I in charge of tech surveillance and security, then yes."

"Well, pleased to meet you," Acid told her. "I'm Acid Vanilla."

Lena giggled. "Yeah, I do know."

The women spread out and faced Nate as he strode over to them. His mood hadn't improved much from earlier, though his anger seemed to subside a little as he glanced between Acid and Spook.

"Did you clear the air, then?" he asked.

Acid gave Abi another wink. "All good here, Nitro."

"I asked you not to call me that," he growled. "I haven't used that name for years."

"Hmm. I wonder why not."

Abi looked away, hiding her amusement. She was warming to this woman faster than she'd expected.

"And…?" Nate continued, still addressing Acid. "You never answered my question. Are you here to stay?"

Acid glanced around, taking in the tense atmosphere and Spook's anxious expression. "I can't go back even if I wanted to," she replied. "Once they find Grimaldi's body, I won't have a strong enough story. They'll know it was me. Hell, they practically set me up for it anyway. So, yes, I'm here to stay."

"That's good," Nate said, running a hand through his hair. "But this is my operation, Acid. I'm glad you're here, but I need you to understand how things work."

Spook snorted. "Come on, Nate. We don't need to do this now."

"Yeah, Nate," Acid chimed in. "We're just catching up, old friends shooting the shit and all that jazz. Relax."

"Relax?" He shook his head, exasperated. "Jesus, how the hell did I let things get to this point?"

Lena looked up from her laptop. "Are you upset because you're the only guy here?" she asked.

"No. It's not that. I just don't appreciate people acting without discussing it first with the rest of the team. It's not planned or systematic. Without a strong strategy, it's dangerous." He turned to Acid, his eyes searching hers. "Is this what it's going to be like working with you and Spook?"

Acid smirked. "Mostly. But it can be very stressful, too."

"All right, enough." Nate took a deep breath as if trying to steady himself. He looked around, his gaze lingering on each member of the group before settling back on Acid. "You seriously want to take down Kancel Kulture?"

Acid's eyes flashed with something bordering on unhinged. "Abso-bloody-lutely."

Nate's jaw stiffened as he eyed Acid with an almost equal intensity. Abi sensed an energy between the two of them that was terrifying and like nothing else she'd ever witnessed. It made her wonder what else these people had seen, what they had done.

"Okay. Screw it," Nate said. "Why not? Do you have a plan?"

Acid stretched her arms, a confident smile spreading across her face. "The plan is the same one I had from the very start. I'm going to avenge The Dullahan. I'm going to kill all those motherfuckers. Now get your organisation in order and let's come up with a strong strategy because we haven't got long."

Nate frowned. "What do you mean?"

"Kancel Kulture have a big job happening in two days," she replied. "It's at a high-profile gala thrown by Titanium Media Group, a way for them to schmooze Japanese investors. Kancel Kulture have been tasked with taking out the three visitors, discrediting the studio in the process."

Abi's eyes widened. "Shit, I've heard about this gala. One of my contacts is part of the team putting it together. It's going to have a lot of security. It's a big event for them."

Acid nodded. "This is huge for Darius too. If he nails this, the client is offering a twenty-million-dollar-a-year retainer for Kancel Kulture to be their go-to team of fixers." She glanced between Nate and Spook. "With The Gorgon and Grimaldi dead, that leaves just the Blood Diamond Twins. That means Darius and Saga will have to get involved in the fieldwork. It's the perfect way to hit him and his crew all at once."

Nate cleared his throat, thinking. "This sounds dangerous, Acid. Not just because of Kancel Kulture, but also the onsite security. We don't have much time to develop a strategy."

Acid grinned. "Then we'd better get moving, hadn't we?"

"Are you sure about this?" Spook stepped closer. "You just took a bit of a beating back there."

Acid shot her a look. "I'm fine. A few bruised ribs aren't going to stop me. That's what painkillers and whisky are for."

Spook's expression didn't falter. "Be serious for once, please. It's going to be risky."

"Yeah, it will be," Acid replied, matching Spook's seriousness. "But you know me, Spooky. I like it risky."

Chapter Forty-Two

Over the next two days, Acid and Spook fell back into some kind of rhythm. It wasn't easy. At times, Acid wanted to tear away and leave, but she swallowed her frustrations and pushed through. The familiarity of their old partnership was returning, albeit slowly.

On Saturday morning they sparred on the patio, their grunts and the thud of fists against flesh resounding over the trickle of the pool filter. Acid's ribs still hurt her, but she strapped up her side and focused on protecting the area. There was no way she was going to complain and have Spook think she wanted leniency.

Yet, she couldn't help but be impressed by Spook's speed and durability. She'd taught her well, but Nate had built on those foundations over the past year. Spook's movements, once awkward and erratic, were now smooth and precise. Each punch, each kick, was delivered with not only force but finesse. She even had Acid worried a few times as they brawled, though she'd never admit it.

Between bouts and training sessions, they shared meals,

these quieter moments filled with a tension that neither of them seemed to want to address directly. They made conversation, but it was mainly focused on the mission rather than their relationship or what happened in Rome, each cautious of reopening old wounds. During a run later in the day, Acid caught glimpses of Spook's single-minded-ness, her eyes set firmly ahead, her lips pursed in concentration. Acid couldn't help but feel a grudging respect for the kid. And, even if she couldn't find the words to say so, it was good to have Spook back by her side. Their friendship wasn't fully mended, but the groundwork was there, being rebuilt through sweat and shared purpose. It was a good start.

Late the previous night, Acid and Nate had caught an Uber into South Central LA to meet a guy Nate's contact had set them up with. Given the quick turnaround and the low price, they suspected the California ID cards he'd agreed to supply wouldn't be top-notch, but they should at least pass a check against the guest list at the venue. As they'd entered South Central, Acid had stared out the window at the dusty, graffiti-covered streets strewn with trash. She'd avoided the area as much as possible while living in Los Angeles. Despite the area being much safer than it had been in the nineties, it still felt grimy and menacing, especially after sundown.

The smoggy LA air had been thick with the scent of garbage as they climbed out of the Uber and headed towards the rendezvous point. They moved quickly, sticking to the shadows as distant gunshots and police sirens echoed through the streets. They met the supplier in an old garage at the end of a dark alley, the flickering strip-light only adding to the disconcerting atmosphere. The man they'd come to meet, a wiry African American with an eye patch and a scar across his throat, opened the trunk of a large black Chevy SUV. Inside were boxes of fake IDs, passports, driver's licences, Social Security cards, and an arsenal of weapons: guns, knives, nightsticks, even a selection of grenades and an RPG.

Acid lifted out two Glock 19s, holding them up like a deprived child in a toy shop. It would be so much easier if they had weapons, but there was no way to get them into the gala undetected. However, that didn't mean there wouldn't be guns to be found once inside. Abi reckoned the studio's security team would be heavily armed – it would just be a matter of getting their hands on them.

Having already agreed on the price, Nate handed over the money, and after a brief inspection of the fake IDs they were on their way. They'd trudged back to Western Avenue, called a cab, and were back in Westlake within the hour. Job done.

Into the night and the next day, the team trained and planned relentlessly. The dining room table was transformed into a mini war room, with the five of them huddled around Lena's dual laptops as they debated tactics, points of entry and exit, and how to handle the security detail once inside.

It was reassuring to discover that Abi, despite her initial reticence, seemed eager to prove her worth. She worked tirelessly for them, her phone glued to her ear as she negotiated with her contacts in the industry, pulling strings to get Acid, Nate and Spook onto the guest list. Also with Abi's help, Lena was able to construct a 3D digital model of the venue, walking them through the layout, noting fire escapes, stairwells, and the points where the security guards were likely to be situated. Nate highlighted potential weaknesses, and with Acid's assistance they outlined contingency plans for various scenarios.

It was the second night, the evening before the mission, when Acid peeled away from the rest of the group and strolled out onto the patio. The warm night air greeted her, carrying with it the distinct scent of marijuana from a nearby house.

She closed her eyes, yearning for a cold beer or a glass of wine. But she'd purposefully abstained for the last twenty-four hours and she wasn't going to break her resolve. This was one of the most important and dangerous missions of recent years. She had to keep her game face on.

Sensing someone was watching her, she opened her eyes and turned to see Nate standing in the doorway.

"Mind if I join you?" he asked.

"Sure." She resumed her stance, staring out across LA as Nate walked over and stood beside her. The city lights, along with the distinct flutter of a police helicopter, were a good reminder of the world outside their dark bubble. They stood side by side in silence for a few moments, but it wasn't uncomfortable.

"Do you think we can do this?" Acid asked, her gaze fixed on the horizon.

"It's your plan," Nate replied.

"It's *our* plan," she corrected. "And this is still your organisation. Although I did think you'd have come up with a bloody name by now."

Nate chuckled. "It's not from want of trying. It's such a pain trying to find something suitable. Every time I come up with one, I talk myself out of it."

"Well, none of that tomorrow night," she said. "Stick to the plan. No second-guessing. You know how this works."

Nate nodded, a hint of a smile tugging at his lips. "And

if we succeed…" He trailed off. Acid raised one eyebrow; if he was waiting for her to finish his sentence, he'd be waiting forever. "What happens afterwards?" he added, finally.

She smiled. "Now, now. One thing at a time, sweetie." Her smile vanished. "We have to be smart about this. We'll be operating in a populated area with plenty of cameras. We can't afford to have our faces captured or put on the news. That would end our careers before we even start. For the last twenty years I've managed to stay off the authorities' radar. No photos of me exist in any police database. I intend to keep it that way."

"I know," Nate said. "We'll do this our way. The old-fashioned way."

"The Caesar way," Acid added, turning her back. She didn't care if Nate agreed or not.

Now there was an awkward silence. Acid folded her arms, contemplating heading back inside when Spook, Lena and Abi appeared, perhaps sensing the gravity of the moment.

"I have some news," Abi said. "I just heard from a reliable source that TMG – Titanium Media Group – is caught up with the mob."

Nate rubbed at his chin. "Shit. That could be a problem."

"Not really," Abi continued. "Apparently TMG have messed up recently and got themselves in trouble with a few high-ranking mobsters. My source thinks that's the reason they're desperate to impress the Japanese investors. They have a lot of debts to pay and need some ready money."

"That's perfect," Acid said. "We can make it look like a professional hit. Orchestrated chaos. We'll hit Kancel Kulture while they're targeting the Japanese. If we play it right, the authorities will think Darius and his crew were the mafia clean-up team, and security took them out."

"What about the Japanese investors?" Lena asked.

Acid glanced at Spook. "We'll try to neutralise Kancel Kulture before they complete their hit, but if we can't…" She paused. Spook nodded, understanding the grim reality. "This way we get the job done and remove ourselves from the picture. Plus, it discredits Kancel Kulture in the industry, leaving a big hole for a new organisation to take up the reins and start pulling in the big clients."

Nate smiled. It was the first genuine smile Acid had seen from him since she'd returned to the fray. "I like that," he said. "Okay. We can do this. Tomorrow night, we're on."

"Awesome," Abi exclaimed, a big grin spreading across her face. "But you'll need to go shopping at some point beforehand," she added, eyeing Acid up and down.

When Abi's gaze returned to hers, Acid was waiting with a glare to meet it. "Why?"

"Because it's a gala," Abi replied. "If you want to get through the door without making a scene, you're going to have to wear a dress."

"Really? I thought I'd go as I am." Acid scowled. "Whatever. "But I'm not wearing a bloody Disney princess gown."

"You are if that's what's needed," Spook said, stepping forward. "You've done it before and you can do it again. Security will be tight, but with Abi's intel we should have no problem getting in – as long as we look the part."

Acid shot a glance around the group, daring any of them to laugh. But the truth was, she'd felt more herself with these people over the past twenty-four hours than she had in the last year with Kancel Kulture. After being embroiled for so long with Darius, dealing with Spook's emotional intelligence and Nate's calm approach to a mission was a massive shock to the system. Yet she felt optimistic for the first time in as long as she could remember.

"All right, fine," she said. "Ball gown or not, tomorrow night we show Kancel Kulture who the real successors to Annihilation Pest Control are. Those bastards won't know what hit them."

Chapter Forty-Three

Darius Duke strode down the winding corridors of Kancel Kulture HQ's second level. His footsteps echoed in the late morning quiet, the sound of his soles slapping against the hard floor already irritating to him. But maybe he was just projecting. Maybe anything and everything would annoy him right now.

Today was the day, and Darius could already feel the weight of the pressure on his shoulders. If everything went according to plan, he would cement his place at the top of the industry. King of killers. Emperor of elite assassins. Screw the likes of Beowulf Caesar and The Dullahan — they were history, relics of the past.

The future belonged to Darius Duke.

Only, things weren't going according to plan. At all. He should be feeling ecstatic right now, ready for action. But that treacherous bitch had screwed him over, not only taking out one of his best operatives but defecting to her old crew. He ground his teeth together, barely able to contain his anger. He'd been up all night pacing his room, fighting the urge to pull his hair out or smash his fist through every pane of glass. He still wanted to. Pity anyone who got in his way today.

Saga walked a few steps behind him, staying quiet for once.

"I want her head," Darius hissed. "Literally, Saga. I want her head served to me on a goddamn plate."

"I understand, sir," Saga replied. "Leave it with me. I won't rest until she pays for her betrayal." He cleared his throat. "But might I suggest we refocus on the task at hand? You know my feelings towards Acid Vanilla. I want nothing more than to see her destroyed. But not today. Not until this is over. Once we get this job done, we'll decide what to do with her."

Darius stopped and sighed. How could his own sister do this to him? How dare she? After everything he'd done for her. He'd wanted her by his side through this, to show her that he was the real deal, better than Caesar, better than anyone. He loved her, damn it. Why couldn't she just toe the line and do what he'd asked of her? Why was she so bloody difficult?

Yet Saga was right. Today was make or break and failure was not an option. He glanced at his right-hand man, whose calm demeanour did little to ease his anxiety. "Fine. I'll put a pin in my incandescent rage, shall I?"

Saga held his gaze without blinking. "If you can, sir. It would help."

"Is everything ready?" Darius asked, as they set off walking again.

"Almost. You just need to sign this off."

They reached the gym, and Saga opened the door to reveal a group of six young people – three women and three men – each strikingly beautiful and dressed to impress for the gala. Their nervousness was evident as Darius and Saga approached, but they stood straight, trying to maintain their composure. None of them looked much older than twenty.

Saga walked in front of them, inspecting each one. "These are our assets," he said. "They're being paid handsomely for their involvement and will handle the preliminary work for us. We'll eliminate the investors' chaperones and let them relax with these fine specimens. They know what to do – they'll keep the Japanese distracted, ply them with drink and drugs, as well as taking as many compromising photos as they can, creating a scene of debauchery and excess. Then we'll move in for the kill and pin the blame on Titanium Media Group."

Darius walked down the line, inspecting each of the young sex workers with a critical eye as if they were livestock or pieces of meat. To him, in a way they were. He pulled at their arms, and ran his hands down the women's legs, checking for stubble. He examined their teeth and prodded their muscles, gauging their physical condition. The young sex workers' eyes were wide with fear and uncertainty, but they didn't flinch.

"Excellent choices," Darius said, scanning the group before him. Each one was meticulously groomed, their outfits chosen to enhance their allure. The girls wore sleek dresses that clung to their bodies, highlighting every curve. One had platinum blonde hair, her eyes a piercing blue. Another had fiery red hair and a deep green dress. The third was an exotic beauty with dark eyes and a golden complexion.

"Something for everyone," he mused to himself. "Well done, Saga."

The boys were equally striking, each dressed in a sharp tuxedo that showed off their physiques. One was tall and lean, with dark hair slicked back. He looked a little like himself, Darius thought, though he considered himself much more rugged and attractive. The other two were fine-featured young men with golden hair and confident smiles. The sort of all-American golden boys he assumed bi-curious Japanese investors might really go for.

"Good," Darius muttered as he completed his inspection. He looked at Saga, who nodded approvingly.

"They've all been briefed and are eager to make the evening a roaring success," Saga said, walking over to Darius. He lowered his voice, turning his back on the others. "I've been up early creating our murder weapons," he whispered, his eyes sparkling. "Ten vials of a quadruple-strength mix of cocaine, speed and heroin. Enough to take out half the guest list."

Darius grinned. What these pretty young things didn't know was that after they'd spiked the Japanese with the lethal concoction, they'd be wiped out with the same mixture. It was a necessary part of the plan, but as he observed these young people he felt a twinge of something unpleasant – guilt, maybe. He quickly squashed it. He rarely got up close and personal with the grim reality of his work, and he wasn't sure he liked it. But screw it. These people were nobodies and their deaths a means to an end. He would shed no tears for them or anyone on his path to the top, including his sister. In this game there was no room for weakness.

"Someone will come and deal with you soon," Saga told the sex workers. The young men and women nodded, making appreciative noises as Darius and Saga left the gym.

As they strode down the corridor, Darius' mind was already shifting to the next phase.

"Will we have to take out security?" he asked, as they reached the elevator.

Saga pressed the call button. "Most likely. But the event will be loud, and suppressors will mask most gunshot sounds. I've also secured us a route in. It'll be impossible to bring weapons through the front, but one of my freelancers has secured a job as part of the catering crew. He'll let us in around the back, through the kitchen."

Darius nodded, impressed. The elevator arrived with a soft ding and they stepped inside. They rode up in silence, each man lost in his thoughts. The doors opened to the top floor and they walked down the plush carpeted corridor to Darius' office.

Frederik and Freek Kriel were already inside as Darius entered, the two of them wandering around and admiring his artwork. Darius took a moment to compose himself, then opened his arms wide and moved into the centre of the room.

"Gentlemen, so good to see you in the flesh. Anything catch your eye?" he asked, gesturing at the artwork.

The Blood Diamond Twins turned to him, their expressions blank. "No," they said in unison, their broad South African drawl turning the word into a sneer. "It's all shite."

Darius faltered and glanced at Saga, whose expression was grim. He was about to speak when Darius barked out a loud laugh, breaking the tension.

"You're right! You're bloody right. It is all terrible," he said, walking over and shaking hands with the twins. Up close, away from the confines of a video call screen, Frederik and Freek were just as gnarly and terrifying as he remembered. Burly and weathered, their tanned leathery skin looked like strips of beef jerky, contrasting sharply with their thick silver wavy hair. They wore matching purple and green silk shirts with huge pouncing tigers embroidered on the back, paired with black army fatigues. As they exchanged greetings, Darius admired their metal teeth, trying to remember which brother was which. He was fairly certain Freek's teeth were gold and Frederik's were white gold, but he chose not to refer to them by name in case he got it wrong.

As they made small talk, Darius noticed Saga wandering over to the corner, swiping at the slim tablet he always had somewhere about his person. The twins' presence was always unsettling, and Darius felt a bit nervous around them alone.

He cleared his throat. "Have you been briefed?"

"Yes," the one who was probably Frederik said. "Saga sent through all the details."

"We've been reading up on the plane over," his brother added, with a hint of a smile. "It's all good. Can't wait for it. The full team."

"Well… sort of, I suppose," Darius replied, feeling a familiar twinge of unease. Three operatives dead and one defected. It didn't look good. "We need this operation to be flawless," he added.

Frederik nodded. "No worries. We know the drill."

Freek's smile widened, revealing both rows of metal teeth. "Just point us in the right direction."

Darius nodded, feeling a little more confident as Saga moved over to stand in front of him, his back to the twins. He leaned forward, lowering his voice. "Can I have a word?"

Darius excused himself and followed Saga to the side of the room, leaving the twins to continue their inspection of his office.

"I've tapped into Acid's friends' communications using a

custom exploit I developed," Saga whispered, the ghost of a smile twisting at his thin lips. "I piggybacked on the signal from one of her team's devices and turned one of their phones into a relay."

"Meaning?"

"That we can track their whereabouts without them knowing." He paused, letting his words sink in. "My intel tells me that this morning they made a curious trip to La Belle on Melrose Avenue."

Darius stared at Saga, waiting for more. Was he supposed to know what that meant?

"A formalwear rental store, sir," Saga clarified. "Dresses and tuxedos and the like."

Darius' eyes widened. But Saga went on before he could speak. "Not to worry though. I have an idea how we can ace this assignment and take out Acid and her little chums in one fell swoop."

Darius felt a surge of excitement. This was more like it. "Come on then, tell me," he said, grinning. "I'm all ears."

Chapter Forty-Four

Acid Vanilla pressed her forehead against the cool glass of the SUV's rear passenger window, taking a moment to compose herself before her work began. It was the night of the gala, and they were just two minutes away from the MacArthur Gallery where the event was taking place.

She sat back and pulled in a deep breath. The strain was getting to everyone, the silence in the car thick with anticipation. They were all lost in their own thoughts, mentally preparing for the task ahead.

Abi was at the wheel, expertly navigating through West-lake's evening traffic. Despite the gallery being only a short drive away, they needed the vehicle for a quick getaway. Lena had rented the large Chevrolet this morning using her fake ID and cash provided by Nate. Everything was arranged to ensure there were no loose ends if things went south.

Lena was up front with Abi, while Spook and Nate shared the cramped back seat with Acid. They were like soldiers in the trenches ready for battle, or football players psyching themselves up before the season's biggest game. It was tense but with an underlying sense of confidence.

"I know we've covered this, but one more time for the cheap seats," Lena piped up, twisting around to address the group. "The doors of the gala open at 8 p.m., which is in ten minutes. The Japanese guests will already be upstairs, having come here straight from the airport at seven. They'll have been taken to a VIP room to be schmoozed before dinner starts at 9 p.m." She paused to let the information sink in. "We believe Kancel Kulture will hit them sometime before dinner, probably around 8.30 p.m. That gives us a thirty-minute window to get inside, reach the VIP room, and set our ambush before KK arrives."

"Understood," Acid replied, her mind already mapping out the steps. She looked around at her team, each of them focused and prepared. "Easy, right? Get in, set up, stay ready."

But it wasn't as simple as that and she knew it. First, they had security to deal with. And they needed guns – as many as they could get their hands on.

"What can go wrong?" she added.

Nate leaned over Spook, giving Acid a pointed look. "With Abi outside in the car and Lena with her on comms, we should be fine. Can everyone check their equipment, please?" He said this last part into his cufflink, his voice reverberating in Acid's earpiece.

She adjusted it, ensuring it was secure. "All good."

"By the way, we do have some firepower already," Abi called back. "I just remembered I have my mom's old piece. She always carried it in her purse, and I took it after the funeral."

"Show me," Acid said.

Keeping one hand on the wheel and her eyes on the

road, Abi fumbled in the concealed shelving in the driver's door before handing over an old snub-nosed revolver. Acid inspected it. It was a tiny, pathetic little weapon – bad range, bad rate of fire, just bad in every way. She handed it back. "Okay, but be careful with it."

Acid made eye contact with Spook who was watching her closely. She gave her a nod and a small smile. It was still slightly awkward between them, but she was glad Spook was here. She was a good kid – no, a good operative – and Acid trusted her. Spook would have her back, just like always.

Abi pulled up alongside MacArthur Park, a minute's walk from the gala venue. The three of them climbed out of the car and gathered on the sidewalk. Nate adjusted his bow tie and smoothed down his tuxedo, looking every bit like a Hollywood star.

"Anyone ever tell you that you'd make a good James Bond?" Acid whispered, leaning in close.

Nate scoffed. "Anyone ever tell you that you'd make a good Bond girl?"

Acid narrowed her eyes at him. He was trying to be flirtatious too, she reasoned, lightening a very heavy atmosphere. But she was no Bond girl. Bond villain, perhaps.

Yet, as she caught sight of herself in a shop window, she sort of knew what he meant. She'd opted for a slinky red number that hugged her figure but was stretchy enough to allow for movement. Spook had gone for the same dress in emerald green and looked about as awkward in hers as Acid felt. It had been a long time since she'd worn an outfit like this, and only then as a disguise. She'd never been the heels and dress type, and as they set off towards the gallery she wobbled slightly.

Spook noticed and smirked. "Not your usual combat boots, huh?"

"Not exactly," Acid replied, grabbing Nate's arm to steady herself. "These bloody things will be the first things to go once we're inside." She dropped the bag she was carrying off her shoulder and showed Spook the contents.

"You brought your boots?"

Acid frowned. "Absolutely, and some for you. We can't run in these strappy things. And something tells me we might need to run at some point this evening."

"I think the strappy things suit you," Spook said.

Acid gave her a withering look but said no more.

They walked the rest of the way in silence, arriving at the entrance of the MacArthur Gallery just before eight. A stern-faced doorman, dressed in a crisp black uniform with gold trim, let them in, his watery grey eyes barely registering their presence. Inside, the entrance hall was grand, its columns adorned with intricate mouldings and a high arched ceiling displaying a large mural that looked Tudor in style but was probably done in the last hundred years. Immense chandeliers hung down over a wide, carpeted staircase that led up to the next level.

They hurried up the stairs as fast as their footwear allowed, emerging into another vestibule with a marble floor and more columns. Doors lined the vast space on either side.

"Over there," Spook said, pointing to an easel displaying a sign that read *TMG Gala*.

"That's us," Nate said. "From now on, everyone stay in character and keep in contact via the comms. Can everyone hear each other?"

"All good," Acid confirmed, touching her earpiece.

"Lena?"

"Got you," her voice crackled in their ears. "I've got the gallery's CCTV feed up. I see the three of you in the main entrance hall. The gala room is to the right. I'll keep tracking you as you move through the building."

"Make sure you do," Spook said. "We need early warning of any problems."

"On it."

They moved towards the grand double doors leading to the gala entrance. Acid took the lead, her heels clicking on the marble floor as she approached a tall skinny man on the door flanked by two security guards. The man barely glanced at her, so she stepped in front of him, flashing her best smile.

"Good evening," she said, in a classy Californian accent. "We're here for the gala. We're so excited to see everyone again, but I'm afraid we forgot our invites like silly gooses."

The man gave her a resigned smile. "Not a problem," he said stiffly. "What are the names?"

"Alana Morgan," Acid replied smoothly, her confidence unwavering. "And this is my kid sister, Zeena Morgan, and her handsome fiancé, Clive Andrews." She turned, giving them the same winning smile. Spook was trying hard not to laugh at Acid's improvisation. Nate, however, looked less amused.

She turned back as the doorman scanned through papers on his clipboard. This was the moment of truth. If Abi's contact hadn't got them on the list, it would require a very fast pivot.

"Ah yes, here we are," the man said after a few tense moments. "Please go through and have a wonderful evening."

"Oh, we will," Acid said, leading the others through the doors being opened for them by the security guards.

"Could have saved myself a thousand dollars," Nate mumbled, in reference to the fake IDs they'd risked life and limb for.

Acid smirked. *That's life for ya, sweetie.*

The main gala hall was as vast and luxurious as she'd imagined. Huge round tables were set for dinner, with crystal glasses and silverware gleaming under elaborate chandeliers. A bar area along one wall was lit by strips of silver and purple lights, and a stage at the far end of the room was being set up with a drum kit and guitar amps. It was only a few minutes past eight, but plenty of guests had already arrived. The room buzzed with the hum of conversations, laughter, and the clinking of glasses. But that was helpful. Noise was good. Crowds were good. The scent of expensive perfume mingled with the rich aroma of food as the three of them moved across the room.

Acid brushed her hair forward to hide her earpiece, satisfied that the connected mic was concealed in her bra. "Alright, we need to get upstairs and we need weapons," she whispered into it.

Lena's voice came through clearly. "There are two armed guards at the end of the corridor to the right of the main room. It leads to a flight of stairs up to the VIP room. They're stationed at the far end, so they'll spot you long before you reach them."

"Got it," Acid replied. She turned to Nate. "You hang back. We'll handle this." Then, grabbing Spook by the arm, she added, "Come on."

They moved towards the door leading out from the main space.

"Lena, have the Japanese arrived?" Spook asked.

"Yep," Lena confirmed. "I've got eyes on the room. I'm working on looping the feed so it won't capture you while you're doing your thing. I need a few more minutes."

"Stay on it," Spook replied.

Acid pushed through the door, immediately slipping into her Alana Morgan persona. "Oh my God," she cried in a perfect Cali drawl, "please, tell me the restroom is this way?"

Spook caught up with her. "I think it is, Sis. For sure," she added, joining in.

They hurried down the corridor towards the two large security guards at the far end. Both men were in their late forties, tanned, with neat military haircuts and clean-shaven jaws. One was slightly taller, the other broader, but they looked almost identical otherwise. Dressed in dark suits with visible earpieces coiling down their necks, each had the unmistakable bulge of a weapon under their jackets.

"Can't go this way," one of them said as they approached, his voice flat and uncompromising.

"Ah, come on, please, doll. I need to take a leak. I'm desperate," Acid pleaded, sticking her chest out slightly. "Take pity on me, won't you? It's hard enough getting in and out of this tight dress."

"There are no restrooms back here," the other guard said sternly.

"Be careful. I've got you on video here," Lena said. "Give me a second."

Acid looked at Spook, then back at the men. "We do really need to pee," Spook said. "Where is the nearest restroom?"

"Back the way you came. Near the entrance to the main hall," the guard replied, irritation creeping into his voice.

"Oh pooey," Acid huffed. "That's so far away. Can't we just sneak past, fellas? I know there's another restroom back here. I'm certain of it. Please?" She fluttered her eyes at them, her voice sugary sweet.

"No, sorry."

In her ear, Lena's voice returned. "Okay, I've scrambled the signal of the camera pointing at you. You've got about three minutes before the control hub gets the feed working again. Make it count."

Acid glanced at Spook, then sighed dramatically. "Well, I'd better take off these damn heels if I'm going to have to trudge all the way back."

"Yeah, me too," Spook added. They both bent down, Acid holding onto one of the men's arms to steady herself. She giggled, playing her part as a ditsy valley-queen to perfection. As she removed the second shoe she sprang into action, driving the heel of the stiletto into the man's neck. Surprised, he staggered back, eyes wide as he spluttered for air. Acid followed up with a knee to his groin, and as he doubled over she snaked her arm around his neck, securing the hold by grabbing her wrist.

She squeezed hard, putting as much pressure on his carotid artery as she could muster, feeling him weaken. Meanwhile, Spook handled the other guard, using the same sleeper hold Acid had taught her. The guy had a bloody welt in the middle of his forehead, no doubt where Spook had struck him with her heel.

Acid gave her a supportive nod as they rode the unconscious guards to the ground. "Good work."

"Thanks," Spook replied, brushing herself down as Nate hurried down the corridor to join them.

"We've got to move fast," Nate said, grabbing one of the guards under the arms.

They dragged the two men through the double doors and out of the camera's view into an empty stairwell. Acid and Spook quickly pulled on their boots as Nate produced a roll of electrical tape from his jacket pocket. He swiftly bound and gagged the guards while Acid stripped them of their weapons. Both men were carrying Colt M1911s, standard-issue sidearms for the United States Armed Forces. Acid handed a gun each to Nate and Spook before saluting the unconscious guards.

"Too long out of the game, fellas," she whispered, as Nate dragged them into a utility closet under the stairs and shut the door.

They moved to the foot of the stairwell, glancing up at the flights of stairs above them. "Lena, we're clear," Spook said. "What's next?"

"You need to go up two flights and then navigate a series of zigzagging corridors to the VIP room," she replied. "I'm still working on the security feed inside that room, but I'm getting there."

"How many guards between us and the Japanese?" Nate asked.

"Four. Two sets. One set guarding the doors immediately at the top of the stairwell and another set at the end of a long corridor."

Acid cracked her neck, feeling the adrenaline surge. "How close to the stairwell are the first two?" she asked.

"You'll come out on a landing to one side of the doorway. They're facing forwards, so they'll be side-on to you as you appear."

Acid pictured the scene in her mind. She had an idea.

Four guards against three of them.

She liked those odds.

Chapter Forty-Five

Pressing herself against the wall, Acid crept up to the second-floor landing, concealing herself behind a narrow buttress on one side of the stairwell to scope out the situation. The two guards were exactly where Lena had described. One was about Acid's height, stocky but not overly muscular, his eyes alert and wary. The other was taller, but his broad shoulders were slouched and he appeared rather docile as if he'd been standing there for hours.

Acid took a moment to slow her breathing. The bats were in flight and they wanted blood. A tapping on her lower back made her spin around. Spook stood a couple of steps down, offering her one of the Colts.

Acid shook her head. Not yet. She didn't want to make any noise if she could help it. Steeling herself, she stepped onto the landing, moving with deliberate caution. She crept forward, hoping for the element of surprise. But as she neared the first guard, the floorboards betrayed her with a loud creak. She froze as the guards snapped their heads to glare at her.

"Who the hell are you?" the shorter guard barked. "How did you get up here?"

Acid shrugged, smiling through gritted teeth. "I'm *sooo* sorry, I must have taken a wrong turn somewhere. Is this not the VIP room?"

The guards stiffened. "We've got strict orders not to let anyone up here until after the meal."

Acid lowered her head, regarding them through her eyelashes. "Couldn't you make an exception? I just want to check it out for a minute or two?"

But the guards weren't buying it. They advanced, their expressions hardening. The nearest guard started to speak into the mic on his lapel.

"Control…?"

Nope. Can't have that.

She lunged forward, striking him in the throat before he could say another word. She followed up with a swift palm strike to his nose, smashing the cartilage and disorienting him. He cried out, staggering into the wall as his partner reached for his weapon.

"Acid!" Spook yelled. "Gun!"

But Acid had already seen it. She moved quickly, dragging the first guard in front of her, using him as a human shield as his buddy fired two shots into his chest. Reaching around, she pulled the guard's gun from his holster and fired a single shot into the second guard's head, killing him instantly. His body dropped to the floor like a puppet with its strings cut.

The landing fell silent after the gunfire. Acid looked around to see Spook and Nate hurrying towards her.

"For Christ's sake," Nate hissed. "We said no shooting people."

"What was I supposed to do?" Acid snapped. "It was either that or let him call for backup."

Acid wiped her hands on her dress, the fabric already stained with blood. This was why she always wore black.

"Lena," Spook said, speaking pointedly into the neckline of her dress as she peered down the corridor. "We need an update. Anything from the control room about shots fired?"

A heavy silence followed. Acid exchanged worried glances with Nate and Spook, her ears straining for any sign of approaching footsteps. The oppressive silence of the corridor was unsettling, but she wondered if that was because it had been soundproofed. These big venues usually were, especially those hosting multiple events simultaneously. That fact alone could be their saving grace.

Finally Lena's voice came through. "We're good. No one seems to have heard anything," she said. "The closest security guards are outside the VIP room, still in position, and they don't look rattled."

"What about the Japanese?" Nate asked.

"They're oblivious, dancing around with some young men and women. They've got music on, they won't hear anything."

"Good. But no sign of Kancel Kulture?" Spook asked.

"Not yet."

Acid grimaced, her instincts screaming that something was off. If the meal was scheduled for nine, she imagined the guests of honour would be escorted downstairs in about twenty minutes. On the one hand, they needed to get in that room before Darius and his crew, so the fact they weren't around was good. But on the other hand – where the hell were they?

"Are you sure there's no sign of Kancel Kulture anywhere in the building?" Acid asked.

"I'm certain. I've got facial recognition running and I'm checking each feed every fifteen seconds. They're not here."

Acid looked at Nate. "Maybe we got it wrong?" he said.

She chewed her bottom lip. No. Something wasn't right.

"The final set of guards between you and the VIP room are at the end of the next corridor," Lena added. "Like before, it's going to be impossible for you to get close to them without being seen."

Nate glanced at Acid. "I have an idea." He removed his bowtie and grabbed the black coiled earpiece and tie from one of the dead guards. He quickly put them on, adjusting his appearance. "What do you think? Close enough?"

Acid looked him up and down. "Works for me. What's your plan?"

"I'll say I'm relieving one of them. An issue downstairs he needs to deal with. Can you take care of him when he comes through here, if I take out the other one?"

"Wait, I've got a better idea," Spook interjected. "Say you're from the control room and noticed his comms aren't working. Tell him he needs to go down and get them replaced. That way, he won't call it in or alert anyone."

"Good thinking, Spooks," Acid said.

Nate rolled his shoulders back. "Okay, good luck every-one." With that, he disappeared through the doors into the windowless corridor beyond.

"How are things your end, Lena?" Acid asked, as she and Spook took an arm each and dragged the dead guards forward onto the landing.

"All good," Lena replied. "I'm still trying to loop the feed in the VIP room, but I'm having trouble."

"What's the issue?" Spook asked, as they finished positioning the guards.

"I'm trying to grab a section of the live feed, but it's not behaving properly. It won't let me record," Lena explained, frustration in her voice. "But don't worry, I've got a few other ideas. I'll be ready when you are and… Shit. You've got company in about five seconds."

Acid and Spook pressed their backs against the wall as the doors opened. A guard in a dark suit stepped through, stopping dead when he saw his fallen colleagues. His hand darted to his weapon, but Spook was already on the move. She rushed at him, smashing the butt of her gun into his temple. He spun almost a full three-sixty, coming to a stop facing Acid, who delivered a brutal elbow strike to the side of his head, rattling his brain enough that he went down cold.

Without electrical tape, they improvised with the guard's belt, hogtying him and stuffing his balled-up socks into his mouth. The makeshift gag was secured with the belt from one of his dead buddies before the two of them hurried down the corridor after Nate.

They found him wrapping tape around the mouth of the remaining guard, who was unconscious with blood seeping from a gash on his forehead. Nate had a cut on his lip but otherwise looked fine.

"How's your guy?" he said, ripping off a length of tape.

"Sleeping like a baby," Acid replied.

Nate nodded, a hint of relief in his eyes. "I mentioned to him we had reason to believe a group called Kancel Kulture had infiltrated the building. Hopefully he'll relay that to the cops when he wakes up."

"If he even remembers," Acid said, shaking her arm. "I think I bruised my bone taking him out. He's going to be groggy and forgetful for a while."

"Okay, Lena, we're outside the room," Spook said, glancing around for cameras. "Any sign of Kancel Kulture yet?"

"No, nothing," came the reply. "I don't get it."

They exchanged uneasy glances. Acid had a sudden sinking feeling. "This isn't right," she said.

Nate's expression was serious, bordering on concerned. "What about the Japanese, Lena? Can we enter the room?"

"Hold on for another second. They're still dancing, still having fun. But... I can't seem to... I don't get this..." Lena's voice trailed off, then she gasped. "Shit. That explains it."

"What?" Acid demanded.

"Why I can't grab a part of the feed to loop. It's not live. The feed I'm seeing is already a loop."

"What?" Spook echoed, her eyes wide.

Acid didn't hesitate. She grabbed the gun from the unconscious guard's holster and, with a nod to the others, pushed open the door to the VIP room.

Shit.

Loud party music was still blaring from the speaker system but there was no longer any fun happening. The three Japanese investors lay lifeless on separate couches. Around them were three men and three women, all young, all dead, their skin pallid, vomit crusted over chins and clothes. As Spook and Nate hurried in after her, Acid stepped forward, her eyes darting from one body to the next, trying to make sense of the carnage. Then the realisation hit her like a punch to the gut.

This was a set-up.

Chapter Forty-Six

The screech from the bats was deafening, a gnawing pressure inside her skull that was almost unbearable. Time ground to a halt as Acid scanned the room, and then suddenly everything snapped back into real-time and she gasped for air.

"Get out!" she yelled. "It's a—"

But it was too late. She spun around to see Frederik and Freek Kriel standing on either side of her friends, guns pointed at Spook's and Nate's heads. The twins' eyes gleamed with a cruel satisfaction, their smirks widening as they tightened their grip on their weapons.

"Not as clever as you think you are, are ya, missy?" Freek snarled.

She ignored him, the bats still screaming in her head as she glanced around, searching for an answer that wasn't there. Her finger tightened on the gun at her side, but the situation was clear. One wrong move and her friends would be dead.

"What do you want?" she asked.

Laughter echoed through the room as Darius stepped out from behind a green velvet curtain lining the walls. Acid turned to look at him, but her attention quickly shifted to Saga, who emerged from the same curtain on the opposite side of the room. Both were holding guns, aimed directly at her.

She looked from one to the other, her pulse pounding in her ears as she fought to maintain her composure.

"Hey, Sis!" Darius boomed. "How are things?" His eyes were cold and predatory as he surveyed the scene. She thought she'd seen every brutal facet of him, but it looked like he'd found another gear.

"I suppose I've been better," she replied, raising her head.

"Hmm. I suppose you're right." He jutted his chin at the .45 still gripped tightly by her side. "I'd suggest you drop that if you want to keep your skull in one piece."

Acid glanced around, the harsh reality sinking in. Outgunned and outmanoeuvred, she had no choice. Releasing her grip, she tossed her only chance of a fair fight onto the nearest couch.

"Take their weapons," Saga instructed the twins, who quickly relieved Nate and Spook of their guns before herding them and Acid into the centre of the room.

"Well, well, well," Darius said, his voice dripping with smug satisfaction as he circled them. "Fancy seeing you guys here."

"Yes, fancy that," Acid muttered.

Darius shook his head, a mocking smile playing on his lips. "I'm glad, actually. This wasn't exactly how the client wanted it, but as you can see, we've already taken out our marks. We can spin it so the studio gets discredited in the investment world, just like the client wants. And now we get to frame you for it too."

He pulled a suppressor from his pocket and began screwing it onto his gun, slowly and deliberately. Given everything that had already transpired, there was no real reason to use one but Darius was all about the performance. He circled the group, making eye contact with each of them in turn. As he got to Acid, he winked. It made her sick.

"And killing us? How does that fit your narrative?" Nate asked.

"TMG has bad debts with the mob here in LA," Saga replied. "We'll make it look like a professional hit that turned into a bloodbath once security got involved. We might even get some of the studio executives sent away. But, regardless, the client gets what they want. Titanium Media Group will be ruined and no longer a threat."

Acid felt a cold fury rise within her, but she forced herself to remain calm. "So four of you, all armed, and us in the middle of the room without a piece between us," she said, knowing Lena was still listening in. "What do you expect us to do now?" She needed to buy time, needed to keep them talking.

Darius laughed. "I don't expect you to do anything," he said. "I'm going to shoot you. Like I should have done two years ago." Acid tensed as he finished screwing in the suppressor nozzle.

"Don't worry, guys," Lena whispered in their earpieces. "I've got this. Keep it together."

"You first, I think," Darius said, aiming the gun at Nate, his finger poised on the trigger.

Spook yelped. Acid's jaw muscles tightened. Nate seemed to hold his breath.

But then a crash shattered the tension. Four security

guards burst in, guns drawn. Acid grabbed Spook, pulling her over the back of one of the couches as the room erupted into chaos. Gunfire filled the air, sharp and relentless, bullets peppering the room as frantic yells rang out.

Peering around the side of the couch, she saw the Blood Diamond Twins going berserk, firing indiscriminately at the guards, their faces twisted with fury and excitement. One guard dropped with a bullet to the head. A second took one shot to the chest and another to the neck. Finally the twins dived for cover as the remaining two guards retreated out the door, trading shots as they went. Across the room, Darius and Saga had taken up positions behind the far couch.

Gunshots continued to echo through the room, the noise drilling into Acid's skull. She was unarmed and nowhere near a weapon. This was bad. Really bad. She rolled back behind the couch as Spook scrambled over beside her.

"What do we do now?" Spook shouted over the noise.

Panic surged through Acid as she searched for a way out. They were down but not out. Risking another look at the situation, she saw Nate crouched behind an overturned table. He'd managed to reach one of the fallen guard's weapons and was taking shots at the twins.

"Acid? What do we do?" Spook asked again, desperation in her voice.

Acid looked at her. The room was a war zone and right now she had no answer. But she knew they needed to do something, and fast.

Otherwise they were all dead.

Chapter Forty-Seven

The VIP room became a battlefield as bullets tore through the air, ricocheting off walls and shattering glass. Staying low, Acid scrambled to the other side of the couch, desperately seeking a way to turn this around as the shootout intensified. There were three couches in the centre of the room, forming a U-shape around a large square coffee table. She and Spook were behind the one directly opposite the door, and she spotted Nate taking cover behind the couch to her left. She assumed Darius and Saga were concealed behind the couch to her right, though she hadn't seen them since the shooting began. The two remaining security guards had backed out of the room and were concealed in the doorway, exchanging fire with the Blood Diamond Twins, who were using the velvet curtain on the far right side of the room for cover.

As Acid watched, Frederik Kriel stepped forward to fire at the security guards but took a fatal hit to the face instead, his head snapping back in a cloud of red mist.

"*Geen! Freddie!*" his brother screamed in Afrikaans. "*Basters!*"

Seizing his brother's weapon he charged at the guards, firing both pistols wildly. A flurry of punishing rounds sent the guards stumbling through the door, collapsing in a heap on the floor. Still screaming, tears streaming down his face, Freek emptied one of the magazines into the guard who had killed his brother, riddling the man's chest and face with bullets.

Acid clutched Spook's arm as Nate emerged from behind the couch, weapon ready. Now it was just him and Freek, both armed and dangerous. Freek spotted him and spun around. Nate's shot hit him in the stomach, but the man didn't even flinch. The lone twin fired back, hitting Nate in the shoulder and forcing him to drop behind cover. Seizing the opportunity, Freek dived behind the opposite couch.

"Nate?" Acid called. "How is it?"

"Not too bad," he replied, though his voice was strained.

Acid quickly assessed the situation, her eyes darting to her gun on the nearby couch. She hesitated, considering the risk, but then Freek's arm appeared over the top of the couch, firing indiscriminately across the room.

"I'll fucking kill you!" he screamed. "You're dead!"

Shit.

This was bad. She had to do something.

As Freek ducked back down, Acid sprang to her feet, dashing for her gun. She grabbed it and fired a few rounds into the couch as she ran back for cover. Spook was there, yanking her down to safety. Acid crouched beside her, readying herself to take out Freek when Spook cried out, "Acid, look!"

She spun around to see Saga and Darius slipping behind the curtain, making their escape. She fired at them, but they'd already gone.

"Go after them," Nate shouted. "I'll handle this prick."

Acid didn't need telling twice. With a quick nod to Spook, they crawled away from the couch, keeping their heads low and moving towards the edge of the room. Reaching the curtain, they jumped to their feet and headed for the fire exit left open by Darius and Saga. Gunshots rumbled behind them as they hurried along a narrow concrete corridor and down a dark stairwell. Acid's dress snagged on the rough walls, but she kept moving, adrenaline pushing her forward.

Peering over the railing, she saw Darius and Saga on the landing below, briefly illuminated by an emergency light above a doorway. Darius glanced up and fired a shot that pinged off the concrete behind her, while Saga yanked the door open and they disappeared out of sight.

"They're on the move," Acid yelled back at Spook. "This way."

They raced down the steps to the lower landing and burst through a door into a vast, low-lit conference room. Rows of identical maroon and gold chairs filled the space, with a projector screen set up at the far end. Darius and Saga were already halfway across the room. Acid fired a shot, missing Darius by a whisper and causing him to spin around and return fire. His shots were wild and erratic, a clear sign of his inexperience. A round whizzed past Acid's ear, another thudded into the wall widely off target.

Grabbing Spook's arm, she pulled her behind a row of chairs as more bullets zipped overhead. Acid peeked around the side of a chair and fired a shot, not aiming to hit but to provoke. Darius and Saga were too far away for a clean shot, but Darius seemed to be the only one armed and she doubted he'd had the foresight to bring a spare magazine. Her plan was clear: draw his fire, drain his ammo, then move in for the kill shot.

But she wasn't there yet.

"They're getting away," Spook yelled.

"Yes, I can see that!"

Darius and Saga had reached the other side of the conference room, where a set of doors opened onto an illuminated corridor.

"Come on. Let's move."

She jumped to her feet and they sprinted across the room, crashing through the doors into the corridor. Darius was waiting for them and fired off another couple of shots that struck the wall to Acid's left. She shoved Spook behind her and returned fire, hitting Darius in the upper arm. He cried out and fired back, screaming in rage before Saga grabbed him and pulled him through another set of doors at the far end.

"Good shot," Spook said, as they continued their pursuit.

"That was just a warning, sweetie."

Darius was using a Glock 17, standard issue for Kancel Kulture since Saga secured a shipment from his Russian Army contact at the start of the year, all with the typical seventeen rounds and no extensions. By Acid's count, Darius had fired fourteen shots since they left the VIP room, which would leave him with only three bullets at the very most.

Almost done.

They chased them into a busy kitchen, the sudden change in environment jarring to the senses. The clatter of pots and pans, the hiss of steam and shouts of startled kitchen staff filled the air. Acid led the way, moving laterally through the narrow space, glancing around as she went. Clouds of steam from boiling pots added to the confusion.

Where the hell had they gone?

The kitchen was a flurry of activity, with chefs and serving staff scrambling to find safety as they realised what was going on. Acid weaved through the chaos, the bats' screams spurring her on.

"There!" Spook cried, grabbing Acid's arm. "By the fridges."

She looked over in time to see Darius pushing through a swing door at the back of the kitchen. They bolted after him and emerged into the rear courtyard of the gallery, the cool night air a welcome relief from the kitchen's heat. Darius had already put some distance between them, but he stopped and turned back.

"Down!" Acid yelled, dragging Spook behind a row of industrial garbage units as Darius opened fire.

One. Two. Three.

She peeked around the side of the unit just as he fired his last shot, the slide on his gun locking back with a metallic click. He pulled the trigger again. Nothing.

"He's out of ammo! Move!" Acid shouted, leaping from cover.

Darius screamed in frustration, flinging the gun at them. Saga grabbed his arm and they fled from the courtyard and into a narrow passage between two buildings.

Acid and Spook sprinted after them. The passage was a tight squeeze, forcing them to crabwalk through the last few metres. They burst onto the street that ran beside the gallery just in time to see Darius and Saga entering MacArthur Park, their silhouettes dissolving into the shadows.

Without hesitation, Acid and Spook crossed over to the park and gave chase. It was shrouded in darkness. Tall lampposts stood at intervals along the winding paths but their bulbs were dim and they offered little illumination.

Acid kept her gun raised, motioning for Spook to stay close. They moved slowly, instincts on high alert, eyes and ears straining for signs of movement. But apart from the distant hum of traffic and the occasional chirp of crickets, the park was silent. No footsteps, no voices, nothing to give away Darius' position.

The park wasn't large, but the path ahead was barely visible, darkness swallowing them as they moved away from the surrounding buildings. Acid turned to Spook, signalling to spread out, each of them taking a different route towards the lake at the park's centre.

"Here," she whispered, handing Spook the gun. "Take it."

Spook glared at her for a moment. "No. I can handle myself. You're a better shot."

Acid was about to insist Spook take the weapon but stopped herself. She still saw Spook as that nerdy young kid she'd met in Paris all those years ago, and that wasn't fair. Spook had changed. She could handle herself. It was time Acid realised that. And Spook was right – Acid was the better shot. With Darius and Saga unarmed, a clear shot could end this in seconds.

The lake's surface shimmered with a faint reflection of moonlight breaking through the clouds as they fanned out, approaching it in a wide arc. Acid kept low, leading with her pistol. As she passed a row of bushes, she heard a rustle and snapped her aim toward the sound. Nothing. She waited for another second. Probably just a critter. She was about to move on when a rush of activity erupted behind her.

Spinning around she saw a dark figure lunging at her. It was Darius. In the moonlight his twisted features looked grotesque, like a Japanese Kabuki mask. He grabbed her wrist and twisted it, trying to wrench the gun from her hand.

"Go to hell," Acid snarled, struggling against his grip.

Darius' face contorted with effort, his eyes wild. He jammed his thumb into the pressure point on her wrist, forcing the gun from her grip and sending it clattering to the ground. Acid retaliated with a heavy punch to his jaw, ignoring the pain shooting through her knuckles. A swift kick sent Darius staggering back, blood dripping from his lip.

"You think you can take me out, Sis?" he sneered. "Not a chance."

Acid didn't respond. She was scanning the area for the pistol.

Where the bloody hell was it?

She stepped back, keeping Darius in her sights while she searched. But the gun was gone, most likely kicked into the undergrowth during their struggle. She refocused as Darius came at her, blocking his punch and delivering another powerful kick to his midsection.

He staggered but remained upright, chuckling to himself as Acid readied herself for another attack.

"Something amusing?" she asked, looking around for Spook.

Darius shrugged theatrically. "I just can't believe you'd be so stupid," he said. "You could have had it all."

"You kept me on a damn leash," she hit back, still on high alert. "I think a part of you knew this was coming. I'd say you're the stupid one, Darius. You really thought I'd join you after what you did. You killed my friend."

"Oh, boo-fucking-hoo!" he sneered. "That old bastard? Who cares? He was on his way out anyway."

"He was The Dullahan. Someone special in this industry. You'd know that if you weren't such a fake."

Darius' smirk vanished. "Enough," he said, drawing a knife from his belt, the blade glinting menacingly in the moonlight.

Bugger.

Why hadn't she noticed the damn knife? She'd been too busy focusing on how many shots he'd fired to assess the situation properly. Her nerves felt like they were on fire as she tightened her stance, eyes locked on the blade and Darius' feet, anticipating his next move.

"Now that's a knife, huh?" he said, winking.

He lunged and she jumped back, startled as she bumped into someone.

"Acid!" It was Spook. But a quick glance over her shoulder told her Spook wasn't in any state to help her. Saga stood a few metres in front of Spook, brandishing a similar knife to the one Darius was holding.

"Looks like we've got ourselves a party," Darius said.

Acid and Spook stood back-to-back, their stances firm, eyes darting between the two knife-wielding madmen.

"Don't worry, kid. You've got this," Acid whispered.

"Yeah? And what if I don't?" Spook replied, her voice shaky.

Acid rolled her shoulders back. "Then we go out fighting," she said.

Chapter Forty-Eight

After everything Spook had endured over the last seven years – all the pain and misery she'd experienced, all the death and bloodshed she'd witnessed – not to mention her extensive assassin training and the fact she'd completed six hits, she was still terrified as she faced off against Stig Saga.

She'd faced danger up close before, a life-or-death situations, but this time it was different. In the past it had been out of her control. But whether she survived the next few minutes was entirely up to her. She had to be strong. She had to fight. Her heart pounded in her chest as she readied herself.

Saga hadn't blinked for a long time. He looked to be sizing her up, his pale skin and sunken eyes even more unsettling in the moonlight. He was tall but lean and probably didn't have much of a weight advantage. Yet he was also lithe, wiry, and a deadly assassin with decades more experience than her. He also had a knife. A big knife. Spook had nothing but her fists and feet.

Saga sprang forward but she shifted out of the way just

in time. He slashed at the air once and retreated, holding the knife up like an Olympic fencer, taunting her.

"Ready to die?" he sneered.

Spook raised her chin, fighting to control her nerves. "You're going to have to work for it," she replied, pleased that her voice was steadier than she felt.

Saga attacked again, slashing the blade in a wide arc. Spook evaded him and danced away, kicking out as she moved, but only managing to graze the back of Saga's calf. He recovered quickly and came at her with renewed fury, slashing wildly with the knife. Spook ducked under the blade and landed a solid punch to his side, knocking him back.

She was finding her stride now, but the fatigue from the chase was setting in. Saga's movements were slowing also, but he still had the upper hand. She couldn't afford to let up now.

He swung at her again and she jumped back, though not fast enough. The blade sliced across her arm, sending a sharp, searing heat through her triceps. She screamed, the pain only lasting as long as it took for her adrenaline to surge, replaced by a wave of intense anger.

Grinding her teeth she stepped forward, dodging another swing of the blade and sweeping Saga's legs out from under him. He hit the concrete hard and Spook stayed in motion, kicking the knife from his hand and following up with a boot to the face, shattering his nose in a spray of blood and snot.

Buoyed by her advantage, she jumped on top of him before he could recover, pinning his arms with her knees and gripping his throat. She glanced up to see Acid and Darius grappling nearby. Acid was trying to get Darius in a headlock but he wriggled free, elbowing her in the head before sprinting away.

Spook tried to call out, but her voice caught in her throat. Beneath her Saga was regaining strength and struggling fiercely. She pressed down harder, keeping him pinned as Acid chased after Darius, disappearing behind a row of trees.

Shit.

Now she really was on her own. Saga continued to squirm, bucking and snarling as he tried to throw her off. Gritting her teeth, Spook squeezed harder on his throat, desperate to end this. She thought she had him, but Saga managed to free one arm and jabbed his thumb into her eye.

She cried out, jerking her head back, trying to bite his bony fingers as they clawed at her face. Saga was now rolling left and right, his hips bucking violently. It felt like she was riding a wild bronco. She leaned forward, desperate to stay on top, but Saga punched her hard in the throat.

Whoa! What the— Shit!

She released him as a heavy pain spread through her neck. She couldn't breathe, she couldn't talk. She felt as if she was going to die. Panicking, she rolled off him and scrambled away, putting distance between them as she fought for air.

Her gaze landed on the dagger, lying a metre behind Saga as he got to his feet. He hadn't seen it. Not yet. She'd like to keep it that way.

"Got you worried?" she gasped, circling him to keep his focus on her.

"I don't get worried about pathetic nobodies," he replied, but he stayed put.

"Oh, I think you are. I think you know you've lost your

touch," Spook continued, keeping his attention on her. "I'm going to kill you."

Saga's eyes narrowed, then he charged, fists ready to strike. Spook tried to sidestep out of the way but he was too fast. Spinning around he drove a knee into her abdomen, doubling her over in agony. Before she could react, something hard smashed into the side of her head and it felt as if her skull had split open. She staggered, pain and fear gripping her. She was losing the fight. She had to turn it around.

Forcing herself upright, she adopted a fighting stance, recalling the training Acid and Nate had drilled into her. She could almost hear Acid's voice in her head.

Aim for the areas people don't expect. The knees, the throat… the groin.

She raised her guard, locking eyes with Saga as he closed in. Then as he got nearer she struck out with a swift kick to his groin.

"*Knulla!*" he cried, bending over to clutch himself.

Seizing the moment, Spook barrelled into him, wrapping her forearm around his neck and squeezing with all her strength. She scanned the area frantically for Acid but saw no sign of her. Saga flailed wildly, but she tightened her grip, feeling his desperate struggle.

Saga, however, was stronger than he looked. He grabbed her around the waist and lifted her in the air before leaning back and slamming her onto the grass. The impact knocked all the wind out of her. Before she could recover, he straddled her, his bony hands closing around her throat.

"Now you will die," he hissed. "Like we both knew you would."

Spook's vision blurred as she clawed at his hands, her air supply cut off. Terror surged as she felt herself slipping away. This wasn't fair. This wasn't how it was supposed to go. She fought on, trying to buck him off, but he was heavier and more resilient than she'd anticipated. Her throat felt like it was collapsing. She stared up at him, bracing herself for the end.

No... Acid...

A sharp crack echoed through the night. Saga's head jerked violently to the side and he slumped to the ground beside her, releasing his grip on her neck. Gasping for air, Spook looked up to see Abi and Lena standing over her. Abi had her mom's gun in hand. They grabbed Spook's hands, pulling her to her feet.

"Are you okay? Anything broken?" Lena asked.

"I don't think so," Spook replied, still catching her breath. "Yeah, I'm fine," she managed. She stared down at Saga's body, feeling nothing but vindication as she saw the hole in the side of his skull. But her triumph only lasted a few seconds as a scream reverberated through the trees.

Spook looked up, her senses firing. That was Acid's scream.

She needed her.

Chapter Forty-Nine

Two minutes earlier, Acid was chasing Darius around the edge of the lake, their pounding footsteps and laboured breaths disturbing the silence of the park. Acid's muscles burned, and the dress clung to her, hindering her movements, but she pressed on, determined not to let him get away. This was it, her final showdown with the man who dared call himself her brother.

"Darius, stop!" she called after him. "It's over."

Even after everything, she still wondered if she could appeal to Darius' sense of family, but the venom in her voice was too hard to mask. Because Darius Duke wasn't her brother. He never had been. And Oscar Duke certainly wasn't her father, just a spectre from her tormented past – a past she was determined to bury forever. Darius carried with him all the evil, all the ego and malice of his father. That man had stolen her childhood and shattered her life. She was damned if she was going to let his son take her future. They might have shared DNA, but that meant nothing. After all, didn't humans share most of their DNA with crabs? Darius had to be eliminated, just like all the others who had dared to cross her.

But he was fast, she'd give him that, especially when running for his life. He vaulted over a white concrete barricade and darted across the wide boulevard that cut through the middle of the park, disappearing into the dense greenery beyond. Acid followed, ignoring the blare of car horns as she weaved through traffic to the other side.

This side of the park was a maze of trees and dimly lit paths, every corner a potential hiding place, every shadow a possible ambush. She pressed on, catching sight of Darius' silhouette against the faint glow of the lamps as he bobbed in and out of sight between the trees. Her muscles burned with exertion, but she pushed through the pain, focused only on her mission. Up ahead, Darius dashed across an open patch of grass and down an incline onto another winding path.

"Darius!" she yelled again. "Stop."

He ignored her, sprinting down the path and across a patch of dry dirt. Four large concrete discs, remnants of long-gone fairground rides, glowed pale in the moonlight. Acid quickened her pace, eyes fixed on Darius as he ran between the concrete circles. Then, as he got to a huge solitary palm tree on the other side, he stopped.

Acid skidded to a halt, her boots grinding against the gravel, when Darius turned to face her. He was nodding to himself and smiling as if suddenly realising a great truth. Raising the knife, he made a show of tossing it aside, like he was surrendering to an armed police unit. Only Acid wasn't armed. And there was only one of her.

"I know you won't kill me," he said. "I'm your brother."

Acid shook her head. "You killed The Dullahan."

"Are you really that bothered about him?" he asked.

"He tried to kill you once upon a time, Alice. He was an assassin. He knew the rules of the game."

"He knew them better than you," Acid replied. "He was an honourable man."

"He was a washed-up old drunk. A nobody. And he was on his last legs. If anything, I did him a favour." He stepped forward, hands raised. "The fact remains, dear sister, you need me. I gave you the life you wanted, the only life you can handle. You'd be nothing without me."

Acid chewed on the inside of her cheek, her mind a storm of dark thoughts. Did he truly believe what he was saying? Was he that deluded? Suddenly, Darius didn't just sound power-mad, he was mentally unhinged. Had he always been like this? Had she? Or had power and circumstance corrupted them both?

She shook her head, trying to clear the fog of doubt. No, they were nothing alike. Never would be.

"I don't need you," she said, her voice firm with conviction. "I don't need anyone."

Darius stepped closer, his expression softening. "I don't want to fight with you, Alice," he said, almost pleading. "You're my sister. I love you."

Acid didn't move. The bats gnawed at her nerves, confusion and mistrust warring within her.

"I hated your dad," she said. "I'd kill him again every time. He's not my father. I don't have one. Never did. Oscar Duke was a rotten piece of shit. Same as you."

"Don't be like that," Darius said, stepping closer. "You and I need each other. I can admit that now. Saga filled my head with lies, made me paranoid. But I'll get rid of him and we'll start fresh. Just you and me. Think of what I've already built, Alice. Together we can create a new organisation. I can give you the world, everything you want. Do you really think those pathetic losers can offer you the same?"

Acid shrugged, feigning indifference as a hundred different thoughts collided in her head. Most of them were chaotic, some were strategic. She knew Darius was trying to save himself, but if she could get close enough, she could overpower him and finish this.

He gestured for her to come closer, smiling, practically fluttering his damn eyelashes. It only fuelled Acid's fire. She lowered her head, twisting her mouth to one side, pretending to consider his request.

"Come on," he whispered. "It's always been me and you, Alice. I lost sight of that, but I see it now. I think you do, too."

She nodded and took a step forward, calculating her next move, assessing her angles.

"Me and you?" she said, with a faint smile.

Darius nodded, almost greedily. "Absolutely. That's all I ever wanted. I know I got caught up in dreams of being number one, and Saga played a big part in that, but screw that anaemic prick, right? We don't need him."

"Damn right. The guy's creepy as hell." Her smile widened, genuinely this time. "I imagine slicing open his pencil neck on a daily basis."

"So we'll start again?" Darius took another step towards her. They were now just a metre apart.

Acid held her nerve, keeping her breathing steady. One step closer and she could strike. She visualised the attack – a swift sidestep, a sharp elbow to the back of his head, then grab him in a blood choke before he knew what hit him. It would be Goodnight Vienna in minutes. She'd keep the pressure on until his brain gave in and his heart stopped.

She was about to move when Darius lunged forward.

The glint of metal caught her eye too late and pain exploded in her side. She groaned, staring at the knife handle protruding from her flesh like it was an alien appendage. The blade was buried deep, sending searing pain radiating through her body. It could have hit an organ. Blood was spreading across her dress in a dark, growing stain.

This was bad. Really bad.

But she wasn't done yet. Despite the pain, despite the blood loss, she still had her rage. The bats weren't letting her give up so easily. She swung wildly, her fist connecting with Darius' jaw with a satisfying crack. He staggered backwards, but she stayed on him, fuelled by pure adrenaline.

The park around them blurred into a swirl of motion and noise as they grappled, fists flying in a desperate struggle for survival. Acid felt herself weakening, the blood loss sapping her strength, but she pushed on, driven by something more intense than pain.

"You stupid bitch," Darius hissed, spittle hitting her face as they clashed. "You've ruined everything."

He grabbed the knife handle and twisted it, sending a shockwave of agony through her body. She screamed. The white-hot pain was overwhelming, but she knew she could use it. Darius was stronger than she'd given him credit but she was a born survivor. Pain was a place she knew. It spurred her on. She kicked at his shins and clawed at his eyes, fighting dirty to gain any advantage.

Darius retaliated by grabbing her by the shoulders and slamming her against a tree. Stars burst behind her eyes but she remained conscious. As he came at her, she pushed herself forward and drove her knee into his groin with all her remaining strength.

He cried out and doubled over. She tried to lock in a

chokehold, but he twisted away, shoving her forward and stamping on her Achilles tendon. She stumbled onto all fours. The ground was cold and hard beneath her, though she barely felt it. Her focus was on survival, on taking out this vicious bastard. The bats. The bats screamed for her to get up and fight.

Then she heard another sound – Spook's voice, shouting her name. Acid looked up to see Darius standing over her. Spook called out again and his attention flicked towards the sound of her voice. He glared back at Acid, hesitation flashing across his face.

"Pains in the fucking neck," he snarled. "The whole lot of you."

He booted Acid in the side, sending her sprawling in the dirt, then turned and ran in the opposite direction.

"She's over here," Spook screamed. "This way."

Within moments Acid's senses were overwhelmed by hurried footsteps and heavy breathing. Three figures emerged from the gloom. Spook darted over and knelt beside her.

"She's hurt," she said. "We need to get her out of here."

Acid shook her head, her vision swimming. "No... Darius..." It was a struggle to speak. "You need to...'

"Forget Darius. He's gone," Spook snapped. "You need medical attention."

"Where's Nate?" Acid mumbled.

"He's in the car, he's okay," another voice said. It sounded like Abi, but as if she was speaking underwater. "He told us what happened. We need to get out of here. The LAPD are on their way."

"Spook... please..." Acid's voice echoed in her head, all but drowned out by the ringing in her ears and the screeching from the bats. "You have to..."

A cold damp hand touched her forehead. "It's okay, we got them," Spook said, from another room, from another universe. "Kancel Kulture are done. We did it. Now, hang in there, Acid. Please."

She shifted, trying to focus on Spook's face, but her features blurred, merging with the shadows. The darkness was closing in, a suffocating blanket threatening to engulf her. She managed a weak smile, her eyelids heavy. "Good work, kid," she whispered. "You were... awesome..."

She trailed off as the darkness came. She fought it for a second longer, holding on as long as she could. Then... black.

Chapter Fifty

Three days later, Spook stood amid the bustling chaos of LAX's main foyer as announcements blared over the PA system. Beside her, Nate, his arm in a sling, scanned the departures board, his tired eyes reflecting the weight of the past week. Nearby, Lena was sitting on the end of a row of seats, engrossed in setting up her new Apple Watch Ultra, which she'd treated herself to during a visit to Koreatown the day before.

Spook smiled as she watched the younger woman fiddling with the settings, lips pursed in concentration. She couldn't picture herself getting the Ultra, but she and Lena were different people with different perspectives on tech. Plus, as Spook kept reminding herself, she wasn't competing with Lena, she wasn't a threat. Because, ultimately, it was Spook who was a different person. She was no longer the timid young tech nerd who had met Acid Vanilla all those years ago.

She'd changed, and she didn't mind that one bit.

"Come on, Spooks, bring it in," Abi said, as she

returned from the restroom, opening her arms and hugging her. "I had a real blast. Thanks... for everything."

Nate scoffed. "Really? You had fun?"

"Well, you know, it was something different to do," she replied, stepping back. "Believe it or not, this hasn't been the most stressful week I've had working in Hollywood. It was good to meet all of you. You saved my life and made me realise what was important. So... thank you."

"No. Thank you," Spook said. "We couldn't have done any of it without you."

Abi jiggled her shoulders in a little dance. "Well, I am fucking amazing, I know that." She tilted her head and grinned at Spook. "Stay in touch, yeah?"

"Umm... that might be tricky, Abi," Nate said, leaning in and lowering his voice. "You know... because of what we do."

Abi rolled her eyes. "All right, big fella, calm down, I get it. It's just what people say. No need to make a big thing of it."

Everyone laughed, even Nate, the tension easing for a moment. Spook glanced at the departure board. "We really should get through security and settled in the departure lounge," she said.

She looked around, spotting Acid sauntering towards them, coffee in hand. Seeing her alive and mobile still sent a shiver of relief through Spook. Her old friend was walking a little stiffly, but she was on the mend. It could have been much worse.

Nate had called in some favours as they sped away from the MacArthur Gallery, arranging for Acid to see an emergency surgeon who moonlighted in the industry and had a backroom operating theatre for such purposes. It had cost them eight thousand dollars, but it had been worth it to save

Acid's life. Darius' knife had nicked her liver, and she would have bled out if they hadn't reached the doctor in time. As she joked after coming around from the anaesthetic, she'd done more damage to her liver herself over the years, by now it was as scarred and callused as her heart.

Spook had smiled at that, though she wasn't sure Acid's heart was as callused - or as callous - as she claimed. She still hadn't brought up what Acid had said to her before passing out, but she had it in the barrel, saving it for the right moment.

"Okay, guys," Abi said, as Acid joined them. "I guess this is it. Safe journey and good luck."

"Will you be okay?" Spook asked. "You know, with your work and everything."

Acid pulled a face and leaned in. "Yeah, sorry about killing your boss," she whispered.

Abi shrugged, a wry smile on her lips. "He was a prick. Honestly, there's always a job for someone like me in a town like this. Plus, now I've got more dirt on people. It puts me in a stronger position."

"Good," Acid said, her expression hardening. "But no talking about us."

"Absolutely not."

"Because I will kill you," she added. "You can count on that."

Abi laughed. Spook did too, even though she suspected Acid was only half-joking.

They exchanged final farewells, then Spook led the way towards passport control, her mind on the journey ahead. It was good to be going home, but it was even better to have Acid with them. They might not have taken out Darius the way Acid wanted, but bringing Acid back had been Spook's goal all along. And she'd achieved it. It felt good.

Chapter Fifty-One

TWO WEEKS LATER

Spook sat with Acid on a low wall outside their Dalston headquarters, nursing cold bottles of beer and soaking up the late afternoon sun. It had been a whirlwind since they returned from LA, but they'd all managed to get some rest and life was now back on an even keel. Well, as even as it ever got in Spook's world. Nate's shoulder had healed, and Acid was looking better, raring to go.

Spook sipped her beer and turned to Acid, finally ready to bring up what she'd been wanting to say.

"You know, you told me I was awesome."

"What?" Acid scoffed. "When?"

"Back in that park, as you were bleeding out. You said, 'Good work, kid, you were awesome.'"

Acid squinted into the sun, taking a sip of her beer. "I must have been delirious."

"Ah, okay." Spook shook her head, laughing.

But it was nice, sitting together in the warmth of the sun as it slowly disappeared behind the rooftops of East London. It had been one hell of a tough year, but they'd all survived it and things were looking up. Nate had arranged interviews with two potential operatives, and with the industry still reeling from Kancel Kulture's demise, business would only get better.

Unbeknownst to Nate, Spook had also been in contact with Abi via an encrypted network. Kancel Kulture had left many angry clients with unfinished business, throwing Hollywood's underbelly into crisis. Still, it was nothing those multi-millionaires couldn't handle. And maybe Spook's organisation would help them out. If the price was right.

She turned at the sound of voices to see Lena and Nate appear from around the side of the building. They sat beside them and Acid bit the tops off two more beers, passing them around.

"How are we all doing?" Nate asked.

"Can't complain," Acid said, giving Spook a look that said, *Don't start.*

"Looks like we've got another three interested operatives," he continued. "I've arranged to meet with them next week."

Spook raised her bottle. "Awesome."

They drank in silence for a moment, each lost in their own thoughts. Spook knew Acid was still angry with herself for letting Darius escape, but she was coping well, not letting her demons take over and maintaining a philosophical outlook. Whether this was just a product of her recuperation or a permanent shift in her personality, Spook couldn't tell. Either way, she was glad to be sitting here with her. There was a time she thought it might never happen.

And yes, Darius had got away. But if Acid still wanted him dead, then they'd deal with it. He was a man alone. A nobody. And they were a team now.

"You know we still haven't come up with a name," Lena said.

The statement was met with groans and jeers, having been a recurring topic for the last two weeks.

"But we do need one," Nate added.

Spook opened her mouth but then shut it again. Maybe Avenging Angels wasn't the best title for their organisation after all. It might have been a good idea once, but not anymore. She was ready to let it go.

"What about Annihilation Pest Control?" Acid said.

Nate laughed. But then stopped as they all turned to see Acid staring off into the middle distance, her face stern.

"What, you're serious?" Spook asked.

"Won't it confuse people?" Lena asked.

Acid didn't flinch. "Does it matter?"

"How about a compromise?" Nate said. "Annihilation Cleaning, something like that."

They all looked at each other, not wanting to be the first to reply. Spook's gaze settled on Acid. "What do you think?"

She pursed her lips. "I suppose it still has a nod to Caesar."

"Exactly. If that's what you want."

She wrinkled her nose. "Yeah, in a weird way, it is. I think it's important to me... somehow."

"So have we got a name?" Lena asked.

"Maybe," Acid said, taking another drink.

Spook leaned back, closing her eyes and letting the warmth of the sun wash over her. Annihilation Cleaning. It was a good name. She liked it. And it meant they were finally moving forward and putting down proper roots. It wouldn't be long before Annihilation Cleaning became industry leaders.

She smiled to herself. What a strange, scary, twisted, chaotic and surreal life this was. She still couldn't quite believe how far she'd come – or who she'd become. But this was Spook's world now, these were her people. And, right now, she wouldn't trade any of it for anything.

Get your FREE ebook

We'll send you a free Acid Vanilla prequel.

Discover how Acid Vanilla transformed from a London teenager into the world's deadliest female assassin.

vinci-books.com/making-a-killer

Also by Matthew Hattersley

vinci-books.com/darkness

They thought John Beckett would be an easy target. They thought wrong.

Deep undercover as a ruthless crime lord's right-hand man, secret service officer John Beckett's mission suddenly takes a deadly turn. When a mysterious data leak puts his life on the line, he must make a choice that will change his life forever.

Darkness On The Edge Of Town
Preview

Chapter 1

Heavy rain pounded on the roof of Jane Isaacs's car as it crept along London's Albert Embankment towards 85 Vauxhall Cross. As the car slowed to a stop, she leaned closer to the window, her gaze tracing up the imposing building to her right – the headquarters of Britain's Secret Intelligence Service, the home of MI6.

A Londoner by birth, Isaacs remembered the controversy that had sparked up when MI6 had moved away from Century House in the mid-nineties to this modern monolith on the banks of the river. The building – an expansive sprawl of glass and concrete – had earned itself a variety of colourful nicknames over the years. Some sneered at it as 'The Lego Building'; others referred to the bold architectural departure as 'Dubai-on-Thames'. But Isaacs didn't mind it too much. For her, it was now simply synonymous with the London skyline. A modern building, like the Shard and the Gherkin, that proved London was still at the cutting edge of design, driven by industry and progress rather than what might look pleasing to the mainstream.

The driver switched off the engine and Isaacs sat upright, preparing herself for what was waiting for her inside. This was her fourth visit to MI6, but her first in the capacity of Home Secretary. She'd yet to be briefed on why she was being called here at 9 a.m. on a Tuesday, but whatever it was, she was determined to make a good impression on those in attendance. She was well aware that the ascension to her new role in the cabinet less than a month earlier had not been without controversy. After a swift cabinet reshuffle, she'd taken over from The Right Honourable Douglas Holmes MP, whose scandalous affairs with two special advisers had propelled him into a forced resignation and a statement read out at the gates of his Kent estate with his stern-faced wife standing supportively by his side. The affair was another grubby matter to hit an already fractious and reeling government, and there were some – many – in the party who felt Isaacs was an unfit replacement. But she'd show them. Her hope was that, under her guidance, the Home Office would reach a level of gravitas and decorum that it had been missing for the last three years.

So, shoulders back, chest out.

She could do this.

The door of her car opened, and she looked up to see Max, the head of her new security detail, holding a large black umbrella for her. It was only a ten-second walk to the main entrance, but she was glad of the cover. Glad of him. His calming presence lessened the anxiety that had been gripping her since she got the phone call at 7 a.m. this morning demanding her presence here today. It was these little things – having an umbrella held for her, being escorted places by a committed security detail – that she was still getting used to in her new role. But she wasn't complaining. She liked feeling both safe and powerful, and most of the time she did. Yet, despite her outward displays of confidence, she was still acclimatising to her new role, and today's high-stakes meeting only amplified her trepidation.

"Ma'am." Max held a large hand out to her.

She took it, offering him a gracious smile as he helped her from the car.

"Will you stay?" she asked, as they made their way to the entrance.

"Of course. I'll be right here when you're finished."

That was what she wanted to hear, but at the bottom of the steps she hesitated. The cold March air hung heavy with anticipation and tension, clinging to her like a second skin. Hard droplets of rain beat down on the taut canvas umbrella as she drew in a deep breath and focused her attention on the glass doors in front of her. Whatever this was about, she would deal with it to the best of her ability.

Gathering her courage, she slowly ascended the steps, Max's presence still a reassuring constant in her periphery. A young woman was waiting behind the sleek glass entrance, and as Isaacs approached, she leaned forward and used her ID card to open the door for her.

"Good morning, Home Secretary," she said, stepping to one side to allow her to enter.

"Thank you. And let's hope it's a good one."

Squaring her shoulders, Isaacs stepped through the door, leaving Max outside with his umbrella. Inside the building, the atmosphere was one of quiet efficiency. Decorated in a modern, minimalist style, the vast atrium was sparse except for a reception desk over to the right, which was manned by three guards who appeared to be making a concerted effort not to look her way. On either side of the space, large canvases hung on the walls, displaying famous scenes from around the capital – Big Ben, the Houses of Parliament, Nelson's Column.

"Would you like to follow me? They are all waiting for you."

The question drew Jane's attention back. "Absolutely. Lead the way."

The young woman swiped them through the security gates and then through a series of double doors. The long, silent corridors seemed to swallow Isaacs up the further they went, each step echoing like a gunshot as her heels clacked against the polished floor. She could almost feel the gravity weighing her down, sensing innumerable secrets lurking behind the closed doors and on the guarded faces of those she passed. Further anticipation coiled in her stomach as they turned a corner and she was faced with a room at the far end of the next corridor. The door was open and she could see Tristan Shepherd, the Foreign Secretary. He looked tired and nervous. At least she wasn't the only one.

Her escort accompanied her to the doorway but no further. As the woman backed away, Isaacs thanked her then stepped inside. Shepherd turned to see her enter and raised his eyebrows as if sharing a moment of grim solidarity. Glancing around the room, Isaacs recognised the director general of MI5, Emily Eastwood – who she'd met with twice since becoming Home Secretary – and also Frank Calder, the incumbent chief of MI6. She offered them both a resigned smile, and got the same in response.

There were four other people in the room, all men. Two of them were seated together at one end of a large round table in the centre of the room, talking in hushed whispers; another was pacing up and down; the fourth was leafing through a pile of papers on the table in front of him. The expression on each man's face was grave, and at least two of them looked as if they hadn't been to bed.

"What's going on, Tristan?" she whispered, as Shepherd approached her and closed the door. He stood beside her and they took in the room. "Are we in trouble?"

He cleared his throat. "I've not been fully briefed, but now you're here we'll get straight into it." He glanced pointedly at the two men sitting at the table. "But yes, Jane, from what I can gather, we're in a great deal of trouble."

They found seats at the round table as silence descended. Glancing around the room, Isaacs was surprised at how plain it looked, almost nondescript in its modernity. There were no pictures on the walls, no exposed pipework or decorative fixtures. There was just one fluorescent strip light that hung from the ceiling, casting the windowless room in a stark white glow. With no windows and only the large table in the centre, it felt spacious and claustrophobic all at once. The air was heavy with expectation.

"Robert, are you going to tell us what the hell this is all about?" the man sitting opposite her asked. "I'm supposed to be on leave. I've got a flight leaving for the Algarve this afternoon." The man looked to be in his early sixties and his features resembled those of a wolfhound. What hair he had left on his head was in direct competition with his bushy white eyebrows and visible nasal hair.

"We shouldn't need to keep you long at this stage, Brian," the man called Robert replied. "This is just a prelim. To fill you in on what intel we have. I'm optimistic we can nip this in the bud before it gets away from us."

"Before we start," Tristan Shepherd butted in. "I think it might be wise if we did introductions. I know most of you, but I'm not sure Jane here has had the pleasure."

Isaacs sat up at the sound of her name, suddenly feeling even more out of place as seven pairs of eyes all turned to look at her. "That would be very helpful," she heard herself say.

She was glad Shepherd was here. They weren't what you'd call friends, but she wouldn't have had the nerve to speak up herself amongst these titans of intelligence. The Foreign Secretary, however, was a seasoned veteran of these sorts of things and was taking it in his stride; in fact, he appeared to be revelling in the unease and chaos buzzing in the air.

Isaacs listened intently, carefully processing the names and titles as the individuals at the table made their introductions. She was familiar with Eastwood, Shepherd, and Calder, but now she added Simon Bryers, head of the NCA, and Brian Somersby, Director of GCHQ, to her mental roster. She'd yet to establish a connection with either of them but there was no time like the present. The remaining two men at the table introduced themselves as Robert Locke and Spencer Bowditch, the chief director and senior officer of Sigma Unit.

Bloody hell!

Like most people in positions of power in the British government, she'd heard the rumours regarding Sigma Unit, yet its existence had always been blurred in ambiguity. From what she'd gathered, they were a covert arm of the British Secret Service's general support branch, whose operatives collaborated not only with MI6 but also with the CIA and Mossad, and carried out clandestine paramilitary operations both domestically and abroad. They were what the Americans called a Black Ops unit – an elite group of former Special Forces operatives who were deployed mainly on 'deniable operations' in foreign territories.

On paper, Sigma Unit didn't exist. Yet here she was sitting metres away from two of its most high-ranking members. And if they were here, something big had gone down. Or was about to.

"Come on then, Locke," Bryers exclaimed, once the introductions were over. "Give us the lowdown. What have you dragged us all here for? We do have work to do over in NCA, you know?"

"Yes, this is all a bit dramatic, old boy," Somersby added, followed by a blustery laugh. "I know you secret service bods like it that way, but couldn't this have been done over the phone? Or in an email?"

Locke glanced at Bowditch, who glanced at Calder. "I'm afraid not," Calder replied. "This is a matter of national security and we can't risk any leaks." He looked back at Robert Locke. "We can't risk *further* leaks."

"There's been a leak?" Somersby asked.

Robert Locke got to his feet and unbuttoned his single-breasted suit jacket with one hand. "We believe so," he said. "But as Frank has already intimated, we're anticipating that we can contain the problem at the source."

Locke was a tall man, with black hair parted on one side and swept back from his face. Isaacs wouldn't have described him as handsome, but there was something intriguing about him. He had a certain charm and he dressed well. He was slim, bordering on skinny; yet despite his build, he didn't seem weak. Far from it. He looked like the sort of person who was constantly wired for danger, full of adrenaline and nerves. He addressed those assembled with stern, unblinking eyes.

"Some of you are already aware that, in the early hours of this morning, one of our elite intelligence analysts intercepted clandestine communications on the dark web pertaining to a potential data breach. This breach has the potential to expose the identities and operational aliases of seven of our operatives." He paused, letting the weight of this revelation permeate the room and the ensuing murmurs to subside. "As you can appreciate, if this intel proves accurate, the security of some of our best men and women will be jeopardised."

"Is it not feasible to extract them regardless?" Shepherd asked. "Provide them protection until we can ascertain the veracity of the situation?"

A muscle in Locke's eye quivered involuntarily. "I'm afraid it's not that simple, Foreign Secretary. Six out of the seven operatives on the list are currently embedded in foreign territories, undertaking deep-cover assignments. Extracting them prematurely would result in the forfeiture of significant strategic advancements and we risk exposing ourselves exponentially."

"But if we don't pull them out," Isaacs spoke up, "their lives could be in danger."

Locke swallowed, his Adam's apple rising and falling visibly. "I believe 'could' is the pivotal term in this context, Home Secretary. Our officers' safety is of paramount importance, but we can't risk confidential information regarding Sigma Unit – as well as countless covert operations – falling into the hands of the media. Xander Templeton, the CIA section chief stationed here in London, is presently in talks with his superiors over in the States regarding the matter. Currently we are at an impasse, anticipating what happens next."

"And what are our options?" Calder asked. "Is containment viable?"

"We remain optimistic," Locke replied. "As it stands, the leaked names have surfaced solely on a dark web forum, which our analysts have already taken down. Bowditch here has just spoken with Jacob Beaumont, our chief analyst at Nightingale House. As far as he's aware, there's no indication that the list of names has re-materialised online. However, we are continuing to monitor the situation and are considering our next move."

An uneasy tension spread through the room. The idea that British Secret Service officers, already putting their lives on the line for their country, could be exposed while operating behind enemy lines hung like a dark cloud over the already charged atmosphere.

"Can you inform us of the whereabouts of the operatives in question?" Shepherd asked.

Locke fixed him with a steely glare, his expression conveying the absurdity of the question. "That information is highly classified and on a need-to-know-basis."

Shepherd bristled at the rebuff. "And don't you think *I* need to know?"

"Apologies, Foreign Secretary," Locke replied, now seemingly more cautious with his words. "However, I maintain that discussing the specifics of the operatives in question at this stage would be detrimental to national security. Many of them have been engaged in deep-cover operations for months, some even years. Which is why I'm reluctant to extract them unless absolutely necessary. Doing so would compromise ongoing missions all over the world. However, there is one name on the list that does concern me."

"Oh?" Shepherd said. "Why is that?"

"He's an exceptional officer," Locke said. "Experienced, highly trained, intelligent – one of our best assets. Yet his current assignment places him in a volatile position. Unlike the other six operatives, he's stationed here in the UK. If the leak becomes public, I'm confident we can swiftly secure the others and arrange extraction. But with this individual, I have my doubts."

Isaacs leaned forward, elbows on the table. "Why?" she asked. "Surely being on home soil makes it easier?"

"Again, I can't disclose too much information at this stage, Home Secretary," Locke replied, his expression unyielding. "What I can say is that this operative has been embedded for over two years, having secured a high-ranking position within a London-based organised crime syndicate. Our main concern is that our lines of communication have gone dark. Jacob Beaumont, whom I mentioned earlier, was acting as his handler but hasn't received any contact in over six months. We suspect the officer in question is working towards a significant breakthrough and has refrained from making contact to minimise exposure. But this also means we have no idea of his current location. If the leak becomes public and the organised crime syndicate find out, we have no means of finding him. Nor can we ensure his safety."

Isaacs stretched her neck. She didn't like the sound of this. The man in question might not have officially existed on any payroll records, but a British Secret Service officer lost on home soil following a data breach was bad optics for the Home Office whichever way you spun it.

"Will they kill him?" she asked.

"He's one of our most skilled operatives," Bowditch added. "He might be able to get to safety. We just don't know."

"And how much does this officer know?" Frank Calder asked. "If he were to be compromised, how much of a threat could he pose to us?"

Locke glanced at Bowditch, his lips pressed together in contemplation. "He's served with us for over a decade, participating in some of our most crucial missions, both domestically and internationally. He knows a lot. A hell of a lot. More than enough to undermine a decade of MI6 and CIA operations if the organised crime syndicate he's aligned with recognises his value and decides to exploit him." He surveyed the room, the weight of his words settling over those present. "But he'd never reveal anything. He's a dedicated officer and tough as hell. He'd die first."

"Can you be certain?" Shepherd asked.

"As certain as we can be about anything," Locke replied. "As you can appreciate, we are exercising extreme caution in this matter, doing everything in our power to contain this breach and prevent that list of names from falling into the wrong hands."

Isaacs nodded, catching Shepherd's eye as she did. He looked as anxious as she felt. "Do we have a name for this operative?" she asked.

Even as she was saying the words, she anticipated a sharp rebuke similar to the one Shepherd had received. Bracing herself for the terse response, she was caught off guard when Locke exchanged a glance with Bowditch, who then offered a curt nod and cleared his throat.

"The officer's name is Beckett," he told the room. "John Beckett."

Chapter 2

Over in Newham, East London, two men walked along a barren concrete gangway that divided up rows of large industrial warehouses near the dockside. It had stopped raining minutes earlier, but the air was still heavy with tension, their confident strides falling in time with one another's as they approached the last warehouse at the end of the row – the one with the dark blue shutters and biometric locking system on its main entrance. Neither of the men had spoken as they walked. They didn't need to. They'd done all their talking in the car on the way over. They knew how this was going to go down.

"Just follow my lead," Rufus Delaney now rasped in a low voice as they got closer to their destination. "Everything has been taken care of. We just need to take it steady and let it play out." When no reply came, he turned to his second in command, casting him a hard scowl as if insulted by his lack of a response.

"Sure, Rufus," he said quickly. "I'm on it. Don't worry."

Delaney stopped and held his hand out across his friend's chest to halt him. "Patrick, are you sure everything is all right?"

The man nodded. "Like I told you just now in the car, I'm fine. I've not been sleeping too well lately, that's all. But you've got nothing to worry about. We've discussed the plan. It's all good. As long as Emree doesn't mess things up."

"He won't."

"Are you certain we can trust him?"

Delaney tilted his head back to take in his taller counterpart. "Why so paranoid all of a sudden? You know who we are. You know what we do. We can trust Emree because he knows what'll happen to him if he fucks this up."

"As long as there are no surprises."

Delaney laughed. Reaching up, he grabbed him by the back of the neck. "You need to get a good night's sleep, my friend. This isn't like you."

"I'm fine."

"Yea" Delaney didn't look convinced. His dark eyes were narrowed as he studied him, trying to read any signs of doubt.

"Don't look at me that way, Rufus," he said, shaking his hand away. "It's me. Patrick. I've got your back, you've got mine. The same as always."

"Okay, good. Let's do this."

Delaney strode off in front, leaving Patrick standing there for a moment with the words echoing in his head.

It's me. Patrick.

And it was. Sort of.

But not always.

John Beckett, the man who'd been living as Patrick Hamilton for the last two years, drew in a long breath. Delaney was right, this was not like him and he needed to pull himself together. But he'd also been telling the truth just now. He hadn't been sleeping well lately. And he knew why. In previous assignments he'd been able to draw a metaphorical line in the sand, leaving a part of himself back in the locker rooms of his psyche to return to once the operation was over. But two years spent as the number two of London's largest and most ruthless criminal organisation had taken its toll. The line between his own identity and that of Patrick had become increasingly blurred, making it harder to keep his moral compass intact. It was unsettling, yet he wasn't going to stop. Not when he was so close to gaining access to The Consortium. Except on days like today, he felt as if the darkness of his current life was eroding his soul.

But that implied he had a soul to begin with.

"Patrick. Get a move on," Delaney called back as he reached the door to the warehouse.

"Sure, let's get this over with," Beckett muttered to himself, shaking off his thoughts and joining Delaney.

They entered through the main door, which had been left unlocked as arranged, and walked through the dimly lit space. At the far end, they were presented with a wall of corrugated iron and a door cut into its centre. Beckett banged his fist against it, and it was opened to reveal a large, thick-set man with a long black beard and hair twisted up into a top knot. He held an assault rifle slung over his shoulder, which Beckett identified as a KORD 6P67. Russian made. Russian supplied most likely, too.

On recognising the two men, the gatekeeper stepped back from the door and beckoned them through. Beckett let Delaney go first, following him into the main space of the warehouse. This room was cold and dark and smelled of diesel and wet concrete. A fitting environment for the kind of business they were about to conduct.

Murat Caliskan was already there waiting for them. He held out his arms as they entered. "You're late," he said, his tone betraying his annoyance.

"We ran into some unexpected traffic," Delaney lied. They'd actually been waiting to get all their pieces on the board before entering the building. "But now we're here. As are you, my friend."

Caliskan grinned. He was a tall, imposing figure with a closely cropped beard and a tattoo of a serpent coiling around his neck. His black hair was slicked back and his eyes were a piercing shade of ice blue that – due to his Turkish heritage – had to be the result of contact lenses. But they only added to his unsettling appearance.

"So...? Get on with it," he snapped. "It was you who was so desperate to see me today. As I understood it, all was going well and we weren't set to meet until the end of the month. Has something happened?"

Beckett studied Caliskan's face. His unease was apparent even beneath the bravado. He raised his head and puffed his chest out regardless, one eye on his man by the door with the Russian assault rifle.

But he was correct. There was no reason for the heads of the Turkish mafia and the Delaney Crime Syndicate to be meeting today. Except yesterday The Consortium had reached out to Delaney and expressed their concern regarding Caliskan's loyalties.

"You know, Murat, I do feel your pain," Delaney began, his voice low and dangerous. "We used to run this city between us, you and I. We were the kings of our respective boroughs. But you know how it goes. Time moves on. Things change. I know the Hunger Family found it hard falling in line when The Consortium took control of London, but I thought you were a savvy old fucker like me. Someone who knew the importance of self-preservation as well as progression. I also thought you understood the potential for opportunity and growth that The Consortium's presence will provide for us all. As well, the consequences for anyone – once again, the Hunger Family, rest in peace – who goes against their wishes."

Caliskan's eyes narrowed, a flicker of doubt clouding his gaze as he shot his man on the door another glance. "Yes. Of course I do. I am on board with the new arrangement. I told them that."

"Really?" Delaney's eyes hardened with cold fury, his voice dripping with scepticism. "Because a little bird told me you've been doing a little extracurricular work over in Riyadh. Is that correct?" He stared intently at the Turk. "What was it, Murat? You thought you could get away with selling a few mills' worth of guns to the Saudis and we wouldn't find out? Tut tut. I had you down as a cleverer boy than that."

"So what if I did?" Caliskan spat back, fear flicking across his face. "What's it to you?"

"It's nothing to me, son," Delaney replied, his tone laced with a mocking bite. "But like you, I work for them now – mostly. And they've tasked me with relieving you of your duties." He lowered his head, his voice a gruff whisper. "Sorry about that."

"Fuck you!" Caliskan snarled. "You don't police me, you egotistical prick. Ozan, show our friends out…"

Three sets of eyes shot over to where the man with the assault rifle had been standing moments earlier. Only he was no longer there.

"Oops," Delaney said with a smirk. "It looks as if your men have deserted you. Clearly, they know what side their bread's buttered on."

"No way," Caliskan snarled. "You can't do this to me. If you kill me, there will be an uprising. The Turkish mafia will take matters into their own hands. You're making a big mistake. You and The Consortium. My people won't stand for this. They'll set London on fire. I tell you. My people will—"

"*Your people* have a new boss," Delaney cut in. "Patrick. Go get him, will you? He should be outside."

Beckett marched over to the door and opened it to reveal Emree Caliskan. The Turkish mafia's new leader, as decreed by The Consortium. Murat Caliskan's younger brother.

Beckett walked with him back to where Delaney and Murat were standing, watching the elder Caliskan as his face dropped and the first realisation of his fate showed in his eyes.

"You fucking bastard," he cried out, lunging at his brother. "I'm going to kill you, you fucking piece of shit."

"No one's killing anyone," Delaney yelled, getting in between the two men. He shoved Murat back and produced a gun from out of his coat, pointing it at him. "Calm it down. Now!"

As Emree and Beckett got closer, Murat stared at his brother, those fake blue eyes ablaze with fury and betrayal. "I can't believe you're fucking me over like this."

"It's just business, brother. Nothing personal," Emree said. "The decision had already been made. I wish it was different, but this way at least we keep it in our family."

Delaney turned to Beckett and pulled a face. "Jesus. Fucking awkward this, innit?" There was mischief in his eyes. He was clearly relishing the situation. Returning his attention to Murat, his face and manner switched back to an icy coldness. "You should go, Emree. The Consortium send their thanks for stepping into the breach at such short notice. They'll be in touch."

Emree hesitated, his eyes filled with emotion as he stared at his brother one last time. Perhaps he was imagining himself in the elder Caliskan's position, Beckett thought. Or making sure he remembered this moment if he was ever tempted to stray from The Consortium's wishes. "Goodbye, brother," he whispered. "I'm sorry. But this is the life we chose."

He bowed his head and hurried away before his brother could respond. He got as far as the door when Murat called after him.

"Fucking traitor."

The younger brother paused for a second. Then he opened the door and disappeared.

Grab your copy….
vinci-books.com/darkness

About the Author

Over the last twenty years Matthew Hattersley has toured Europe in rock n roll bands, trained as a professional actor and founded a theatre and media company. He's also had a lot of dead end jobs…

Now he writes Neo-Noir Thrillers and Crime Fiction. He has also had his writing featured in The New York Observer & Huffington Post.

He lives with his wife and young daughter in Manchester, UK.